TUND

THOR GARCIA

EQUUS

Equus Press
www.equuspress.com

Equus Press
Birkbeck College (William Rowe)
43 Gordon Square, London, WC1 H0PD, United Kingdom

Cover, typeset & design by lazarus
Printed in the Czech Republic by PB Tisk

ISBN 978-1-9996964-2-9

Cover, typeset & design © lazarus
Cover montage: *Ranxerox* © Stefano Tamburini & Tanino Liberatore (1980)
Author photo © Marc Brown

for Matsuya Takenaga

BAYCITY

Thinking back, it seems I can actually remember my first day in Bay City.

It was about 10 o'clock at night, say, the end of January 19—. I'd driven since the afternoon, seven or eight hours up from Windy Tree. I'd spent the night before there at my brother's, sitting around with him and some of his people. I'd hit the road the next afternoon, racing the sun in full free-fall. It eclipsed me an hour or two out, then I'd stopped at one of the classier roadside burger joints, of the type with plastic walnut tabletops and gold handles on the bathroom doors. That had left my stomach crammed with a four-dollar plate of fried cheese potato skins; a side of fries; Pepsi in a glass, with ice. And a lot of ketchup.

My car was full of sand, socks, and three or four boxes of my best and greatest record albums. Everything else was about exactly 100 percent on the dot. My dollar-green sportscoat had brown patches on the elbows. My t-shirt was cuffed up and the color of peach paint. My pants, brown, flared at the ankles and seethed with white checks. The shoes: Spang maroon wingtips. My hands smelled like gasoline from all the fill-ups. I was halfway through a pack of new cigarettes.

I punched the car lighter and stoked up a fresh one, clean and lean and from one of the very top advertised brands. I had wanted it this way, I remember thinking – just like this. Smoke curled around my face and I blew more through my nose. I sucked again and blew, loving each tasty millimeter.

The city was finally coming up. I'd seen all the signs.

I recall steering leisurely, but also with a certain rapt surety, as I shot through a brief mountain pass. The road seemed to pause, ever quite so slightly, before suddenly surging to the left. My concentration ambled, but did not wander. It seems I had an inkling about what was coming.

I careened out of the pass, whipping over the nubbled highway surface.

A sheen of sweat lightly lathered my face. The radio was off. I'd nixed the tunes back near Converse Bay. A cruel trade-off, granted – but one against which I dared not quibble.

I recall these things with vibrant alacrity, and the agenda that lay behind them. I had wanted to keep my mind clear. Keep everything peeled, keep it perked. Keep the bubbles shining. Keep the desktop clear, the papers in their right stacks. My notion was to vacuum it in, each and every micrometer. ALL OF IT. Because each second was beyond totally crucial.

I was jack-knifing into Bay City, the world trailing after me. The beginning and the end of many, many things.

I keeled ahead, drumming across the lanky highway.

I saw my hair flutter, ever so swiftly, as I risked a final lightning glance in the rearview.

MY LAST LOOK BACK.

Then suddenly.

Bay City just fucking emerged.

She busted out from behind the cover of those cresting, sloppy hills. She tore away that veil of blank nightness – and erupted. Like it was the most natural thing in the world. Like it was what she was supposed to do.

LIKE SHE WAS WAITING FOR ME.

Bay City.

She was straight ahead, filling up half the gamut before me. Wall to wall, side to side, up and down. I hurled into her flickering gold gulf, an aching burning racing up the back of my neck.

I torqued into a torrent of twinkling skyscrapers. I saw lights and bridges and warehouse paddies, starboard and leeward. Cola billboards, whiskey signs, a tower of giant shining pantyhose. Ads for the people on the six o'clock news. All of that.

This is it, I remember thinking. This is the one.

The city and I: A conflagration in the happening. In the happening now.

In the mix.

I was 23 years old. Twenty-three – and I wanted it straight like it came. I wanted it straight, I wanted it deep, I wanted it lengthy. I wanted it ponderous, blue and heavy. I wanted it fast like karate and steep like the Poconos.

I wanted to screw it on. I wanted to screw it all the way over.

Nothing more, mind you; but not a filthy crumb less.

Or let me put it this way: I wanted in. And I wanted it now.

Things hadn't always gone right. Heck, heck no. But they weren't supposed to, they never did. There was always a shakedown, and there had always been. A tall man standing there with unflinching lips and waterless eyes, shaking his head, a sheaf of unknowable documents in his hand, giving him the legal right. He was the devil dog, the bastard in bastard's clothing. He would always be there. That was the way it went, the world over, and no one got away, no one had a prayer. The ones who thought they did were wrong. The worst type of wrong.

I was past thinking otherwise.

Yet how can I say to you? From what perspective may you best discreetly discern?

Now was time.

Now was time for the grope and the run and the stabbing thrust toward the green water.

Now. Not a chance of it later.

Grope and run and stab. Grope and run and stab. Winner take nothing; loser taking even less.

I looked around savagely, drinking it all in as fast as I could gurgle.

The city was cloaked in her darkling robes. She seemed oddly moody, a shade petulant. But that classy lady sparkled too, yeah, she was bright. The bitch couldn't hide it – not from me, not on this night.

Ah, I say to you! I was not mistaken when I ascertained Bay City was glowing with the force of some unquenchable interior furnace, some white-hot core which leached far into the extremities to burn and burn against the gloom.

I could tell it even then, that first feckled night – just driving into Bay City for the first time.

Remember, I was coming in from the south highway. That road doesn't carry you above or below her, like some, but throws you smack into her, neck-to-neck, face-to-face.

She was spangles and cheroots, Bay City was – all uptown horns and downstreet shifteyes. She was left-of-center, right-on-top, and flush down the middle. Everything up front and all at once. Brass and tacks and show-time. Hanging wires and sharp canny cornices. Feathery pouches and blunt, angular curbsides.

I was just driving in there, into Bay City. No one could say a damn thing about it.   Bay City. I was taking that woman on. I was rattling her chain and she was straightening her whip, tracing it across the ground with a wet, svelte hiss.

The intensity was high, I remember it being very high – it was a tango, a mambo, a two-step, a tete and a tete.

I whirred down the window and took a whiff. Sultry Bay City gushes wafted around my left arm: Warm and voluptuous and thick, but with a gilding of the bitterest cold – the residue that glided in from the ocean and the various bays which bloomed on her every side like glittering wings. I snorted, taking in a good deal of exhaust and fumes, ripe and pungent – along with the unmistakable aroma of steak on the fry, a scent of peppery falafel.

Bay City!

I was getting in. I felt it for sure then.

At that moment.

I liked her look, from the get-go I was liking Bay City.

Her press was no good, certainly, this was true. It was said she was filled with crude murderers and half-wit bandits, chockablock with predatory jades and eponymous ruffians, booted no-jack hustlers who found their solace in perversion and perving – who drew on the puerile vigor of the innocent foolish for their vile and craven sustenance.

This could not, of course, be doubted, and I did not do so. My people had warned me in this regard, repeatedly and with looks burdened by a dozen formless but ferociously loquacious fears: DON'T GO – STAY WHERE IT'S "SAFE." You don't know what you're getting into. Those people will skin you like a Thursday night tripe, and won't even notice when you're gone. YOU DON'T HAVE A JOB.

But suffice it to allow me to declaim: I didn't care. And I did not care. Not a damn penny whit.

I felt it inside, this feeling. It was there. It was every which way.

Bay City, hah. I would bash the bitch before she sucked my blood.

I'd decided it long beforehand. It was my premiere testament, my opening foray. I had declared it months in advance. There would be absolutely no turning back.

That was the one bargain. The one I had made with myself.

The way I looked at it, the gig was simple, basic. A question of execution, as based on general principle. Like a walk-on tryout for porn movies or such. Beer for the ballgame. A kiss for grandma. A boxful of labrador puppies.

I'd laid it all down way ahead of time.

Even if she turned on me, I would never let Bay City take me for a blind sucker.

Yes: She had industries and executive suites; tramps, trollops and troubadours; Chinese and stuntmen and art deco; drug war and turf war and sex war; poets and prelates, primates and prefab; football teams and baseball; dogs in the park and sludge-on-the-seas; grey-templed men; FBI field offices, Securities and Exchange Commission, Ad Hoc Offices of the Ex Officio; nuclear and Navy Intelligence; Armenians and Irish, Turkmen; shrimp burritos, advanced sharkskin; engineering software conglomerates.

All of this. And all of this.

I had one thousand two hundred dollars, but my balls hung like gunnysacks.

I saw my off-ramp and veered toward it, pumping the gas then letting off. I rode the thundering reverb, my every sensor tuned to the pinging hum of my pulsating V-8 Thunderbird, Gold Series.

I was coming in. Deep in now.

I was socking it to Bay City, I was knocking her left and right. Right from the go-gun I had her on the run.

Suddenly there were curves. The off-ramp flung me around at a 320-degree angle. Then it plunged, rolling steep in an awful hurry.

I jerked the wheel left. My teeth clapped. I struggled to keep the car from skating the highway rail. I yanked the wheel with most of the guff I could bring to bear.

I hit the brakes. There was a squeal followed by a squall, but no impact. Only minor skidding and a slight bouncing. Then it straightened, yeah, she went candid.

And there I was.

In.

All lights vanished as I vroomed ahead, still on a slight fall. I slid into a cavern of concrete, tons of metal and girders and implacable cement on all sides.

Then I was out of it. And then I knew I was really in.

I was there. I had landed.

The stoplight read red. I hit the brakes. My vehicle brayed and did as commanded. I checked myself, glances over both shoulders, fore and aft, reverse and counter. I was out of breath.

Reflexively, I lit a new smoke. I took a look around.

There wasn't much. Tattered old houses and apartment blocks, row after row of them. A few trees and strips of sidewalks, bus benches, billboards shrouded and peeling. Very dark too, hardly any streetlights at all.

Suddenly, I had no idea where I was, or why.

Then I remembered. The light changed to a most pearlaceous green. I gunned the Bird, rearing myself forward, whirling into the lurking melee.

My breast mottled over with joy. I was in Bay City at last. Stalking armored in my gold thunder fowl, probing for the vortex of the action.

2

The plan was to bunk up with some buddies, Steph and Andy, pals who'd been living in Bay City for a year or more. They were my advance guard, the recon crew, the research team. They had said it would be fine if I stayed at their pad for a few weeks – that is, until I secured my own digs, and began the project of my fortune.

I followed the directions they had given me. A left turn, then right, another left, another right, then onto a broad main thoroughfare.

There was action here, lots of it, and I liked it. I was in now, and this what it meant: Liquor stores, people walking around in a haze of dull neon. A maze of sidewalk café tables and chairs, bums and trash of all kinds. A ratted purple sofa, half in the street, half on the sidewalk. Cardboard boxes, a gaggle of skateboarding kids with goatees. Designer purse stores with merchandise from Europe on all the major intersections. And there, to the right – a few nice fires, in a few nice trashcans.

I gandered some frolicking neon: 24-HOUR RUBBER GOODS.

I gulped it all in. I rinsed out, gargled, gulped again, and felt my eyes get bigger.

A dark swirling figure spun into the street, directly in front of me.

Bam!

I slammed the brakes.

I saw it to be bearded, a man, deeply tanned or possibly dirtied. An odd cap sat on his head, Santa Claus-style, with a long swinging element to it that hung almost to his shoulders.

But it was his hands that drew my immediate attention.

There was something flashing and silver in one of them. The fellow gestured at me crazily and made a kind of leaping motion, up and down, up and down. A patchwork of grimacing lines getched around the opening that was his mouth.

He darted toward me.

It was all happening very quickly. I could not help but think: O God, O God, here it comes, here it comes – the unleashed fury-hell of which I had been warned.

And so very, very early.

I saw it clearly. In terrible, vivid, color focus. Here he was coming.

I saw it all in less than an instant: This fellow would rip me from my vehicle.

He would knife me first, surely, then drag me off and rape away at me frenziedly in some alleyway. I would beg him NO PLEASE NO. But it would mean nothing, to him. He would slap angrily at the back of my neck, as if I were some loose red-headed woman – *his* loose red-headed woman. I would shriek and cower as he pulled my shirt from my back and lashed me with enraged swipes. Onlookers would hoot down from the apartment blocks, giggling and turning up the television as my assailant pounded away, clubbing away into oblivion all my tender beliefs and chivalrous instincts.

I'd be lying there. He'd take my car, loot it, sell it, spill my record albums into the streets. Punks would look them over scornfully, then ramble them over with their skateboards, gleefully yelping as the vinyl splintered and the priceless covers tore. He'd try on my clothes, only to discard them as fraudulent garbage he couldn't be bothered with. He'd hogtie me, truss me, bloody me, leave me freezing and utterly shattered, wishing it had all been a dream – my youth, schools, my foolish craving to come to Bay City, everything.

There would be no police, no figment of an officer until it was far, far too late. That was a given, and darn tootin'. If I was lucky,

I'd be able to call the police myself, crawling bloody from the alleyway, trailing an intestine, begging disinterested bums for a quarter.

Oh, it was coming. I could see it so clearly. He was almost at the door.

I jerked around and looked for the lock. It was UP.

UNLOCKED.

Why, why?

My annihilation was so very close now.

Forward he raced.

Closer.

CLOSER.

Ah, shit. Oh shit shit. Shite. Shi'ite. Poopy poop. Poopy pee poopy.

Here he was. Here. I could almost feel his breath at my ear, hot and rather mildewy. Smelled like a week's worth of onions and cream cheese, mixed in with a crate of cheap appleberry wine. But that knife of his would surely be the sharpest of all.

And still he came.

Then I almost laughed. The guy jumped back, stood still, and took a deep drink – from a silver can of beer. He danced off to the other side of the road, whining and waggling his hands at something else, cackling at the moon and whatall else.

I swooned, then crumbled.

No, no murdering fiend here, friend. Indeed. Just something slothy and baggy, with his teeth curled in the mud. Just a born crow who couldn't fly anymore. Just some old crust, some neck-deep fly fisherman with no top for his convertible left out in the tornado.

I gunned the car and sped through Bay City, lights of all colors and kinds raining down upon me.

A few more twists and turns and I found Steph and Andy's neighborhood. It was a hilly and steep place, but the parking was surprisingly easy.

I stomped the emergency brake and got out, whipping shut the door with a crack and a boom. It was different out here – cool and quiet and comfortable, the houses old and in the style of Victorian castles, cast in soft blues and browns, red bricks and white trim, many with yellow bulbs in the porchways. Corner Irish bars and laundromats winked gamely from the top of a nearby ridge.

I took another look around, drinking in mouthfuls of the air – Bay City air.

Yeah, I thought. I could do with this here, like this.

It felt right, I could feel it inside me. I was getting in.

Check that – I was already in.

3

I found the number and climbed two flights of rickety wooden stairs. The steps were covered with a multitude of dead bugs, but I didn't care. I would take all the dead bugs in the world at this point. In fact, I would demand them.

I rang the golden bell. Steph and Andy opened the door together.

Both were beaming.

Me: "Is this the fuck pad?"

Indeed, they said.

And in the next second I was inside that bright and warm place. It was a two-bedroom number, kitchen and fold out futon-style couches together in the main room, a window view of a wood and brick house on the catty-corner.

Steph and Andy had two fresh six-packs of beer in brown and green bottles – according to the packages, brands from Alaska and Ireland.

Hello, hello, Bay City!

Immediately we drank a few down. Steph stepped over to the stereo and yanked the trigger on some key Pooh Sticks. And there we were all of a sudden, talking and drinking them down and blasting the Pooh Sticks.

Andy quickly went into a story about the lesbians who lived next door, one of whom was a reporter for one of the local papers.

"I'd like to fuck her," Steph said merrily. We had a few good laughs about that.

In due time they laid down some rules for me: NO SMOKING in the apartment, only on what they called "the porch," and no loud music after 11 o'clock, except on Fridays and Saturdays, when you could go till midnight but no more. Sure, I said – sure, no problem. After that they both said they had to get to sleep.

Work in the morning: Steph taught computer-training downtown; computer-data input for Andy at a longshore shipping company, Procurement Dept.

Okay, for sure, I said – and the same goes for me: Sleep and then looking for a job and an apartment, first thing in the morning.

They shut the doors to their bedrooms.

And there I was alone – in Bay City.

I soon saw that five beers remained.

I cracked one of the Alaskans, stood around awhile, then walked over to Steph and Andy's bookshelf. A bunch of bologna on it. These guys, I said to myself. What *the hell* was going on over here? There were things up there like oversize paperbacks by 37-year-old lit-seminar graduates, going on about sex with a cousin and mom's drinking, stories about blind girls dreaming of Mozart while romping with Isaac the professor's German shepherd. And the rest of it. Also, there were a seeming great many thin cartoon-type volumes about ways to kill your girlfriend's cats, and joke politics and various pranks, how to put bombs in mailboxes, etc.

I walked out to the "porch" for a smoke. It wasn't really a porch, but a kind of landing at the top of another rickety flight of stairs. Nothing but chipped paint, a few cracked wood planks. Splinters. I lit and looked.

Bay City – she was chains upon cris-crossing chains of lights, veritable trellises of lights, white and yellow and orange, bits of pink popping there and again. Office towers stood staunch and blocky amid the mist-foggy fray, bathing in sultry ochres, simmering aquamarines, burning lavenders. Solitary red lights blinked atop a good half dozen of the buildings, who knew what for.

I took it all in – her, Bay City, the one. I felt myself gently swaying as I stood and gazed on her. I was in now, or close to it – very, very close.

I looked up and saw the sky to be swimming with all manner of helicopters, airliners and single-engine bi-planes. And there, over to the left – a police searchlight. No, two police searchlights: one on some blown-out ghetto building, one aimed at the ground – probably on some punk thug who deserved a beating, by some cops who deserved to give it.

Love it, I thought. LOVE IT.

Bay City, I sneered. You bitch. You lying whore sack of come. You four-on-the-floor mother-cunt. Come on, you filthy bitch. You cheap whore. You dirty lying two-dollar strumpet.

Come to daddy.

I looked Bay City over. People were out there in her, running through her legs, streaming through her hair, scampering through her dank and wondrous jungles. And she was humming, Bay City was, I could hear it, even at this hour: A hanging hum, a whispered whir, a rousting about; clanging and hoots.

All kinds of folks were out there. Maybe they didn't know it yet, but I was coming for them.

Me, I was coming. A new shriek across their horizon.

Excitement purred and throbbed within me. I would meet some of these people. I would meet them and put their necks to the stone.

They would be evil and insane, and I would expose them. They would be kind and generous, gracious of intent and exacting of mind, and I would hoist them onto my shoulders, shouting invective at all comers, throwing elbows at anybody who tried to stop me. They would be dried like broken-off forlorn roadside wood husks, shriveled on the inside and ravaged by rot. I would fluff these to the side from the outset, deny them any specter. They would be tender and tingly – and we would tangle, together, raw, till the red moistness of dawn.

And I saw it: Someone would hand me a million dollars and thank me for the honor. A man would take a picture, and it would be of me. It would be printed in 300,000 copies of a glossy magazine, and delivered to the doorsteps of discriminating idiots.

Me. Me *in there*.

I sighed. Bay City. You filthy lying worthless dog-doing she-slut. You cheap slattern whore. You dirty dyke. You wench. You filthy no-good lying head-jobbing queen of fuck-fuck.

Come to poppa.

I walked back in and opened another beer. I drank it down while flipping through some computer magazine that had Steph's name on the address label.

I wrenched the top off one more beer. I'd originally favored the Alaskans, but all that was left now was the Irish. A bitter brew, most certainly. I downed a long suck.

There was just one left now, one beer. Hell, I thought, I'll pay those guys back later.

I drank it. I sat on Steph and Andy's futon-couch and drank it, and then, still sitting there, I lit up a smoke. Hell, I thought, those guys won't notice one smoke in here, so long as it's smoked in peace.

And I did smoke it in peace. I ashed in one of the empty bottles.

Steph and Andy had left blankets out for me. I was tired, my head spun. I unfolded the futon-couch. I was in Bay City. I looked at some drawings of dead cats, and passed out.

RABBIT COUNTRY

1

Munger dropped back in the afternoon and we rode together. The road led to a hill, then leveled out on a long plateau. It was clear and hot up there, the sun blasting down, the weeds fringed white and gold. Just a few lazy clouds, laying about like wasted ladies.

We came past a shack. A kid in a white t-shirt was out front, fifteen, fourteen years old. Watching us, a stick in his hand. It was very quiet. Nothing much but the squeak of our wheels, the knobs of the tires against the road, a bit of a breeze.

Suddenly these two dogs erupted from beneath the shack. They snarled and woofed, tearing across the dirt at us. We stood on our cranks and began to pedal. Most dogs you'd meet were harmless, but still you tried to outrace them. There was a feeling that something could go wrong if you let them get too close. But nothing ever had before.

The dogs clicked along the pavement. So fast they had made it to us. They were right up next to us, right there in the road with us. I kept expecting one of them to jump, to try to take a snap at my calf or whatnot. That's the sort of thing you were always worried about. But they never did.

One of the dogs was medium-size and brown, some kind of a shepherd mix, I guessed. He flew past me and went neck and neck with Munger, who had stretched out a lead by now.

The other dog was little and white, shorthair, probably some kind of a puppy. Maybe just small. He was running smack next to me, shoulder to shoulder, trying his hardest to keep up. He had these little black spots on him, about the size and shape of raisins. He looked over at me from time to time, his little tongue hanging out.

I saw a car coming at us in the other lane. It was a good ways off, but it was coming. I saw it rocking up and down over the road surface. It was brown, a station wagon. When I saw it I didn't think anything too special – just another car.

There was a honk. I flicked a glance over my shoulder. A car, right back of us. He wanted to pass, he didn't want to wait. Another honk. I nudged over to the farthest edge of the road. Ahead, I saw Munger do the same.

This wasn't unusual. The roads there don't have much of a shoulder, making so that sometimes you had to scootch over to the lip of the pavement if somebody wanted to pass. But normally the guy still had to swerve some to avoid you.

I didn't think it could possibly happen. It seems like there should have been too many variables that should have prevented it. I thought something would stop it before it got that far.

I looked at the pup. We had eye contact. His tongue flopped out of his mouth.

Right as the car came up behind, the station wagon rolled past the other way. It was like that, exactly like that. The little dog couldn't do anything.

It was very noisy, the sound of two cars coming up on each other like that.

From the corner of my eye I saw the little white dog disappear under the car, as it came up from behind us.

Then both cars were gone, completely sped away.

It was quiet again, the only sound the clicks of my rear wheel turning.

*

There wasn't as much blood as I thought there might be. Some was coming down the pup's nose and out his mouth. There were black smear marks on his fur, from where he'd been smashed along the road. He was lying there on the highway. His eyes were closed.

Munger picked him up and carried him by his two front paws over to the roadside. He lay him down beside some bushes and weeds. We stood and looked at him.

I got jumpy. All over my body I could feel my blood whipping through the veins, the arteries, where ever it goes. It was almost like I could hear the blood plunging down between my shoulders, roaring around my chest. I felt drops of sweat on my cheeks, sweat rolling from the top of my head down onto my eyelashes.

We hadn't done anything wrong that I could tell, but somehow it felt that we had. Somebody had to be responsible for this. I looked in all directions to see if anyone was coming, coming to check things out. But there was no one.

Munger said maybe the little dog wasn't dead. He bent down over the little guy. Maybe, he said, maybe he could hear him breathing. He wasn't sure, but maybe. Maybe he was still alive.

I didn't like that. If he was alive, I didn't know how we could help him. There was no way, we didn't have anything. But anyway, he couldn't be alive.

I asked Munger what he meant.

He said he'd heard of such things. Like where something very young, like a puppy or even a child, gets hit hard but manages to survive. Car crashes, a fall from the tenth story, run over by a backhoe. They get knocked out by the impact, but because their bodies are still undeveloped and lightweight, not a lot of bad damage is done. Something to do with the bones being soft and not fully formed, in which case they don't break or damage the internal organs.

Maybe, I said. But it had looked to me like the car's fender had hit the pup smack on the back of the head. But as I say, there was no obvious indication that his head had been crushed or anything.

I looked around, still expecting to see somebody coming. But there was no one.

I saw the other dog that had chased us, the bigger brown one. He was standing up the road a piece, snuffing at the ground.

Munger tapped me on the shoulder. He wanted me to check to see if I thought the little pup was alive.

I got down on a knee.

I didn't know, I couldn't tell. Maybe there actually was a little breath coming out.

But – maybe it was the breeze, or some sort of amplification of the breeze, through the ear holes of my helmet. Maybe I was only thinking it. The rocks and gravel were pressing against my knee. I told Munger I didn't know.

Finally it dawned on me. We could see if the pup's heart was still beating. That would let us know for sure.

I bent back down. I put my right hand around the little pup's ribcage. It was warm, even hot. Fit in my palm perfectly, a little smaller than a softball.

But I couldn't tell. It didn't seem like any heart beating. There was some kind of beating going on. But it seemed like it might be only my own blood, thumping through my hands. After a while, my thoughts of it got all mixed up. I couldn't tell anything from anything.

Munger tried. But he also couldn't say for sure. He said it was possible the pup was still alive, but the position he was in was preventing the heartbeat from getting through to us. Something to do with gravity and angles and the way blood flows in a body. But he didn't think it would be right to move the pup again, because that could injure him more, if he really was still alive.

I looked around. It had gotten late in the day. It was turning purple on one side of the road, and pink on the other. We got on our bikes and rode away.

2

In my last year of school I faced a vacancy in my apartment. A tall brown-freckled blond girl not long out of high school ended up moving in. Her last name was German and she worked in one of the clothing shops in town, trying to save money so she could enroll in the university. I met her for coffee and we agreed on it, shaking hands there in the café.

Her mother arrived with her the day she moved in. I helped carry in her trunk and boxes; her stacks of second-hand dresses; the plastic milk crates containing her music cassettes; these little cut-glass jars she had, filled with spices and incense and dried-up flower petals; and a two-foot plastic yellow wristwatch, which she immediately hung on the wall. There were also containers of various art supplies. The mother declared that her daughter loved to paint.

The mother and I sat in the kitchen talking over coffee. The mother had a frizzy, dried-out sort of look. Her eyes were watery, she sighed often. She'd probably been complaining the last couple years about how tired she was. I pictured her wearing a hair net to her work, at a bakery or shoe factory somewhere. Things would have happened. She would have relationships with a certain type of bleary older man. He would move in from time to time, then out. He would generally be traveling light. He would be the sort with a mustache or goatee, until the day he would shave it off, making him look like he'd just been released from prison. He'd always be turning up in a different used car; he'd continually be surrounded by used cars. He would talk about the cars, about the men he was trying to sell them to, the problems that were involved, various parts of the cars, mechanical difficulties.

An image flashed of the mother licking her lips in front of the television. The room was dark. In front of her was a water glass and a bottle of wine.

We talked. She tried to be skeptical about her daughter moving in with me. She made a point of asking a few questions: What town was I from, what subjects was I studying. Did I work, what were my "long-range" plans.

I did my best to reassure her. I told her I was rarely at home, and that when I was, I preferred quiet. I had to study a lot, I said, because I was behind and taking extra courses to catch up, which meant a lot of time at the library and computer labs. And yes – I had been working a part-time shift, taking cash at a parking lot downtown.

The mother left. The girl worked in her room, hanging her calendar, unloading her trunk, whatever else she did. I walked up to the store for a twelve-case of beer. The girl was giddy. By midnight I was asleep, naked on her sheets, sweating and exhausted after three ejaculations.

We carried on like that for some months. On the one hand, I appreciated what seemed to be my good fortune.

Even today, I continue to maintain she was essentially good. It was probably impossible for her to be anything else, at this juncture. She was a ripe and ready fruit, but like so many of them, bruised in spots. She had a clearing complexion and a bouncing energy, a gymnast's type of energy. She couldn't sit in one place for very long, but she never seemed to move very far. She was fixated on particular rock stars, mostly British.

She said one day that she'd had her "first date" on her thirteenth birthday. She smiled as she said it. She was vague. I remembered the girls like that from high school. How they had so suddenly slipped away from their existence as one of the girls, to assume a kind of mythic stature, draped in a mixture of longing, loathing and rumors of birth control. One day they would disappear from the school, never to be seen again. You might hear a story later about how they had wound up in Arizona.

In the sunlight from the window, her hair was nearly transparent. We spent sweltering afternoons in her room, the drone of news radio crackling on and on. Wars in Africa and floods in St. Louis, Tennessee tornadoes and the car wrecks of drivers from Gardena.

There were difficulties. I began to be troubled by some of her characteristics, which included drinking coffee from a cup the size of a small bowl. She was always making pasta dishes, which she would never throw out but leave sitting in the refrigerator, sometimes for a week or more.

We never went out together in public, and never once did I see her lay a brush on her paints. She had slender hips, a beautiful long back, hardly any breasts at all. I answered a great many questions, mostly of a technical, mechanical nature. Sometimes she smelled. She said it was infections and viruses, of the kind exclusive to women.

The end came quick. It was a combination, but mainly I felt things were getting too comfortable, too sit-on-the-couch. So fast it had happened – I didn't like that. Also, every time I looked at her I was seeing a bit more of the mother here and there. Nothing very specific, and maybe it's unfair to look at somebody that way – but I was seeing it.

There was yelling one afternoon and I walked out. I went to the park and sat a couple hours, talking and drinking 40-ounce bottles of beer with a few of the local bums. They told me a bunch of lies. One of them, for example, claimed to have had two consecutive wives from Yugoslavia. Both blonds. He said they had been great and jealous lovers, but neither would tolerate his socks on the floor. Neither. It was the funniest thing he'd ever heard of.

I returned to the apartment. Me and the girl had a talk, after which she proposed, in her way, to make things right. I let it happen, for a few minutes – but I was tired, I was fed up. I pushed her hand away. It upset her. She ran out, tears in her eyes.

A couple nights later I came home and found her sitting at the kitchen table. There was also a young man there, someone I'd never seen before. Lord, how I hated to see that. There was shouting. This was my house. A chair was pushed over. They left.

She took scissors to a few of my shirts and left them in a shredded pile on the floor. She scrawled a little note, leaving it beneath the shreds.

3

Munger had got his money saved and gone to Portugal, for at least a year, he said. I was living in a place newly carved into the hills, and had started work at a small establishment. Mary was a girl who also worked there. It started at one of these Saturday work parties. People standing around outside at the barbecue, then sitting around with the music inside as the beer dwindles and it gets dark. People starting to leave together in groups. Then there you are kissing this girl next to your car. You look around in the middle of it and the night is so fine and clear, so warm and tree-smelling. Here is this girl, laughing at everything you say. You get in your car and follow her over to her apartment.

Mary was Republican. She would talk about it, she was always talking about it. The internship she'd had in Washington a few years ago, something they were saying in the papers, the friend who had dated – or was still dating – a Congressman. Her brother who was hoping to join the FBI.

Mary. Oh, Mary.

I never took her to a restaurant or movie, we never went to a bar together. But she never applied sanction or guilt, she never flung it, she never made a mention. It was only all over her face – in the way she held it as if to say everything in the world was nothing if not always 100 percent completely fine.

At work, I rarely acknowledged her. There was plenty of talk already, those people didn't need anything added. I would maybe nod and say "hi" to her, that would be all, yet end up driving over to her house that night. Or she would call to ask if she could come over. If it was late enough, I would almost always say yes. My roommates would be in their rooms, meditating in front of their computers, working on their photography. If they happened to see her, I would play it off as some kind of crisis that needed my intervention. My roommates would always buy a story about a Republican girl with a crisis. I would tell them it also involved her Christianity.

But I don't think I've ever been in as bad a shape as when I would sit around at my apartment, wondering why Mary hadn't called for a few days, or sometimes as long as a week. And getting really frustrated the times it was only her answering machine that picked up when I dialed over to her place. If I called and she herself answered, I'd immediately hang up.

One Saturday morning, I just went over there. It was humid and overcast, the streets still black and wet. She was tentative and crisp toward me, but I convinced her to drive us out to the beach. I must admit, I was saying some funny things, and that had helped. I was badly hung over, there'd been next to no sleep, and you can say some pretty funny things to the right person when you're in that kind of shape.

We stopped at a gas station. I bought a newspaper, a styrofoam thing of coffee. Then we went out to the sand. Mary had a diet cola. We sat there in our jeans and our shoes off. I smoked one cigarette after the other, flipping through the paper and saying hardly anything, waiting for the worst of the shakes to pass. I could feel her staring at me, watching everything I did, but I don't think I looked her way for almost 40 minutes. She sighed, kept crossing and uncrossing her legs. Once she got up, put her feet in the water, and came back with some broken brown seashells. She said the water was cold. I giggled but didn't say anything.

I came to the racing forms. I started reading her off the names of some of the horses. It wasn't much funny, but Mary was laughing.

I leaned over and kissed her with a full cigarette mouth. I stuck in the tongue, wiggled it around. I pushed in extra saliva, breathing through my mouth. I wanted her to get all the cigarettes that she could.

She met me full on. She didn't back down. She grabbed me around the ear. She kissed me heavy, wrapped her mouth around my tongue and pulled it in. I rolled on top of her. I pressed the back of her head into the sand. I fell between her legs and kissed her on the beach.

My dick started to rise, my head started to pound. I was breathing hard, I was running out of air. Behind me I heard the roar of the surf. Ahead of me, cars whistled by on the highway. I went dizzy. Two boys walked by, one of them whipping a stick in the sand. I rolled off and had a laugh.

I led the way to the liquor store. I got a 12-case of cans, three large bottled beers, more cigarettes, a bag of salt and vinegar potato chips. We went out to the pier, past the restaurant and the line shop, out to the very end. I felt loose and sweaty walking out there. Black spots blipped on and off in my eyes.

Mary refused one of the large bottles but took sips from one of the cans. I started to drink. We sat on the wood stumps and talked. Fishermen were casting on both sides. Some of them left, new ones came to take their places. I finished the bottles and started on the cans. I jogged off to the restaurant to take pisses. Maybe I lectured her for a time, could have been about anything, but I don't think it went on too long. Then it was over and Mary was laughing again at what I was saying, looking at me in her way. I was always finding her staring at me, no matter where we were, no matter what I said. But the beer was good, the cigarettes tasty. I didn't mind.

I was standing against the pier railing and she crawled under my arms and kissed the corner of my mouth. Her breath was warm against my ear as she whispered. I kissed her for a while, lit a smoke, kissed her, took drags off the cigarette, kissed her, drank some beer, and kissed her again.

The sun was going down, we'd been there all day. Mary said she was getting cold, shouldn't we go. I said no, the sky was going pink, it was too beautiful to go.

A black guy and white guy couple were fishing near us. They'd come later in the day. They had beards and overcoats and a rusted old blue Coleman cooler. They may have been bums, I don't know. They saw us kissing and started in with some comments. We laughed and joked with them. I kind of shocked myself when I said we were in fact getting married. Mary didn't look at me when I said that, just nodded her head like it was true and laughed at the two guys. I looked at her standing there, jean fabric tight over her thighs, bare feet in low black heels.

The guys asked for spare smokes. I gave them out. I gave them beers. The black guy took out a fifth and passed it over. It was whiskey, third of the bottle left. I lipped from it and more went down than I meant to. The guy saw it. The look on his face said he wasn't happy, but he didn't say anything. Maybe he'd been saving it for later. I felt sort of bad about that. I passed them out more beer. Then the guys started telling stories, amazingly funny ones. We were laughing so much. I don't remember anything they said now, only it was so funny.

We were leaving. Mary was leading me by the hand. It was dark out now, except for the little pier bulbs that were hardly worth anything. I looked behind me and saw the two guys. They were next to my torn bag of booze. My newspaper was flapping in the wind. I was a little confused, but I just followed Mary.

We came past the restaurant toward the shore. I didn't see it start, but a fight had broken out in front of us. A muscley guy in a tank-top and tiny mustache, taking swipes at an old fat fisherman type who was much shorter. The younger guy hit the old guy twice in the side of the head, then once on the shoulder. The sound was these hard loud pops, which shocked and scared me. I started yelling for it to stop.

People were moving on all sides, murmurs and shouts. I pulled free of Mary and rolled into the two guys. I tried to grab the younger guy but couldn't get a hold. I glanced off him and fell to the wood planking. Something hit the back of my head, I don't know what.

Mary was helping me up. She grabbed my hand and we started running. We ran all the way to the street. We got to her car and drove to her apartment.

We went in. I fell on the couch. She brought me a glass of cold water from her bottle tank. I drank it. I got up and went to her fridge and pulled out a can of light beer. I heard Mary in the bathroom, putting a tape into her player. An English band, big a few years ago.

I took the beer into the bathroom and sat on the closed toilet seat. Mary was in her bra and panties. She helped me stand, took the beer from my hand, and lifted the shirt over my head. I flipped off my shoes and socks. She clipped up her hair behind her, first holding the clip in her mouth as she twisted her hair like a rope. The shower came on. I went in first. She went down on me as I stood, my ass shivering against the cold bathroom tiles, steam flowing around her head.

I went straight to the bed, still wet. Mary toweled and then came in. Her skin was soft, the softest I'd ever felt it. She rode me first, and kept riding until I'd gone soft and then hard again. And so I was hard again. I flipped her over. I had to work to make the third time happen. It was long strokes, then short stabbing ones, and sucking on her earrings, her hair, her neck. Finally it happened.

My chest was panging. I was thinking about a cigarette but didn't see myself getting up to find it. I'd given about everything. The back of my head was throbbing. I closed my eyes. Mary curled herself close. She started crying. I said what, what. It was woman problems. Some test they'd done which had had bad results, at least ones that weren't perfectly right. They were checking again, but possibly it was serious. In a worst case there might have to be an operation.

Mary cried and cried and then she stopped. Her tears were on my chest. She kissed me and rolled over, pressing her ass against me.

I held her, I held her. And I didn't know, I didn't know.

THE DIDDLING OF THE IMMENSITY

t was at one of the trashier class establishments, in one of the middling rungs of the upper downtown. He was there with a buddy. She had come with a number of friends.

Out in the night, bikers roamed yelling in dirty leather. A tassel of bums hacked each other with rusted shivs, rolled, spat, got up again. Under a coppery yellow streetlamp, a gang of sexually-active children assaulted a poor, haggard woman. She stumbled, collapsed and sighed in the alleyway. While on the other side of town, commando vans loaded with police in armor motored with steely professional determination, en route to a Neighborhood Watch meeting that had gotten out of hand.

Inside the classy trash establishment, they drank.

She was gorgeous, stunning. Tall, mid-twenties, blondish and stunning. Slender, slim, bronzed, delightfully svelte, and tall – her hair a golden gush of blondish-brown. Her face possessed the smooth lines of a calm and natural sensuality (if brokered, some said, by the merest hint of brutality that seemed certain to grow more pronounced with age). Even so, her cheeks were often quite pink. In the center of her face were lodged a pair of sumptuously carved and cleaned nostrils. And when she smiled, well. When she smiled her left cheek mole might wriggle; her jaw might jouncingly jut; her head might slightly cock; and something not unlike sunlight would pour through that throbbingly delightful carmine cavity. And her chalky dark blues, perhaps imbued with a suggestion of vulnerability, would shimmy and slash at whomever lay in the immediate vicinity.

It was said she'd been a swimmer in college.

She did no work that anyone could cite (rumor had long loosely linked her with a certain design institute), yet was able to live in a comfortable neutral area of the city – somewhat beyond the lower rungs, yet rather snug against the highly cosmopolitan homosexual district.

But it was really her beauty – ah, her beauty. She was the kind who provoked both sexes – men and women alike. She was ogled at, moaned after, despaired over in passing. Yet hers was not the beauty of skin-moisturizer adverts and network television alone. That wasn't enough anymore: not in these times; not in this town; not with this bunch. Indeed: She was apt to don the rare Ecuadorian beanie; the occasionally unexpected brown argyle; the suddenly appearing German high-collar; the vaguely unfashionable Vietnamese sandal.

Or, as on this night, the flimsy cloth summer floozy dress, which she'd snapped up for eight dollars at the refreshingly dilapidated K-Mart downtown.

None of this, however, obstructed the fact that her breasts sat up – they didn't stick out. Likewise, while her hips were rather wide, they didn't quite protrude. Her buttocks did, however – just slightly more than was perhaps too far. The twin insane globes of that device heaved, they quivered and juked. They jiggled and jimmied independently, but also in supernal, near preternatural concord.

Her legs ran long, while her ankles were virtually non-existent. What ankle there was had the curiously decadent and profound character of knots found in the stems of Hapsburgian champagne glasses.

She was no slouch in the intellectual arena, either. This was evident from even the slimmest swipe of conversation.

Dan said something to his buddy, Greg Hernandez. Greg nodded – and muttered something himself. Then he just went over there – Dan Bunn did. He moved himself next to the gorgeous woman.

She was positioned at the bar, sandwiched between a few friends – Edith and Shalamar and Peg, to be exact, and also her housemate Enrico, who professed to read only Asian babes. Enrico and Shalamar smoked platonically on light cigarettes. Shalamar's was a menthol.

Dan Bunn strode up. He ignored the rest. He honed in on the beauty. He went and straightaway plucked up the woman, even as she stood amid her percolating partisan throng.

Dan was like that. He had the confidence. It wasn't completely unearned. He was pretty tall himself, and on the lighter side of darkly complected. His face was slightly wider than was perchance the norm; chin was brief but firm, with an indentation the shape of a corn-nut in the center. His fingers were of average length, but of a somewhat abnormal thickness. His hair fell in controlled swoops to just above his shirt collar. His eyes hinted of grimly tender chestnuts, which nevertheless were wont to sparkle. He could play them well.

Dan focused in. Within seconds she'd spoken her name: "Janice."

"That's a pretty name," Dan Bunn said.

"Thank you."

Dan paid, unfumblingly, for a round of drinks. He hoisted a foaming beer to his lips. Janice smiled and lifted a goblette of lambent wine.

Dan gazed at Janice, grinned, spoke. Janice, glittering in the hazy neon dimness, bantered back. When the dialogue paused for no more than half a second, Dan looked around for his buddy Greg Hernandez. He saw with satisfaction that Greg was talking to Shalamar. Dan also caught Enrico's eye – or Enrico caught his – but only for a fraction of a second.

Dan returned to Janice. Leaning forward, she risked a further statement. Dan seized the opening to chance another observation of his own. Janice, her neck mildly pinkening, lifted her eyebrows. Dan chuckled, burped softly and glanced at his watch. He then said something that caused Janice to convulse with laughter. Dan, taking the cue, took the opportunity to convulse as well.

The dialogue was severely in motion. Dan liked the way Janice's mole wriggled when she smiled. Most girls – most women – didn't have such things on their faces.

*

The evening was at last drifting to pieces – disintegrating into a chaos of hugs and shouts. Everyone had languored into the region of the parking lot. The noise of speeding long-distance trucks, whipping nervily along the nearby interstate, could be discerned atop the eddying tides of fervid spring air.

Dan put his lips to Janice's unlipsticked mouth. He raced his hands over Janice's bare shoulders, over her bare arms. He brought his hands up and gently massaged her breasts. They were robust, resolute breasts of medium to medium-small size, smugly cosseted in a bra of gunmetal gray.

"Oh, God," Dan moaned. "Oh, babe."

"Oh Christ Jesus," Janice said softly, whisperedly. She licked a single stroke against Dan's underlip.

"Come here," Dan said, huskily.

He grabbed Janice by the hand and maneuvered her among the cars. He pressed her against the rear wheel hub and trunk of a rusting and pitted yellow Mustang. He threw his face against hers. He plunged his right hand under her flimsy red skirt, pawing at the top of her legs. Janice loosened her hips just enough to let Dan slip two hot fingers between her thighs.

"No, Dan, no. Not now," Janice said weakly. She squirmed briefly and tried to bring her thighs close together. Her lightly mascaraed eyelashes fluttered.

Dan panted, scampering his lips along Janice's neck. His right hand worked frenziedly, but Janice had locked her hips and he made little headway. He brought the hand up, scraped it against her breasts, then returned it to the panties. One finger crawled over the elastic edge of the panty rim, tested the intensity of the tension, then withdrew. His left hand squeezed a vealish chunk of Janice's upper thigh.

At that point Shalamar yelled.

She and some of the others were standing on the sidewalk, about 30 yards away.

"C'mon, you guys!" Shalamar shrieked. "This is no time for playing hide the soup spoon!"

Soup spoon?

That stupid girl, thought Dan – yelling out in the street like that. He heard Greg Hernandez laugh drunkenly. Enrico and Peg tittered.

Dan Bunn hesitated. By the time his pause was complete, Janice had slipped from his grasp. She was out of his reach, smoothing down the flimsy floozy dress.

"Oh, God," said Dan, rushing his fingers through his hair. "Oh, God. Let's go somewhere. Now. My place maybe, yeah?"

Janice laughed but said nothing. Launching a brief smile into the night sky, she turned and scurried toward the others. Dan, flush with exhilaration, moved after her.

*

Dan was standing, thinking. His mind touched briefly on the pair of special-frame sunglasses he'd purchased at the new sunglasses store. It grazed over the braided shoelaces he'd recently installed in his burgundy wing-tips. It glanced over the texture of the roasted sunflower seeds that had dotted his lunchtime salad. And next, for the 888th time that day, his mind feasted a blinding few seconds on Janice. In his mind's eye, Dan had frankly seen himself crawling under Janice's warm naked body – his tongue groping and stabbing, groping and stabbing, wherever and whenever it saw fit. And that was pretty frequently. Janice's tongue appeared again, flashing wetly in the darkness, in the navel vicinity of Dan's nearly hairless belly...

"Yes, that's right, Bob," Dan found himself saying all of a sudden. "It *is* a kind of intelligent gel. An intelligent plastic, if you will."

Dan was at the chemicals company. He surveyed the members of the Investors Group Associates (IGA) conference. A ruddy-faced balding man raised a hand. Dan eyed his seating chart.

"Yes, Richard Stevens?"

"Dan, I'm impressed with your work – quite impressed, actually, kudos to you – but when can we expect to see the first wide-scale commercial application? Realistically, how far away are we?"

"Good question," said Dan. "Perfect. I'm glad you asked."

Dan reached under the wooden, sharp-cornered table and grinned. He winced, licked his lips, and brought out into the open a sleek, glinting blue roller-skate of fine engineering. A built-in stand was attached to the appliance. Dan set it upright on the table.

"This prototype model is, as we speak, being test-purveyed at a number of retail institutions," said Dan. "East coast – Boston, New York, Connecticut, Miami, that region. Just shipped from the factory at the start of the month, I believe. Totally legal-vetted and regulatory-cleared. It's got the gel right here in the ankle. Responds, as you know, to the body's natural heat to make a full conformed fit. Your chip is located right here in the front of the toe, nobody knows a thing… and off you go."

Dan spun a wheel. The men murmured.

"But gentlemen," Dan continued, "the thing to remember is: This is just one of the potential applications. This is a *roller skate* – a thing with wheels that one puts on one's foot. I ask you, respectfully, to think about that fact carefully. The truth is, we're only at the top-most tip of the proverbial iceberg. I think you'd agree the potential licensing options/opportunities are darn near boggling."

The men murmured. Dan swiveled and snatched a folder from a white and beige stack two feet high.

"Gentlemen, we've compiled some technical-research data for you and your lab folks. On page fourteen, I believe, you'll find the composites framework, followed in succession by the application index, estimate portfolio, cladding/coating funicular, regional matrix, liability extract and facility redux…"

*

Later, work was over. Dan went to Greg Hernandez's apartment. Greg was spread out on the couch, watching a video on his home computer.

"Did you bang that chick yet?" Greg asked, staring at the screen.

"What chick?"

"You know, whatever her name is."

"Oh, Janice. Yeah, I banged her."

"I thought you would."

The video showed a naked brown woman with black hair, an archipelago of gold and jade hanging from her neck, situated on all fours upon a platform in the center of what appeared to be a warehouse or auditorium. Dozens of naked men of all races and creeds, some still wearing socks, queued around her. A few did excitable calisthenics-type moves, while most of the rest stood blank and slump-shouldered, apparently dazed as they stared at the stage action. The film showed the men pulling and squeezing at implements of diverse pigmentation and structure, sometimes helped along by lips belonging to the members of a small crew of friendly, tired-looking bikini-clad aides.

The camera went close-up on a red digital counter: *56... 57... 58... 59...* Time was up. Four or five fellows who had been variously entering the woman were led away by a team of men in white T-shirts and green ball caps. One team member ran up to the woman and, using a yellow sponge, wiped her shiny, unsagging buttock cheeks. The movie cut to a shot of the woman smiling. Vim and hearty, her eyes somewhat low-lidded, she flicked her tongue between her lips, rolled her eyes, brought the tongue out again. She flashed another huge grin. Her breasts, filled with cellophane, tumbled in a controlled jumble between her elbows.

Five or six fresh naked men stepped forward and took position. The camera cut to a slick floor littered with slack glistening condoms and torn condom-wrappers. Good promo for the condom companies.

"Is this real?" asked Dan Bunn.

"Yeah, you bet," said Greg. "C'mon, it's on the internet. New World's Record. Hooray."

"Hip, hip hooray," said Dan.

Greg gulped from his beer, then put the beer down. He cleared his throat and said, "So when?"

"When what?"

"When did you bang her?"

"Who?"

"The Janice chick."

"Oh, yeah. After we went out last week."

"Where'd you go?"

"Took her to that Italian place, you know the one. Then we went back over to her place. Did it there." Dan nipped from his beer.

"Nice apartment?"

"Yeah," said Dan, shrugging. "I guess it was all right. Not too shabby."

"Yeah, probably. She suck you?"

"You know it, bro."

"You shoot off in her mouth? She swallow?"

"Yeah," said Dan. "I mean, I think so. I tried to. She went to the bathroom right after."

"That's cool," said Greg, lifting his bottle. "What about the gay guy?"

"The roommate guy?"

"Yeah, him."

"He was around when I went over there. Then he disappeared somewhere. Probably some gay thing."

"Yeah, probably," said Greg.

They sat and drank a while. It got dark. The beer ran out. Dan went home.

*

Dan Bunn strolled through the downtown business district. It was the early evening. Cars sped, people walked, joggers suffered. Dan walked, thinking about not very much at all.

He was tired but a good ways from exhausted; he was perhaps a shade indolent, but far from shiftless. A brisk, balanced economy, consisting of a splendid affability and an ecumenical imperturbability, attended his mindset. Work was over for the day, after all. It was over. Already he could hardly remember what had gone on.

Dan walked. His gait was sure and forward and contained a slight rocking motion, making it half a quiver short of a swagger, four-fifths of a full strut. A blast of faintly sulfurous city breeze ruffled his hair. It swept a wad of yellow newspaper across the plaza and into a swollen, sleeping bum. It lofted a child's shout far down the colorfully pullulating boulevard. Dan looked up at the glinting pandemonium of skyscrapers that encircled him. Whippets of breeze flayed and flared his eyelashes.

A truck painted in the blue and yellow striping of a well-known wafer company hustled down the broad avenue, its clutch grinding with a slight diffidence. Dan observed the vehicle and was reminded of his friend Greg Hernandez. Hadn't, Dan wondered, Greg once worked for the corporation that controlled that particular company? Indeed, perhaps Greg still worked there – now, today, at this moment.

Greg Hernandez, of course, continued to "temp" – often for computer companies, sometimes food conglomerates, and sometimes, for frugal weeks at a time, for no one at all. He'd been doing it for about three years now. While Greg often remarked that he "liked it," the young man also maintained an official policy of alertness for "a good full-time position." Over the years a couple jobs had looked possibly promising – but nothing had ever quite converted into a permanent placement with benefits.

Jeez, Dan mused, nobody'd ever offered Greg a full plate. It was a pity, really, a darn shame. To think of it happening in the strongest and richest and most spectacular nation in the world – in the history of the world. In the gobstobbingest bad-assed nuclear mutha of them all. To his good friend, Greg Hernandez.

Dan forced bursts of air from between tightly held lips, causing a phtupt-phtupt sound.

Well, thought Dan, but Greg was all right – really all right. Heart of gold, that guy, and funny as hell. No, Greg would do fine, in the end, Dan decided. It would all work out. It always did – most of the time. Shoot, Greg had even been hanging out with that girlfriend of Janice's, Shalamar. A cute little one she was, Shalamar – small but busty, compact and squeezable, that type. Yeah, hell, thought Dan – it would all work out for Greg Hernandez. Eventually – sooner or later. It always did, for most – for many people. More or less, to some extent.

Dan passed out of downtown and into the first of the outer regions. Flat-eyed youths coasted on bicycles and skateboards, maintained security around trashcans and dumpsters. Dogs sniffed; cats shrugged; men pushed shopping carts stuffed with rags, cans and hangers. Inside overheated cafes, slow-moving kitchen workers spread aging tuna salad across recently toasted bagels. Young fellows in expensively ironed t-shirts huddled together silently, punching buttons on individual mobile phones.

The declining light fired the buildings and hardened the shadows. The blues seemed very blue, the tans and browns lustrous. It was as though all the sun that had been soaked up during the day had risen to the surface and was now seeping back into the air. Lights began to burn in apartment windows, radio sambas traipsed into the avenues on tin feet. The smell of cooked food wandered out, fast-food together with prickly ethnic herbs, everything mixing with bus exhaust. The buses honked. Some of the cars went too fast around corners, screeching their tires as they went.

Dan saw a girl, a group of girls, near the corner. They were standing next to a beat-up low sedan that had dirty white primer smeared on its front end. Older guys were in the car – a goateed fellow up front, backward ball caps in the back, a murky tattoo on a bicep out the window. Dan looked at the girls. Cut-off shorts and tights snaking up their asses, chunks of bare ass and leg hanging out. Not a bra on a one, it seemed. Tits sticking out like that.

*

Dan moved on into a particularly neutral area of the city and knocked on Janice's door. Her housemate, Enrico, answered. Dan handled it well, he always did. "Gay guys" didn't bother him. In fact, when he thought about it, which wasn't all that often, he rather admired them. For one, they dressed well, generally, and their level of education and income was high, collectively. Indeed, it seemed that overall there was less to "worry about" with gays than with the rest of the population. Because gays were good citizens, good people, caring people, and solid voters. Dan had read articles.

Janice appeared. She wore a pure lime mini with low black heels. Dan glimpsed the outline of her underwear elastic embossed upon the dress. In a lightning spasm, his eyes tracked the entirety of her legs – from the acme of her hip-waist combine down to her epicurean and delicately crafted ankles. He looked into her face. Her eyes were radiant, her lips seemed to have been recently moistened. Her arms were slender and bare, but for a silver, intricately-notched Honduran bracelet dangling sweetly over the petite and insolent knob of her left wrist.

She smelled, too. The way she smelled – it was so fresh. A definite freshness, yet of the hovering and elusive kind. There was absolutely no telling if it was a commercial scent or something divinely her own, something preciously primal, perhaps inculcated from the ocean aeons ago.

Dan handled it well. He did these things well. He didn't think about it, it came naturally. Almost reflexively he grew a quick briar of repartee; fabulated a fuscia bursting with bonhomie; puffed off a patch of pun-based by-products. Janice and Enrico laughed, effortlessly and seemingly quite genuinely. Because Dan had the timing.

Dan grabbed Janice by the arm. They bid Enrico ciao. Adieu. They were off to an Italian restaurant.

The place was called Tony Zack's. They sat in the immense trellised Main Room, beneath a giant pearly flower of a chandelier made of molded plastic and steel fittings. The restaurant specialized in wilted radicchio and sage, honey-balsam calamari, California chicken and oyster linguini. Crusty bread came with each table. The waiters wore black pants and pleated shirts. Combined, these things were enough to make Tony Zack's, located adjacent to the downtown sector proper, crowded almost every night. Dan had made the reservations a day in advance.

Janice had the sautéed tilapia with caper berries, fergola, arugula and hazelnuts, while Dan had opted for a grilled filet on Sicilian potato cake, with Sardinia peppers, cauliflower sauce, chick peas and, uh, parmesan polenta. The waiters whisked the mess away briskly, and what crusty bread crumbs they hadn't whisked, Dan had – with swift kicks of his forefinger while Janice used the restroom. Dan had talked some about his work, and Janice had talked some about her family. "Dad" was an orthopedist or orthodontist, while an older brother was posted with The Foreign Service – Guatemala or Guangdong.

A waiter cantered by. Dan signaled. Another bottle of wine? he queried of Janice, hopefully. She blushed triflingly. No, she'd had enough for now, thank you. How about dessert then? Well, maybe a little – but not a whole one for herself. Ice cream? Dan nodded to the waiter. They would split a peach-lemon sorbet.

Well, and so they dined. The dialogue ensued apace. Intimacies were revealed, a certain rapport established. Inevitably, the discussion veered toward sex.

"Me too, I've always enjoyed sex," Janice Ungmann said. What seemed to be the pinkest part of her tongue moved between her teeth – only to vanish as though it had never existed. Her chalky blues glistered.

"It's so… *natural*. You know?"

"I know," said Dan. "I *know* it is. That's what makes it so… *great*. It's totally natural. You know?"

"I *know!*"

Dan studied her with an intent, really-wanting-to-know-you gaze. He asked questions, supplied a quantity of personal data, laughed apparently shyly, asked more questions. Janice replied, often mercurially and frequently with dexterous humor.

"No, really," Janice said, her lips curving into a perfectly symmetrical smile. "Don't get the wrong idea or anything. I'm a nice girl. I really am. I like kissing and petting, foreplay and doggie-style, all that stuff. I mean, that is, unless you got a couple of whips and rods handy, some handcuffs and a blindfold, hot wax and a mature donkey…"

Janice let out a whunt of laughter. Her tongue flourished brazenly into the open – before making a thrilling retreat nearly as fast as it had sprung. She swept her tongue along the entirety of her upper lip. A fresh frosting of pink seemed to re-tinge the tans of her face and neck. She regarded Dan with a pleasant and puissant acuity.

Dan forced himself back into the linguistic volley. His mind groped for something appropriate to say – or better yet, something just the right bit inappropriate. He came very near a few such things, but all he could muster was a tight, quick smile. An awkward half-second it lasted – until Dan caught up and put some solid chin in it.

Under the table, Janice's knee shot forward. It caught Dan on the inside of a thigh.

"Sorry," she said.

"No problem," said Dan.

They paid – or rather, Dan did – nodded in unison to a graciously bowing and tuxedoed Tony Zack, and left the restaurant. Standing on the walk, they simultaneously offered each other the privacy to check their phones for messages – a good sign. Dan, thinking about whether he should suggest they see some jazz, hailed a taxi.

*

Dan set his tumbler of pulpy cider on the coffee table. They were in Janice's wineless apartment, which at this hour smelled faintly of pollen and hollandaise sauce.

The dialogue, post-jazz, had been continuing apace.

Dan Bunn lifted a forefinger and switched off the porticoed end table lamp.

"What are you doing?"

Janice's voice was not the least bit curious.

"Come here," Dan said, striding toward her through the dimness.

He swept up Janice's hand. He led her out the open sliding glass to the balcony. The city lights were strewn, xanthic and twinkly.

Tufts of warm ocean breeze attacked from the left, right and center, whirling up Janice's skirt even with her panty line. Above, clouds swirled and seethed, mixing and mutating in inscrutable patterns. Dead leaves skidded and scratched along the pavement in ineluctable harmonies. Trees flapped, heaving and shaking their branches.

Dan grabbed Janice at the waist with both hands. He stuck his mouth to hers. She drew in her breath suddenly; tightened her mouth; and loosened it as Dan's tongue entered. Her lips slackened; then firmed. Dan worked his way in. Their tongues probed, tasted, discerned texture, pulled back. The tongues rushed forward once more.

Dan pressed Janice against the railing. His left hand caressed her midsection, pressed against the restraining bodice of her bra, wandered amongst the snugly bunched breast tops. His right hand climbed purposefully around Janice's neck, his fingers trawling through her soft honey-brown.

The sky flickered. Over the ocean, a low rumbling gave forth, spreading delibly across the city. The winds quickened yet again. Tree branches banged. Leaves skittered and fled.

Dan closed his eyes and wove deep his tongue; he brought it out; he licked the space between Janice's upper lip and nose; the space between her chin and lower lips. Janice thrust herself into him, her thigh roughly massaging his testicles.

"Jesus," she whispered. "Christ Jesus, I'm wet. I am so goddamned *wet*."

"You're a dirty bitch," Dan panted. "Whore."

Dan nailed the timing. God, he did enjoy saying that. Every time he had the chance. It didn't seem totally right to him, not totally – but no woman had ever complained. Why should they? That's how it was these days. They liked the dirty talk – apparently, they liked being called bitches and whores. It made them feel all sexy and hot. At least during sex it did. Timing was everything. Outside the bed, say in an office or restaurant – probably not so much. You might even get sued. Hell if Dan knew why. But it had been announced in all the female magazines. *Go ahead, try it*, they said – *when you're chowin' down on your man.*

And Dan supposed so.

Dan shoved Janice against the railing, pressing himself between her thighs. Janice gasped. Dan gnawed and sucked at her chin.

Thunder boomed over the city. Electric discharges danced unseen through the air. A penetrating smell stung at the nostrils. The boomlets recoiled. Then Dan felt the wetness. A drop, three drops, on his wrist, which lay against the back of Janice's head. A flurry of wet pellets shattered against Janice's left shoulder, broaching the lime fabric, re-depositing themselves in new configurations on her skin.

"Let's go in," Janice whispered, her mouth ashine with saliva.

"No," said Dan, breathing through his nose. "No… Okay."

She led him back through the sliding glass, into the darkened sitting room. Dan grabbed her lower hips from behind. He tumbled them both to the couch, which was clumped with numerous cherry and walnut-toned pillows. He climbed atop her and rejoined their mouths.

After a moment, Dan Bunn felt Janice Ungmann's fingers slip over his pants waist. Her hand writhed inside Dan's grey-brown slacks. Her fingers snapped and dived within the heated confine, narrowly missing contact with Dan's emboldened, outstretched member, which lay wretchedly against his thigh, strapped down by a swaddling of cotton brief. Dan lunged himself upward and forward. But still the hand failed to make contact.

Dan roistered miserably. He groaned and brought a hand to Janice's chest. The hand flapped madly at her breasts, pulling and manipulating, struggling vainly to free the pliable, delectable items from their meshy lime carapace.

Janice squirmed. "Oh, God," she said, and moaned.

Contorting and swiveling himself violently, one knee and then the other landing against the carpet, Dan succeeded in maneuvering his mouth to the crotch of Janice's silken peach-colored panties. Dan sucked for a time, through the fabric, his tongue poking about wildly. He was buffeted by Janice's heat, the scent of her – the vaguely vanilla, variously oniony taste of her through the panty fabric. His tongue knocked against the insides of her thighs. Her hips began to buckle and refract, to gently and rhythmically contract. Dan felt Janice's fingers against his eyebrow, against his forehead. He looked up. She was calling him. He lifted himself and scrambled forward.

"Lay back," Janice commanded.

Dan did. He lay back. Within seconds a metallic ring resounded – a certain *ping* it was, discernable above the furious din of the fandangoing winds, the retching trees, the falling rain outside the window.

His belt buckle.

Janice's hands seeped through Dan's underwear – and brought him into the clear at last.

However, her labors were preciously brief. Dan felt her pressure cease.

"Just a minute," her voice said.

A particular warmth and a peculiar affection, along with a slight dollop of lightness, cloaked her tone. She rose. Dan heard the gentle, stylish patter of her footsteps. In the hall, a light went on. A door shut.

Oh, Dan thought – *of course*. She's gone to get a condom.

Dan Bunn lay there, considering the option. He listened to the per-plap of the rain – he listened for Janice. A thin layer of perplexion fell upon him, followed by a more substantial coating of befuddlement. At last he found himself enclosed in a jelly-like nimbus of bewilderment.

Several minutes elapsed. Dan had begun to slump. He blinked several times in rapid succession, trying to pick out and identify objects in the room. He interpreted the outline of the mahogany roll-top desk, the curls and pouts of the hanging rhododendron against the sliding glass.

Janice did not return.

Dan sat up on the couch. He looked down the hall and saw light leaking out from one of the doorways. He clasped the top of his trousers. With gruesomely tender steps, he began to walk down the hall.

He came to the door with the light coming out from under. Dan knew – it was the bathroom. Ah, she was undressing, yes. And doing girl things. Dan smiled.

He continued down the hall. He stopped in an open doorway. In the dimness he saw a bed. He ducked in and slipped off his shoes. He tore off his shirt, slithered out of his trousers, and sat on the edge of the bed. He sagged. A water bed. He giggled and slipped out of his briefs. He lifted the covers and wormed underneath. The covers smelled newly washed – a springy, blossomy scent.

Dan lay back on the pillows and waited. A wide, blissful smile elaborated itself upon his face. The length of tender flesh that was his penis throbbed.

*

Dan Bunn was at his desk at work. He'd returned from lunch and was due for a meeting with Mr. Rudikoff, the elderly co-founder of the company.

His desk phone beeped. It was Rudikoff's executive secretary, Elaine. He was to go see the old man immediately.

Dan floated down the brown-carpeted hall. He entered the corporate chief's chamber.

"Good morning, Dan. Have a seat, if you would."

"Yes, sir," Dan said, moving toward one of the dark chocolate leather chairs.

Rudikoff appeared grim, irritated. Perhaps agitated. The old man picked up a sheaf of printed papers and straightened them with an impatient rustling. He beheld Dan Bunn with unblinking sanguinary eyes. Dull window light glinted off Rudikoff's lined but tanned forehead. A cloistered armada of skyscrapers shot up sleekly and greyly behind him.

"Now, Dan," he began, "we try to run a pretty above-board conglomerate here. I don't need to tell you that – you're already well aware of it. And I've got nearly, what is it" – he looked at his watch – "nearly 35 years of my life invested in this corporation. As you well know, I was here at the very beginning with Dr. Sanderford. Do you know what that's like, Dan? Thirty-four-plus years in the chemical plastics adhesives business?"

Dan started to speak. "I, uhn – "

The older man cut him off. The executive's voice was heated and pitched.

"Save it, Dan. Seriously, just save it."

Dan inhaled sharply. Rudikoff glowered.

"You haven't even been alive 35 years, so just save it. Hell, Dan, your daddy probably barely even knew what a pussy was 35 years ago – let alone think about putting his four-point-two inches inside your mommy. God bless her."

Rudikoff crossed himself quickly. He sank his eyes once more into Dan.

"Thirty-five years," Rudikoff continued. "An awful lot of blood and gristle goes into 35 years, Dan. A lot of putting yourself on the line and building up a reputation. Any idea what that's like? You don't go from nothing to a high-ass listing on The New York Stock Exchange for nothing. You got to keep your heart hard and your cock clean, don't you? Your nose clean. And Dan, we're on that New York exchange. We're up there. And Dan – you don't get high-ass classified government clearances – crissakes, man, I've got a security clearance that can take me straight into the White House lobby at a moment's notice. Crissakes, half the government spooks themselves aren't supposed to know the things we're supposed to. And let me tell you – that's not beans on toast, young man. That's not shit on a plate."

Rudikoff clapped his hands down on his desk. His jaw shot forward.

"Young man, are you listening?"

"Y-yes," said Dan. "Of course, sir."

"So perhaps, Dan, you can understand my concern when I see this – " Rudikoff knocked the sheaf of papers " – when I have to put my eyes on something like this report, let me tell you, boy, it is really something."

Rudikoff gave a slow wag of his head. "You, one of our finest employees. You. We believed in you, Dan. We were almost ready to hand the keys to the place over to you. We were preparing to hand them straight over to you one day. You were the guy, Dan. None other than."

Rudikoff shook his head again. It was a sad shake.

Dan looked at his boss, struggling to control the suddenly unbearable twitching of his nose and lips. His mind strained to decipher what Rudikoff was talking about. But he could think of nothing. Unless –

Rudikoff re-straightened the papers. He cleared his throat and began:

"On the evening of April –, a one Daniel Walter Bunn was observed in the dwelling of a one Enrico Eugene Cowen, a known and confirmed homosexual. After loitering with a one Janice Michelle Ungmann, a young Caucasoid female, in the sitting room and balcony of the residence, Mr. Bunn was observed undressing to the point of nudity. He then entered the bed of the aforementioned Mr. Cowen. Shortly thereafter, Mr. Cowen emerged from the bathroom wearing a white terry cloth bathrobe. Mr. Cowen entered the bedroom, removed the bathrobe, and joined Mr. Bunn in the bed. The two men began a conversation, at which point Ms. Ungmann, entered the bedroom. After a brief discussion, Ms. Ungmann joined the two men in the bed. She proceeded to remove her clothing, including undergarments. The three individuals including Mr. Bunn then proceeded to roll around upon the bed together for nearly fourteen minutes. Mr. Cowen was witnessed using Ms. Ungmann's genital undergarment to restrict her from speaking, while Mr. Bunn was seen in apparent flagrant violation of her genital/anal precinct. Use of even minimal prophylactic prevention to guard against disease and female impregnation was not detected. Mr. Bunn and Mr. Cowen were then violated orally and internally, by each other, while Ms. Ungmann, still gagged with her own undergarment, was witnessed violating Mr. Bunn with a purple object of an estimated plastic origin. Use of prophylactic prevention was not detected. Soon thereafter, Mr. Bunn exited the bed, reapplied his clothing, and exited the apartment house."

Rudikoff glared.

Dan Bunn said, "But wait – "

Rudikoff cut him off savagely, clapping his hands down on the desk.

"No, sir," the business chief said, his eyes boring into Dan Bunn. "Just no. Not today, sir. In no way."

Rudikoff held up a page of the report and crushed it in a palm. He tossed the wad toward a cheap circular trash bin. The wad hit the rim, bounced, caught the rim again, then rode about halfway around the circular ridge before plunging and disappearing from view.

"Let me explain, Mr. Bunn. This is via satellite – a paid-for top-dollar certified security-technical assessment. Do you *understand*, Mr. Bunn? Crissakes, Dan, pay attention for once. This isn't some game – it's the so-called real world, my friend. They got triplicate copies, photo, video, whatever the hell it is, and they are prepared to provide that to us… Should it come to that. And I sincerely hope it never does. I never want to have to lay my eyes on something like that. Let alone bear the responsibility for bringing it into a civil court of law."

Both men looked down. Neither said anything.

At last Rudikoff spoke. His words contained a meditative, reflective quality.

"I'm sorry, Dan. But being sorry doesn't change a damn stupid thing, does it. I've got to do what I've got to – to do what I've got to do. A person in my shoes just can't ignore it. Too many people know by now. The board would never sanction it."

"Listen to me, Dan," Rudikoff continued. "We are prepared to give you a fairly generous severance package, which will include the first six months of your therapy costs. Then we'll seal the documents forever. That will be the end of it. You can get the help you need, we can move on, and no one else will ever know. I personally guarantee it. You've got my word on it."

"But – "

"Dan – *just no.*"

Rudikoff's words shot forth in a rasping whisper-growl. The corporate leader stared, his dry, milky brown eyes locked on Dan Bunn.

"Dan," he continued after a long pause, "now you listen to me, and I mean it. My very serious advice is: Take this deal. Do yourself a favor and take it. You drag us into court; you want to be a funny guy; you want to fight it – crissakes, man, we'll have so many attorneys down your pants you won't know what hand you pick your nose with. And that's not happy stuff. We'll bring in the reporters from all the big papers and TV. Mainstream media, helicopters, internet, the whole damn crazy works. It'll happen so fast your head will fuck-friggin' spin. We can get it done – believe you me, son. We've got the people. We've got the resources. We've got the machinery. We can make it happen."

Dan was speechless.

"Here," Rudikoff said. "The paperwork's all ready already. I would advise you to sign it. I think it's your best shot. Sign and you've got a good chance of getting a fresh start. Anybody calls us, we'll say you worked here, you were competent, you left on your own volition. That's what the paperwork says. All voluntary. You'll be able to get another job when this is over, somewhere. I really think so, Dan."

Dan realized Rudikoff was holding out a pen. He rose from the chair, took the writing instrument between his fingers, and shakily signed his name.

"Fine, Dan, fine," Rudikoff said. He sighed, inhaled tartly, and licked his upper lip.

"Now go to lunch. You've already had lunch? Go again. Go out and get yourself a nice hot bowl of chili, two scoops, you'll need it. I'll have the secretary make your copies. You come back, clear out your desk, and that'll be the last of you. I'm sorry it had to come to this, but a man in my position – well, perhaps you understand?"

"Okay," was all Dan could muster. His voice was thick. His eyelids batted uncontrollably…

*

The phone buzzed. Dan shook his head, blinked, shook his head once more and picked up the line. It was Rudikoff's executive secretary, Elaine. Rudikoff was ready to see him. He rose and entered the corporate captain's chamber.

"Dan, my man, nice to see you," Rudikoff said, smiling.

The old man stood from his leather swivel chair and gave Dan a taut but lingering handshake. Behind him, out the wall-sized window, the city sat bristling and majestic in the wan afternoon sun.

"And you, sir."

"Indeed." Rudikoff grinned warmly and leaned forward. "Indeed, indeed. Well, well. I won't take too much of your time.

How does a nice performance bonus sound? To the tune of about 50,000 U.S.D.A.-certified greenbacks?"

Dan gasped. He softly gasped.

"How about stock options?" Rudikoff went on. "Feel like any? How about unlimited stock options to the extent the federal law allows? How does that sound? That's not chicken-fried steak by the pound, now is it? That's not ham and Hawaii pizza, I don't think."

Dan's mouth hung open.

"Actually," Rudikoff said, "forget how it sounds. In fact, fuck it. Fuck it all, young Dan, that's what I say. It's yours. The cash has already been transferred to your account. Nothing you can say about it. Everything's already been cleared by the bozos in accounting and the personnel goons. You're out of the loop, my friend."

Rudikoff leaned back and laughed.

"Excuse me, but are you serious?" asked Dan.

"Serious my ass," Rudikoff said, letting out a fresh yowl of laughter. "Ha, shit-dippy I'm serious. Our stock's gone out the roof the past year, and it's thanks to guys like you, Dan. You're out there meeting the folks, aren't you? You're the one pressing the flesh, as they say – if you get my meaning. My drift."

Rudikoff chuckled. "Anyway, the fact remains, our stock just keeps going up and up – *up-up-up-up!* And there's no sign of it coming down, maybe not ever. That's what the jerks tell me – not the way the world is now, the line were in – this *stuff* we do. Don't ask, don't tell – ha ha, get it? Do you get it? Ha! Dan, do you *get it?* Ha ha!"

Rudikoff leaned back and let out another blurf of laughing. "Doesn't it feel great to be rich! Shit-dippy it does!"

Dan swallowed. "Gosh, I don't know what to say. Thank you, I guess."

"Don't say nothin,' Dan." Rudikoff's face was reddening now. "Just keep doing your little bit to make us a big old smelly old mess of old messy mess money. In fact, take the rest of the afternoon off. I insist. What's a good young man like you doing around here anyway? Go out there and get yourself a nice slice of clean pink pussy, Dan. Crissakes – go get a nice slice of pussy! Already got a nice slice? Hell, then go buy *her* a nice slice!"

Rudikoff cackled. "Pussy for everyone! *This is the goddamn free world!*"

Dan sat there. He wasn't sure what to do. He thought he should probably do as he was told.

Rudikoff, laughing, began to cough. Dan, breathing heavily through his nose, got up and walked out.

*

Dan went home and ate half a can of low-sodium chili. He called Janice Ungmann's phone and set up an appointment for later. He then went over to Greg Hernandez's.

The young men sat in straight-backed chairs, looking into Greg's home computer set-up. The computer was hooked on to the internet.

They watched the computer. It whirred and clicked, hummed and banged.

THE BLUES GUITARISTS
HAVE BEEN CRUCIFIED

I will tell you, there was no more "getting it." We understood already, we had got it a long time ago. Why we were where we were. The hell, it was no place for people. It never is, shouldn't be, will never be… and if there is a God, and if, and only if…

There we were.

Cal had a job. As brilliant and beautiful as she was, it should go almost without saying that her work involved drunks, rapists, sodomites, thieves, degenerates, suspects and little bad boys who couldn't keep their pee-pees in their pockets or pay their gas bills. It was shelter work, "social" work for the unsocial, an after-the-fact place set up and left to hang on by some dead man. The state university had trained her for it, and she liked it as much as anyone could and probably a little more. And they paid her about two bucks. It wasn't enough.

I didn't and still don't know how good she was at it. I don't know if you can ever really know in this line. But in any case, now she'd taken the test, and done pretty good on it, and met the people, and shaken what she thought were the right hands – and maybe, maybe, The Government was now going to hire her.

Yeah, all right: A step into the big time – in this "industry." It would mean something like $34,608.42 per year, before taxes, after "benefits." Not a lot of cash, to some folks, and hardly any, when you take a square look at the world and add it all up. But yet, to us… ah, I say to you. It would mean a little air, wouldn't it. Some water, probably. Not a small amount of dirt. And I didn't know or care about any fire – it was already pretty hot around here, and not just because of the heat.

She was supposed to find out on Friday.

Me, I needed a job. I needed it bad. I needed it real bad. It had been so long, too long, but no one was going along. Not the agencies. Not the personnel-people. Not a single expert from Human Resources. Nobody like that.

The company people looked at me wrong, and that was wrong. I don't know, maybe I really didn't get it, but I don't think so. Still, I guess I didn't understand. I mean, I couldn't quite figure it. I was smart. I was all right looking.

The hell, I was the smartest. I was incredibly good looking. I could stand and talk and move my hands. I could do all these together at once. I could sit and stare. No, and it wasn't "the economy." The economy was going bang. Bang-bang it was going. Historic highs and lows, stocks punching the ceiling, "economic expansion" yimmie-yimmie. You couldn't take two breaths without somebody announcing how bang-boom it all was. No, and it wasn't the war. There was no war. Only warlords. Only "conflicts." Only terror. Only madmen.

Yeah.

Okay, they were bastards, cruel and unusual and stupid. Or maybe not so unusual, now that you mention it. Whiz and bang was what they wanted, fireworks and "presentation." I.e., take your personal-worth; multiply by flapdoodle; add in fudge; flimflam squared; cosine poppycock; clientele doo-dad; divide by approximate exchange-value. All so you could bust in someplace, get in there, sit in a swivel chair and start picking at your hands and playing with your face. All so you could jump in there with the rest of the hogs and start kicking around the pork. All so you get in there and get started plotting to get out of it.

Oh, but I had Cal. We belonged together. We belonged like the wind and the leaves. Like stairs and tall buildings. Dogs and the park; fields and open spaces. Color and pictures; police and crackling radios; justice and blindfolds. Hammers and nails and wood.

*

I was in the kitchen. I was standing before the sink. The cold water was running down on a dirty yellow pile of half-shorn potatoes. The peeler dropped into the sink. The beer bottle was in my right hand.

My hand was squeezing this brown bottle. It squeezed very, very tightly. Squeezed and kept squeezing until little black somersaults were cartwheeling in my eyes. I looked down. The hand was going white, white, white… I was telling myself, this bottle will have to break before I make another move.

Then I heard Cal crying again. And it was all different again.

A big bunch of air fluttered out my nose and mouth.

"I'm sorry, baby," I called out. "I'm bad. I'm sorry. I won't do it again."

She sobbed. I could hear her out there on the couch.

I pulled the beer from the counter, drank it. I stood in the middle of the kitchen, looked at the water stain in the corner of the ceiling, and drank the beer. It was hot in there. It was hot everywhere.

I didn't mean it to, but the thing had just popped out, about a minute before. That kind of language is what I'm talking about. Names and so forth, various oaths, what have you. It was never the right thing to say. And I'd heard the drill, thought the thoughts, seen pictures of the scene – thought it, seen it. But sometimes… no, it's still never right.

But what she told me, Cal… I don't think I'll ever forget it.

It had started right after I'd driven her home from work. I'd gone into the kitchen with the idea of cooking for a change. I knew Cal would like that, and she had. Things were going fine, yes… and then we'd started in with the usual sort of chat – which "somehow" ended up in the same usual sort of place: When was I going to find work. You know: When was it going to come together, was I looking hard enough. Was I doing the right things to make it happen.

I don't know, maybe I got irritated, going through it all again. The same chat, you know. I was pretty tired of it. And maybe I really didn't care any more. That's what I said, actually. I believe I said it in a calm, maybe even lazy voice. And maybe the look on my face was a laugh, but without the laughter sound.

"Maybe I don't care any more, babe."

A long dirty curl of potato skin peeled away and fell into the sink.

"Maybe no one will hire me. I guess if it gets bad enough, I'll just have to start cutting lawns, blowing leaves or something. After they kick me off welfare, of course. That wouldn't be so bad, would it? There's plenty worse things, hon, you know there is. Just take a look at this world. Hell, I can stay busy just taking care of things around the house. There's more than enough to do here. You know how it can get."

Before I knew it, Cal was up from her place at the table. She crossed the kitchen lickety-split. She was right up there on the end of my nose.

Her hair was swinging in her eyes. Her cheeks had these burning splotches they get. Her eyes dark and smoky, lips spittle-spacked. The words flew out of her mouth like little blades, cutting me all over, in ways I didn't know how to handle. Couldn't even think to handle. I was standing there with the peeler in my hand.

She said: "Well, I don't know what *you* think, but don't expect *me* to support you on my own. That's the *last* thing that'll happen. God, I can't believe you'd even think such a thing! Forget it! *Just forget it!*"

Something like this, and it went on longer than you might think. I stood and took it. I stuttered and fidgeted, shook, trembled and rattled. I stood there and took it. Well, and when she was finished, I don't know – I guess the bad words were just ready to spill out of me.

I mean, what she said… No, there's still no excuse. But it was a heck of a thing, a dang damn heck of a thing, to hear from your wife. Your mother, maybe, at some point, if things ever got really awful and it came to that. But – never, never your wife.

I mean, Cal has always been one to slug it out. And really, it's good. Nobody really wants a woman who'll let herself be pushed around like a load of half-cooked onion rings on a plate. But, it's… it's that you never think of it happening like that.

Now she was crying again. Cal. She cries a lot, but never for show, I don't think, never just to get you. There's always something true behind it, I've never doubted it, and she would kill me if I did. I mean, she cried every day for a week when she knew "for sure" that she had AIDS, before the test came back saying that she didn't.

I left the beer and went out to her. I sat down, put my arms around her, and kissed her wet cheeks. We didn't say anything.

*

Okay, yeah, and now the bastards were really arrayed. The snakes were uncoiling. The artillery was exposed. The helicopter gunships were refueling for another rocket sortie. The dirty calumny bastards were starting to put their thick grubby hands all over the box.

I sat there next to Cal and I thought. We sat there, me thinking, Cal doing what she does. We sat there and I still didn't like any part of any of it.

We sat there and the phone rang. I sprang from the couch and caught it in the middle of the second ring.

I listened to the agency chick. I grabbed a pen and started jotting. I took it down. She was done.

"Work tomorrow," I said, throwing myself next to Cal back on the couch.

"Where?"

"Hell if I know. Some place…"

"How long?"

"She said at least one, maybe two days. Wooh, two days, honey!"

I shrieked, stamped my feet on the floor. I stung Cal on the upper and lower lips.

"Yeah," I went on, "and she said they might be looking for a full-time person. She basically said that if I do a pretty decent job, they might want to take me under consideration. It's just a possible though – nothing official. But she said they might be thinking about it."

"Yeah, they might," Cal said. "How much they going to give you?"

I said, "$7.83 an hour."

Cal seemed pretty okay with this, more or less. I myself was shaking again – but different.

We waddled together back to the kitchen and finished making the dinner. We mixed the potatoes with strips of salami and bell pepper, dusted the whole thing with the last of our package of jack cheese. It baked and we ate. By then it was almost dark – not that it had cooled much.

Cal went into the bathroom for her nightly hour-plus. I sat in the quiet for a bit, then got up to clear the table and rinse the dishes. I soaked and soaped and rinsed with a general thoroughness, then lay everything out to dry on our special flower print dish rag. I took extra care to make sure all the glasses were in straight queues; that no lone wolf knife had acclimated itself among the spoons; that no curving tail of wet cheese had insinuated itself to the wall of the sink.

I came out of the kitchen. I walked to the shelf, removed my pad, pens and pencils, and sat back down at the table. I had the feeling it was finally time to do something. I'd been getting this feeling at least once a week, and sometimes three or four times out of seven, for a long time now – you know, that it was finally time to do something.

I sat in the chair at the table and synchronized the pens and pencils into a straight line. I wet my lips with a deliberate tongue swipe. I gave the pad a staunch, slow-blinking gaze.

At length I selected one of the pens, a blue ballpoint with gold company lettering on the barrel, and positioned it amidst my fingers. I inhaled a quick, professional snort through my nose, re-moistened my lips. Just as I was preparing to savagely dash the pen against the pad, I heard the bathroom door click open.

Cal walked out in a warm mist.

I tossed the pen. It landed on the pad with an audible plap.

She came up behind me on bare feet. She hung a kiss on my left ear. I turned and saw her pink and shiny, slick of hair and cheek.

"It's getting late," she observed. She traced a finger from my ear down my neck to my shoulder. "Work day tomorrow. Maybe you should think about coming to bed."

Her voice was weary and soft – but not without a certain persuasive logic, or so it seemed, curled in its concept.

I let the sentence drift. I let everything drift there and looked up at her. Her eyes were still a little red and sort of puffed, as were her lips.

"You know, that's not a bad idea," I said.

Her back was already to me. I watched her and her haunches and her towel go off to the bedroom. I watched her damp shank of straight-cut hair bob and lap and dance across the top of her shoulders. Her long clean legs sort of slightly whispered against each other, winding along the dark and flattening sea-green shag…

I didn't go anywhere. Far from it. I looked at the pad. I never did get around to stabbing it. I stayed at the kitchen table, sweated at a low burn, and looked at it. I stayed at the kitchen table and fingered the little fuzzy dent between my nose and lips.

After a while I got up. I put the water on the stove, shoveled some freeze-dried, sat back down with a cup of instant. I got back up, went to the cupboard, found the Early Times, and poured some into the coffee. Hell, it was late now. I needed to settle down, loosen up. I did the same one more time, then a few more times, and when the Early Times was gone, I happened to find one last bottle of beer.

I drank it down slow, feet on the table. The night breeze finally nosed through the drapes, coating my legs, arms and cheeks with a bit of overdue cool.

It was after three by the time I walked across the creaking shag, got naked, and crawled onto the bedcovers. Cal was sleeping hard – a swath of sheet across her midsection, knees and elbows to the four corners, toes and tits to the moon. One of her "psychology" casebooks was open. I snapped it shut, flipped off the talk-radio, switched off the night lamp.

Green glow from the clock radio reflected on the tip of my nose. My testicles lay drying against the sheet. I guess I finally slid away, listening to the blood whoosh around my ears.

*

The alarm hit. Cal rolled off and headed for her kitchen/bathroom bit in the morning. I lay there and didn't feel like moving.

Couldn't move, in fact.

It lasted I don't know how long. It lasted until I remembered me and Cal were supposed to kill them: Blow them away, crush them, defenestrate, blow them out of the water and that's right: *Kill them*. Until I remembered that the longer I lay there, the more secure their artillery would become, and the longer it would take for us to launch the lightning flanking maneuver which would blow them back to whence they had slithered. And until I remembered that the longer I lay there, the longer I would lay there.

I rolled off finally, hand gripping a tall hard morning one, and that felt pretty good, that was an all-right sign. I went in for a shower. When it was about over, Cal peeped in for a kiss. When I strode from behind the curtain, she was a naked big girl in front of the mirror, squeezing at something small and red on her chin.

Ten minutes later I was sitting at the kitchen table, one slightly trembling hand hovering around a cup of instant. My eyes felt quite tiny; the head was dinging away; I was stuffed full of aspirin; but I was fully dressed.

Hair slicked and the rest of it. Brown sportscoat with lighter brown chevrons. Skinny red tie with black Big Bens. Dark swirling confetti shirt. Cracked black leather belt. Navy polyesters, snug across my hind side, long over the hobnails. Stomach tight, breasts sleek, biceps rock, brain marbled…

I sipped at the coffee. I sipped and looked at the spoon sitting in Cal's empty yogurt box. Five minutes went by in a series of difficult eye-blinks. I finished the coffee. I took the empty coffee cup in one hand and palmed the yogurt box in the other. I got up and set the cup and spoon in the sink. I dropped the yogurt box in the paper-in-the-plastic trash sack hanging from the doorknob.

I yelled to Cal, "How you doing in there?"

She didn't say anything. I walked to the hall and saw her in the bathroom mirror. She was still naked, only now a white cream was on her face.

I kicked open the front door. Skies throwing down blue, tree leaves showing green with brown spots, yellow lawn dewy, asphalt gray, glass in the gutter three or four colors. I sat on the step and whiffed the morning still-cool. Somebody down below was up and cooking eggs.

I came back in and looked at the clock. It was time to go. In fact, it was past time.

"Honey! We got to go!"

Cal's coffee was still in the kitchen, chilled now. I took it down to the bathroom. By now she had her slacks and bra on, but the cream was still on her face. Her hair was still up. A love song about how they had broken each other's hearts was on the battery radio.

I stuck my face in and said, "C'mon, sweetie." I winked, then did it again.

She gave me the steel stare.

I took her coffee out to the stairs and wolfed it. It was around this point I started to get a janged-up kind of feeling, fingers plinking and tinking the iron stair rail. I wasn't sure why. But then I figured it out. Yeah, I knew plenty well.

It would be no good to be late. No one hires a guy who's late on the first day. Anyway, hell, I needed the money. No, I wanted the money. Okay: I wanted and needed some money. I was good enough with nickels and pennies by now to drag out a couple days' worth of job for as long as a few weeks. Cal's check was almost good enough to cover the rent, utilities and whatever stuff she needed. But I just hated to stick it to her for things like "gas" for the car. Just hated it. She didn't like it either. I really needed some cash, at least for unleaded.

Yeah, and maybe I was a bit uneasy about what kind of "assignment" they might try to throw me. I never liked that idea, going into these pay-by-the-quarter-hour arrangements. Sometimes the people thought you were some maths genius who could handle complicated computer programs which involved purchasing back-ordered cardiograph assembly fixtures from Singapore. They acted like you should know, in fact, like why *don't* you know this information? What do you *do* anyway? What do you think you're *doing*, coming around here? That had happened. Other places acted like you'd never seen a tie-on shoe before. "Hi there, good morning," they'd tell you, "and this is what we in our industry call a 'word processor.' It's kind of a typewriter, combined with an automatic salad mixer and anesthetic device… you've seen, yes?" Either way, it felt too jokey. Like, you could never quite believe you were in there – you know, that it was actually happening.

But – right. Cal was going to get that job tomorrow. Well, no – but we couldn't bank on it yet. Dear no. And since we couldn't…

"Aw hell, Cal!"

I walked back in. She was finally wiping the cream off.

"Dang it, babe, we're going to be late! Hurry, would you!"

She stuck her tongue out.

God, and then things got all crossed together again. My lips flapped and my tongue flared, and I said some more things. Maybe I shouldn't have. No – I just shouldn't have. But what did she think? Here I was, all ready to go, all ready to go out there and poke it to 'em three ways…

"I'll be out in the car," I said.

I went out back to the hulk. The rusting lumpen mass was still there – still caked with crud, but she was still gold. I unlocked, stepped in, and lit her up. She chugged, fired, backfired, roared, idled and finally hummed. I held my breath as a flag of black rose out of the tail end and floated across the top.

It was another six to eight minutes before Cal showed. She was crying, or close to right on it. She opened the door and sat down. Even with the sunglasses on, her face looked like it could probably fry two steaks and an omelet just then. And maybe have enough juice left over to singe a side of fries.

"Aw, babe, c'mon."

"Shut up. Just shut up.…"

I clipped it tight. Her face was doing the puckering. That always made me sick. Made her sick, too, you could see it, she hated to have it happen to her face like that. Made me sick seeing her so sick of it and hating it so much. Shit.

"I'm sorry, honey," I said.

She rolled down her window and looked out.

Okay, yes, she was right, perfect. Her husband… okay, this and that, what have you. Things so far hadn't really gone as she'd expected, and I don't blame her for it, I don't, why should I? All those good intentions, waiting for college to end so she could go out there and do the good things, and her mother... that old liberal bitch.

Well, at least I knew Cal was keeping whatever hard times we might have been having mostly to herself. Otherwise Al and Rita would have been over a long time ago... I could see it happening, I'd run it through front and back: Al "guiding" me outside to poke his finger in my chest and snap his spearmint gum in my face; Rita all ashen and grim and weighing, seriously *weighing*, whether to call the police. And Cal crying, crying, completely helpless now that they'd come... at which point they the three of them would drive away in their car... God, and I'd be there, all alone. That would be the worst – night falling, shadows on the march, a stiff breeze against the back of my neck... And no Cal, no money, no nothing... then maybe after all, a police or two, stopping by, tipped off by Rita, showing up to take down a "report" and ask me what it was "all about."

See, that's what I'm talking about. These bastards, they show up one day, and they try to tell you. They show up and they say, *Here it is, eat.* It's over, sit down, all done, made it this far, finished – now *eat*. C'mon, boy – wear this, wear that, sit down – *eat*. Comb your hair, shut your mouth, and *eat*. After all that wrenching and twisting and pulling from the day you were an hour old, all to make you resemble something that can get into college – all that effort to make everything tidy and fit and fine, so you can take your right place in line and not bother anybody too much... and hope to sweet mama Jesus you don't wind up on Skid Row or Death Row or with the no-hair hari-haris – all of that, all of that hard work on your behalf, and now you want to say something? "Well, there he goes," you can hear them saying. They might mutter, "Careful, don't let that happen to you, young fella," to some poor kid standing there.

Well, but there was at least one way out. I'd figured this out before, it was so damn obvious, but sometimes you'd forget. But it was always good to remember:

The first step was to surrender.

The second was to give up.

The third was to toss in the towel.

The fourth was to relinquish all hope.

The fifth was to forget any of it had ever happened.

We drove to Cal's place. The joint was swarming with shopping carts and guys who looked like they'd just crawled out from winter under a beer truck. She got out.

I thought about saying something like, "Just one more day, babe," but that phrase didn't come out of my mouth. No. They wouldn't hire me to find sand in the Mojave, but I wasn't that dumb. Hell, they wouldn't trust me to find trash in an alley or hardbacks at the library – but I wasn't a total ass. No, I couldn't get a buck to find zits at the high school, pills at the old-folks home, hell, white folks at a gun show. None of that. Oh hell no. Forget it, just forget it. But I wasn't that stupid.

Anyway, I had to hustle. It didn't look like I was going to make the 8:30 start time.

*

Traffic wasn't heavy. It wasn't light, but it wasn't heavy, and I couldn't blame it. So there wasn't much to blame – unless I was going to get up and blame Cal, which I wasn't going to do. Was not going to do that. In any case, the sun really hotted up during the drive. Sweat puddled at my temples, slid down the sides of my face, sank into my collar, rode the ridge of my spine.

I read the address off the paper scrap. Another a few blocks went by and I found myself in a field of glass and brick and adolescent green saplings. I scanned for addresses, saw my number, dinked a left-hand shot across the lane and into the parking lot. A low long place, not old. Unfinished gray stone and roof solar panels, a net of power wires stretching yon and near, hills of yellow poppies over tilled earth up front.

I unbuckled, checked the hair in the rearview.

I said to myself: Be a nice little man, would you? We want the "money" – you need the money – that's all. Everything you don't like, all your nice ideas about everything that's no good – it gets left here. It stays right here in the front seat of the hulk, in the big sloppy package it came in. I visualized a panel on the top of my head flipping open, and the big bunch of the things being lifted out and set onto the fissuring naugahyde. Yes, I said, all of it stays – because you need to make it through. No, you do.

I took a deep breath.

At door-slam time the car clock read 8:39.

It couldn't have taken me much more than 35 seconds to jog the walk to the smoked-glass front doors. Which is why I was sort of more than stunned when the big red digital on the wall behind the chick at the desk read: 8:47.

She said, "You must be from the agency?"

"No," I said in a whisper-hiss. "Moloney sent me for the maps and ball bearings. This the right place?"

No – I told the chick: "Yeah."

I gulped and sighed. I gushed and gestured.

"Wow, I'm so sorry I'm late. I guess I've got a slightly different time than you guys." I looked at the nonexistent watch on my wrist, shrugged and shook my head in shell-shocked befuddled bafflement. "I mean, it's just so… *totally weird.* You know?"

"Oh well," she said, "don't worry about it." She delivered a small grin while simultaneously grabbing up a sheaf of papers. "C'mon, I'll take you to your work space."

I walked around the plastic oak barrier and followed her into an empty white hall. Through one doorway I saw a few heads hunched and bobbing, along with a couple others stretched and toothy, but we didn't go in there. Instead, the chick went left into a room about the size of wide-screen television. It had a desk, a chair, a computer set-up, a potted tree, a short brown carpet, grey-white venetians against the sun.

I sat in the chair and listened to her explain it. Behind her on the wall I noticed a big blown-up color picture, silver-framed, an aerial view – Giants stadium or some such, standing-room only, college oom-pah band on the field, Saturday afternoon football game probably.

I didn't like it. Some geek had put it up there. Some middle-aged guy who'd probably tell a long story about it – about how he was in the helicopter when it happened, or his buddy was, or what a big astonishing game it had been, how unique the photo-technology was, how he'd been the second coronet player in the marching band, back in, uh, what's-it-called…

The chick was done talking.

"So basically," I said, "what you're saying is, you'd like me to type this list of addresses into the computer?"

"Yes. I mean – as I explained."

"Right. Those little codes by each name. They've got to go in, too. And I've got to make sure I hit 'Enter' after I've typed each one in. Otherwise, it won't be in the machine."

"Right."

"I think I got it."

"Good. Just holler if you need anything."

"Sure thing," I said, nodding. And smiling. And feeling, yeah, like doing a bit of yelping and yodeling then and there. But no, she couldn't help me. Not she. Not no one. She was who she was, and that should have been okay. And it was. I had come there on my own.

She walked out.

I suppose I didn't think much about anything, not immediately. I was actually a bit relieved – the lateness factor, the explaining and so on, was over. Yes, everything was fine now. I was alone. And work – typing to be done. Clear enough. Very clear, as it turned out. No obvious gray areas that needed immediate focus and handling.

It was very cool in that room, verging on cold, you could hear the hum of hidden air conditioners. I tossed a hank of hair out of my eyes and looked over the stack. A computerized listing of addresses – various companies, along with a few individual names. "Clients," one would figure. By each was a handwritten code, consisting of a few letters and numbers, which was to be entered in a particular field on the computer screen. Each of these codes had been highlighted in a garish blue, green, orange or yellow ink – why, I don't know, as I hadn't been informed re: purpose of color highlighting. I thumbed the sheaf. Looked like 20, 25 pages or so. A day's worth, a day and a half, depending.

And so I began. What I mean is, I buckled down. My eyes flicked dangerously between sheaf and computer screen, in furious, inexorable, lock-step tandem with my flexed and flapping fingers.

I was probably on about the third page when I palpably and for goodness realized it.

Like I was saying, you can never expect some of these things. Just too jokey. A real caper jape spoof, you know? I mean, there had been times previous where it had been similar, but never quite this, never quite exactly like this – addresses! Yeah, and it still wasn't supposed to be, it would still never be, and now the bastards –

*

In my various tests with the agencies, I have recorded – depending on the day – typing speeds of between 65 and 85 words per minute. It cannot be excluded that I skirted the edge of perhaps 90 "wpm" on this morning.

I worked with a stormy diligence and a stony assiduousness which left my lips smarting from the intense pursedness with which I held them. I got up once to use the restroom. When I did, it appeared that the air conditioning had completely dried out my nose and left my ears cotton-stuffed. My insides didn't feel too good either – not nearly enough grease or what have you. But it wouldn't have mattered if I were hemorrhaging, so long as I was standing. I downed three more aspirin from the pile I'd dumped in my pocket.

My fingers flew, they attacked the keyboard.

Aided by the surprise fact that more than a few of the pages had most of the names and addresses crossed out, I blitzed completely through the stack by 12:07 (wall clock time). I took a moment to double-check what I'd done (one fix), then walked back up front to the desk chick.

"Okay, what's next?" I said, setting the sheaf on the desk.

"Finished?" said she.

"Yep."

"Already?"

"That's right."

"Wow."

"Yes."

She thumbed the sheaf – then unloaded a happy little grin-type thing.

"Well, huh, let's see," she said.

Her eyes swept across the desk, fluttered, and landed back on me. "Actually, I don't have anything else. That's it. You're free to go home, I guess. Or go to lunch. Or wherever you need to go."

She gave the grin thing again, adding a little laugh. She shrugged her shoulders, blinked, gave a tilt of her head.

As if that were the end of it.

I think my mouth paused in a half-open position for several seconds. Then I said:

"You're kidding. I mean, the agency said you would need me for at least two days. Maybe even longer."

"Well, exactly. We thought we might. But, you know – wow again. You really made quick work of it today. Really."

She shrugged, grinned again and very quickly signed the timecard. She stuck it out for me to take.

"Here you go. Thank you very much. We'll be sure to keep you in mind if anything comes up in the future. Your name's on the list."

"Thank you," I said.

I stood there and took it from her like that. I stood there, feeling vaguely achy. I stood there, wondering what Cal would say, and I took it.

∗

I got back in the hulk.

All the stuff I'd put in storage was waiting. I tried it out again. It all still fit pretty good – If maybe a little tighter than before.

I looked at the timecard. The chick had cut the difference. She'd given me the 8:30 start time, but signed me out at noon straight up. I did the calculus: Three and a half hours, minus probably a whole two-thirds of one hour, at least, for taxes…

I suppose I sat a while, with the windows up, and sweated. Time happened. My chest pumped and the sweat ran down – over my eyelashes, down my cheeks, over my lips and down my chin. Pressure pushed against my face and shoulders – but I couldn't move to roll down the window. I felt a warm bead of sweat snaking down, smack between my buttocks.

Sitting there – it was a little too familiar. Okay, then I saw it. Like the same as – okay.

Sitting in the car, burning up but way too tired. Like the one day, a month or so after our wedding, during which Cal had disclosed the information about her "two-year" affair with the "married" patrol cop. It "began," of course, when she was seventeen and still living at Al and Rita's. And, well, it had been her "first," but by the time it was "over" they had most certainly "done everything, more than once" – and wasn't that interesting, wasn't that enchanting? And I had sat there and listened to her say this, listened to her talk about the weekends where they "never left the hotel room," but how she "didn't really love him," sat there and listened – and I didn't know whether to rush that little girl into the bedroom and nail off the door, or drag her into the bushes and paddle her behind and wring her neck…

The desk chick walked out. Pleated tan pants, white oval-neck, gold necklace, watch crystal flashing. Black wraparounds across the face, maroon leatherkin purse over a wrist. Tan multi-strap sandals. She walked around the side of the building, disappeared a moment, then re-emerged behind the wheel of a white hatchback two-door. Not new; not very old.

She came to a stop at the drive; leaned her head forward; looked both ways; and drove on to the street and away.

I watched this. And then I watched myself start up my own car; back out of the space; sidle up to the driveway; look both ways; and drift out on to the street.

The hatch was maybe one hundred yards ahead. I whomped the gas. Shortly I was but 35 yards behind, with one car in between.

We rolled into a mall lot. The chick got out of the hatch and headed for the big supermarket, depositing her keys in her purse as she walked. I saw that – and then I myself was parking and stepping out into the afternoon haze. I was probably 25 feet behind her as she parted the glass and walked into the air-conditioning.

I strolled the aisles. There she was, bent over, about two feet high, in front of a display of cat food. "Super Sale Days," a sign said in an electrified ice green font. Below it she was piling can upon can into a red plastic hand-basket, seafood flavor and chicken and vegetarian, all the varieties. She paused to look at the label on a can, at the little print that lists the dietary/caloric information.

I stood there I don't know how long. Then I turned, stumbled a step, looked up. A surveillance camera was sticking out of the wall. It was pointing at me. Entirely white – same color as the wall.

*

Friday.

No early-morning calls from my agencies.

I put on long green shorts, a red t-shirt with yellow advertising, thin blue work socks with black and red pine cones. Drove Cal in to work. She was crying, but just a little – the big day and all, I guess, and maybe also a fresh snag on the pantyhose.

Something like that. You know, and just a matter of hours before knowing how it was going to work out – but no big. She was able to clamp it up pretty good by the time we got there. All was pretty fine – time to go. She got out, said she'd call, first thing she heard.

I went back and got the paper. Not much there, just the usual – military and police and peacekeeping, a massacre or two, hardline bully factions, prayers for the schools and gun rights, along with another dose of new special geniuses who were busy rearranging our world and everything in it – and of course, not to be left out, never – another revolutionary TV show. Also, not much around for breakfast. However, it was Friday – shopping day.

I glimpsed it, for a moment, there in the kitchen. I got flecked up and jumpy – just standing and thinking it through.

I'd pick Cal up, the job wrapped in her arms. We'd run to the store and buy it up, buy it all: Meat and lettuce and tuna fish, carrots and sweet green bananas, ice cream and wheat bread. And the hell with it – I said crap on it: A bottle of champagne, too. Why not, celebration day. Then head out for a while – maybe drop in on a movie, yeah, and maybe not, probably not – movies were fakes. Maybe just a visit to that open-air bagel cafe on the boulevard, with the ferns and art-student reject art on the walls. Then maybe a roll down the alley to The Sixkiller – unload a cocktail or nine, spin Cal around a few dances at the jukebox. Why not? Screwy heck what Cal said. Why the hell not? Celebration. Then back home – ice cream, coffee – bed.

I cracked a tin of the 39-cent automatic biscuits. I spread them in the oven, crafted a cup of instant.

So damn hot in the house suddenly. The sun whacking down, not even a cloud. I threw open the front door and all the windows. A breeze stirred the drapes, once – but nothing more.

The buns came out. I socked them with the margarine, pelted them with the last dregs of the honey.

I gunned the last of the coffee. It burned, still too hot.

I needed to calm down, relax. Drinking coffee so fast like that. Now no more coffee to drink. Too many cheap muffins too fast. I took the paper out to the stairs. It was too bright. I went down to the car for sunglasses and came back. It was too hot.

I stood on the stairs. It was late enough by now for the people to be out. There they were: The cart guys wrapped in plastic, looking for aluminum and more plastic; the younger guys in hoods, hands mashing into pushed-low pants. It was too hot to be wearing hoods. On the right, the other pack of guys – working on a car – cars, three or four different ones.

So quiet. Standing there. The sky peeled open like that. Not a cloud, not a thing. The sun crashing against the rooftops – the rooftops dark and corroded, stretching and angling…

I was down the stairs and running. Two blocks, then west past the brick elementary school, the scoreboard-style bank clock, past the lounge bars and greasyspoon, into the intersection and across. The heat rose off the oily blacktop. A car honked, a motorcycle screamed.

Finally, into the park. An empty cool quietness, four square city blocks worth. Basketball and tennis courts stamped out in the appropriate corners. Broken glass and dirty paper, right where they always were. Morning wet still on the grass tips. A bush frosted in white; a tree frothing with pink.

I strolled, lifted my head and inhaled. I watched the swaying trees. I labored across the grass, shuffling through the perfume.

I came along the top of a slope. Somebody was at the bottom: A mom and two kids on a blanket it looked like, forty-fifty yards away. I watched. The mom took a plastic bottle from a bag and twisted. The pop and fizz crackled across the quiet. It boomed, bounced, zinged over the lawn and tickled under my nostrils. The kids laughed, the noise exploding, caroming along and over the hills.

I lay in the tree shade, my face heavy with a studge of sweat. My eyes closed. When they opened, the mother and the kids were gone. The studge had vanished.

A light brown ant was crawling on my wrist. I flicked him down, rolled, shook the grass from my head. I got up and headed over the hill, down for a look at the pond and the duck.

*

I went down to the hulk and fired it up. Windows all the way down, radio all the way up. Cal had got the news and decided to cash it in for the day – Friday and all. Her bosses were casual. It was no secret. The bums would never notice the difference.

She wasn't crying when I got there.

I peppered her with kisses, ran my hands over her shoulders. I said, "Cal, fuck, I'm sorry, babe."

You know, I didn't know, and I still don't. Right off the bat like that.

"Fuck, you're sorry, babe? 'Hi, honey. Fuck, I'm sorry, babe.' What does that mean? 'Hi, honey. Fuck, I'm sorry, babe.' Fuck, you're sorry, babe? What is that supposed to mean? Fuck, you're sorry, babe?"

Tough. *Tough.* I roared toward the market. Cal's hair swung as we took the road dips. I was thinking: Get her inside, get her shopping. Start "the recovery," the getting "over" it, the moving on to the next thing, the next steppppppp…

A bit of a delayed reaction. Typical. Because before too long at all, my heart was going chigger-boom, chigger-bam, chumpa-chumpa. And I was thinking: The fucking lousy *bastards.* The cheap fucking no-account scurvy *bastards.*

Some bastard cut in front of me, then slowed down. A serious nix – you don't pass and cut, just to slow down. I hit the horn, Cal yelled. I jerked us up and around the bastard. We muscled past him, drubbing the train track as we rumbled. And another honk, and a bit of a blur, and then – there we were at the Safeway.

The place sat on a full city block like a huge brown castle, ringed by palms that were stuck against the sky like green twirlers. A tiny right and into the ocean of pavement – the lot was jammed, nothing was giving. Two laps, three, sweat pouring, into number four – then finally a spot at the end of the strip off the Main Entrance.

We got out and strode among the pocked stone pillars and plastic lawn chairs. Cal was a good ten feet ahead of me. I knew that had to change, I knew it had to change pretty quick if we were going to make it through the next ten minutes. I snatched her hand as we headed into the machine air. We were in the store now, at last, and that was good, it was fine, it meant something to do. We yanked a cart and swam out onto the linoleum.

Cal likes to get the fruits and vegetables out of the way first, so we started in that section. I hung around as she gathered the oranges and lettuce, but she was taking too long picking out her apples. Maybe they were bruised or whatever, something quite understandable – but it was taking too long. I nipped her on the cheek, said I'd catch up with her.

It seemed like a good idea. Give us each time to spread out, get in some deep breaths. I hunted around and selected a few items. It felt swell, the cool dry store air blowing up my shorts.

I met up with her in the toiletries region, amid a knot of women sniffing at the air fresheners and bowl spritzers. Okay, sure, and I don't know – maybe, again, I should have seen it coming. But after a letdown like we just had – were still having…

Cal rolled her eyes and let loose with it: No money for this junk and the other about it – right there in the aisle, if you can believe, right there in front of all the people.

I set down the champagne bottle, the 12-pack of beer, the armload of cookies and tortilla chips. She kept going – and going.

And that was all for right then, because then she was pushing the cart the one way and I was going the other.

We linked up again at the register. I tossed the stuff on the conveyor as she ran over to the machine to take out a couple twenties.

It was then that I noticed him. He'd been there the whole time, I guess – something so big and obvious and matter of fact you'd never give it a second thought. A big guy and tall, must have been close to sixty or even older. Wearing the white store shirt with the blue logo, the blue store smock. Thick head of jet white hair, wavy, straight-cut at the ears. White walrus-style mustache, lightly stained. Boulder-style shoulders, set high and back. Barrel chest, fire hydrant forearms, devices which resembled redwood stumps for hands. And the face – oh, the face. A terrible bronze scape of wrinkles and folds it was, a cruel bedlam of creases, crags and corrugations…

"Paper in the plastic, please," I told him, following his inquiry.

"Yes-sir," he said.

He whisked to the task, but there was no hurrying. He was brief with the bags, but far from careless. His hands were rapid, but his movements elaborately composed. His eyes rang out in clear clanging blue from the jagged craters that were his eye sockets.

Cal was back with the cash. The guy looked at her and said three or four words. I don't know what they were: Hi there young lady, nice day isn't it, hot one, good for lemonade, there you are, fine, yes I think so, thank you very much, something along these lines – but she smiled at him. Lord, but she ripped one – eyes sparking and prancing, big and round as pancakes, giggles and sighs, the works. I stood there and watched her give the guy a smile like it was the first time she'd ever done such a thing with her mouth – like it was the first time she found out that beautiful curvy red split in her face worked like that.

*

I wheeled the cart out into the sun and fumes.

We didn't get more than ten steps before I saw the hulk. She was down on the rear left. Way down. Flat down. Cal and I both saw it, but nobody said a word until we got right up on it and confirmed it was in fact so.

I let go with a few good ones.

Cal spluttered some herself, ending with: "Why do we only have this piece of junk car?"

I took it standing there, without a word in reply. Just stood there and took it clean, like a bulldozer of bricks, without ado of any sort; let it lay and pound me for a good twenty seconds. I breathed in and out, looking at the hulk – letting it roll, kick and squirm and pound me.

Then, as if I'd never heard it, I flipped the trunk and started rooting for the fix-it gear.

I don't know, a lot of time went by, I guess. It took me a while to figure everything out – the order things were supposed to go, the machinery of it , the process, the technics.

Cal sat on the curb, chin in her hands, while I worked on it. Down on my knees, with nary a finger of breeze to ripple the sun. With gawkers and jokers walking by, the overly curious bird asking if we needed some "help." No thanks, got it handled, pal buddy unselfish helper. Just a little flat, you understand, no sweat, very routine. *Very.* Don't worry, be finished in two seconds, really, just about done, everything coming together…

∗

I fell down to a knee, gasping. I spun dizzy for a spell. I looked up. The sun mauled away at me – creamed me flush on the nose, pitched against my neck and chest. The angles seemed to shift; the kilters got all twitchy. The giant supermarket sign glided across the sky. The palm trees tilted and started to wave, started to go round and round.

Just two of the whichisits that keep the tire on were left.

I got up, wiped the sweat, sucked the haze. I gripped the screw deal and delivered unto one of the rusting bastards another furious wrenching twist.

There was a scraping sound, followed by a moaning. The hulk slid forward. Then it sort of jumped.

I rolled as far and fast as I could.

"Cal! Hey!"

"What! What!"

"Hey!"

We stood there and watched it.

Cal said, "It's going to fall, isn't it."

"Fall?"

I got back down and examined it. The thing seemed to be hanging, hanging by the merest –

I felt the shadow, behind me. Didn't see it – felt it.

Then I saw it. He was there.

I turned, looked up. I saw the face, the craggy craters. He took a puff from a cigarette, exhaled through his nose, dropped the butt almost on my hand. A spark or two nicked my wrist.

He: "Help you with something?"

"Oh God, yes," I heard Cal say.

A boot, black, came down upon the butt.

"If it's possible," I said, rising.

I said, "Gee, the car almost fell. It's the jack, bending, just about to collapse – hope it's not too serious. It's an old one, you know, old car. It's these nut things, the tire, flat – over here – yes – "

He nodded. He sank down, without a word, and snatched up the tools.

I looked at Cal, looked at him, heard the tools tinkle. The hulk went down a ways. The gentleman grunted mildly.

The hulk began to go back up.

A drop of sweat rolled from my nose and splashed the parking lot.

He was back in front of me, swallowing my hand in his. The hulk hung upon the jack. The lousy tire was on the ground, quiet and shrunken, a little tail of silver radial sticking out.

"There you are," he said. "Just put your spare on and away with you you go."

I started flumming at the mouth again – Cal too – thanking him and so forth. But all he said was, "Forget it. I'm on my break."

He nodded, flashed a crinkled wink at Cal. He walked off.

It took seven-ten minutes to screw on the skinny replacement wheel. I tossed the gear in the back, we loaded the bags and got in. I tripped the fuse. The hulk gurgled and spat and roared.

We limped along the roadway. We darted through the purple pools of evening shadow springing from the streetside trees and buildings. We fled on straight lines and tight corners across the blueing pavement. I clasped Cal's hand, and she squeezed mine.

TONY AND POOF

Tony was at Grandma Lorraine's again. Tony's mom had gone down to the shore with Ron, a man with curly black hair who had picked them up that morning in his car, a purple jeep with many long scratches.

It was yet another sun-blasted day. Tony sat in a kitchen chair under the deep porch awning of the back yard. To his right sat Grandma Lorraine, swaying in the wooden swing. Tony was holding a new paperback book.

"When's your mother coming back?" asked Grandma Lorraine, though she had asked that question of Barbara before her daughter had departed.

"I don't know," said Tony. "Probably before night." He shrugged.

"I hope so," said Grandma Lorraine. "I don't have all day."

"Neither do I," said Tony. He flipped one of his legs in the air. The leg came down, Tony's rubber shoe bottom smacking against the porch cement.

"C'mere, Poof," said Grandma Lorraine.

A coal-colored poodle the size of small ham ran over from the red brick wall where it had been snuffing about. The dog's tongue hung out. Its collar and tag jingled as it hopped on to Grandma Lorraine's lap.

"Want some?" said Grandma Lorraine. She held her can of Hamm's to the dog's mouth. The canine lapped at it. "Sure you do, sure you do. You're my little baby."

"Don't give him beer," said Tony. He giggled and grinned, rocking his head against the back of the chair.

"Oh, poo," said Grandma Lorraine. "A little beer's not going to hurt anybody."

Poof took a few more laps from the can then hopped down from Grandma Lorraine. He ran back on to the yellowing lawn, wagging his matted string of tail.

"Beer's not good for him," said Tony.

"Oh, poo," said Grandma Lorraine. She slunk back in her swing, her thin lipsticked lips scowling. She waved a hand. "Your mother tell you to say that?"

"No."

"Yes she did. Oh, foo. Beer never hurt a little anybody."

Grandma Lorraine took a swig from her can. Tony opened to the first page in his book. They sat in the heat. It was about two p.m. The backyard was quiet, save for the squeaking chains of Grandma Lorraine's swing, flies buzzing under the fiberglass porch awning, and the rare vroom of cars down Bennis Avenue. Grandma Lorraine's three-bedroom house sat at the elbow of the tree-lined street, which formed the twisted spine of the subdivision across the main boulevard from Charles Babbage High School.

Grandma Lorraine looked at Tony. "You hungry?"

"Um, sure," said Tony.

"Well, don't get too excited," Grandma Lorraine said. "All I got is crackers and tomato. That good enough for you?"

"Yes."

Grandma Lorraine took in another mouthful of Hamm's. She let the beer sit on her tongue as she looked out over the yard. She closed her eyes and swallowed before turning to face Tony again.

"You still want some?" she asked.

"Yes."

"You sure?"

"Sure," said Tony, unable to hold back a little laugh.

Grandma Lorraine took a last drink from the can, then gave it a single squeeze at the middle. She stood from the swing and walked to the back door. Before entering she dropped the can into a paper grocery sack, which sat next to a low wicker basket. The basket contained a musty flannel blanket, numerous fleas, and the rough stench of flea-killer. On the wall nearby a rust-pocked sign was posted: BEWARE OF DOG.

Grandma Lorraine was a wiry eyelash of a woman who wore her auburn-dyed hair in a makeshift salad of roll-curls and bangs. She prided herself on being quick on her feet, and those she viewed as "slowpokes" frequently bore the brunt of her chopping tongue. An avid sun-worshiper in younger days, the skin of her twig-like arms and legs was a scaly mosaic of brown spots and purple lesions.

On hot days such as these, the tissue paper-like skin of her cheeks became smudged with streaks of near-maroon. Her standard uniform, winter or summer, was a pair of cutoff jeans and a loose, colorful blouse. Owing to the fragile state of her skin, Grandma Lorraine was prone to receiving a bleeding gash where others would have escaped with a bruise. Often, therefore, she spent many an afternoon holding Kleenex to a shin or forearm wounded in a minor encounter with a chair or stool.

Tony watched Poof. The dog was again snuffing, this time in the square pebble garden that occupied the middle of the back yard. Willie, Tony's grandfather, had many years before constructed an elaborate wooden playhouse on the site. Grandma Lorraine had taken a hammer and personally torn it down, shortly after her youngest daughter, Jan, had entered her first and last year of high school. Grandma Lorraine had since placed dozens of unexpected heirlooms and oddities on the site, many of them acquired at yard sales or, every so often, from alley trashcans. These included giant wind-spun plastic sunflowers; a chipped and faded ceramic statue of a bearded hunter with a bow and sling of arrows; a plaster hen in a cowboy hat; an owl, one side of its hollow body gashed open, wearing a pair of blue sunglasses; a scarecrow constructed from bottle caps and zebra-striped cloth ribbon; and a variety of old stone turtles, plastic bunnies, cartoon mice and carved wooden ducks.

Poof stopped his snuffing and jogged over to a slender leafy tree Grandma Lorraine had recently planted in the south corner of the perfectly rectangular back yard. He began to paw at the dirt at the base of the tree.

Grandma Lorraine exited the house, carrying a small cocktail-waitress tray. The tray held restaurant packages of saltine crackers, a tomato sliced into seven strips, a glass of water with one ice cube floating in it, several napkins emblazoned with the red Kentucky Fried Chicken logo, and a fresh can of Hamm's. She set the tray atop a milk crate and picked up the Hamm's. She pulled the tab and took in a drink.

"Here it is," she told Tony.

The boy sat looking at the first page of his paperback book.

"Hey there," said Grandma Lorraine. "Don't expect me to bring it over to you. Don't think we're on an airplane or anything."

"Okay," said Tony. He yawned and made no effort to move. Sleepy all of a sudden.

"Hey!" Grandma Lorraine shouted. "Poof! Dog!" She gritted her teeth, bunched her face in a scowl.

Poof was digging at the young tree in the corner. On hearing Grandma Lorraine's voice, he began to dig faster, his tiny paws kicking up dirt which splashed against his chest.

Only after Grandma Lorraine had set down her beer, stood up and lurched on to the lawn did Poof retreat. He ran toward his master with a guilty little smile, wagging his tail. Grandma Lorraine scooped him up in her arms and carried him back to the swing.

"God, that's the third time he's done it today!" Grandma Lorraine said. She squeezed Poof in her arms and gently shook him. "Darn it," she said. Her face was damp with sweat and her eyes moist, giving her the expression of a crumpled and anxious wet rag.

Tony got up and walked to the cocktail tray. He took the glass of water and two packages of saltines back to his chair. He sat down and opened one of the cellophane packages. Crumbs from the crackers fell down between his legs, a few darting into the space between his shorts and legs, where they lodged in the soft pudge of his inner thighs.

Inside the house, the phone rang.

"Shoo, it's the phone," said Grandma Lorraine, bunching up her face once more. She moved to stand, Poof leaping from her lap with a jingle-jangle. She set her beer can on the tray.

"Make sure Poof doesn't get that tree again," she told Tony. She moved swiftly inside to answer the ring.

Poof wandered back on to the lawn. He noticed a sparrow pecking at the dirt along the south wall and took off after it with playful run-leaps. The bird skirted away, up and over the wall. Poof snuffed around where it had been.

Grandma Lorraine talked on the kitchen phone. Tony heard her make several wails, followed by a sighing "Oh, no." He finished the first saltine and fished the second from the wrapper.

A moment later Grandma Lorraine came out the back door. She was wearing sunglasses and had a purse hanging from one wrist. She shook the keys in her other hand.

"It's your Aunt Jan," she said in an urgent yet weary voice. "I'm going to go send her some money or something. I'll be right back." She looked across the yard. "And watch Poof! Don't let him get that tree."

The back door slammed.

Tony looked over his shoulder. Through the large bay window that backed the porch and yard, he saw Grandma Lorraine open and flit through the front screen door. The door banged shut. He heard the slam of a car door, followed by the roar of Grandma Lorraine's car starting up, and finally the sound of the car being driven away.

Tony put another piece of cracker in his mouth. He lowered his head to focus on page one of his book.

But it was too hot. Tony's concentration broke and he looked up. He saw Poof digging at the young tree.

The boy watched the dog for a time, then glanced away. He noticed the sliced tomatoes on the tray next to Grandma Lorraine's beer can. He stood and walked over.

Tony studied the arrangement of items. Moving with extreme caution, he took hold of the beer can with his thumb and forefinger. He hoisted it, slowly, to his nose. He heard the fizz of the carbonation, listened to the ping of bursting bubbles echoing inside the thin aluminum skin. He cringed at the sour, sharp smell of the beverage.

Tony set the can down. With two careful hands, he next picked up the napkin containing the tomatoes. He felt wetness on his palms – the tomato juices leaking through the paper fiber. Cradling the tomatoes in his hands, Tony stepped across the porch and on to the lawn. Dried, dead grass crackled under his hi-tops. He felt the sun's heat bounce from the grass onto his shins and calves.

In the sun the tomatoes glittered like strange jewels. Tony stood, mesmerized by the sight. Of particular interest were the golden seeds that lay in the thick film of the tomato innards. He'd seen tomatoes before, of course, but none, it seemed, as glistening and bright as these.

He convulsed his hands, watching the tomatoes wiggle in response. He imagined they were the guts of some animal – or maybe even the heart of a person. Probably the heart of a baby, he reasoned.

The sun bore down, weighing on Tony's shoulders, searing the outermost part of his biceps.

Placing the tomato napkin in his left hand, Tony lifted one of the slices with his right. He threw the slice at the section of brick wall in front of him. It was a weak toss. The tomato hit with a soft splat, clung briefly to the pink surface, and dropped to the dirt.

Tony aimed at Poof with the next slice. It was another lackluster throw, however, off to the right by a few feet. The slice didn't even make it to the wall. It skidded in the dirt, a plume of dust rising at the impact. Poof, digging at the tree, didn't even seem to notice.

Tony, now feeling a little more limber, decided to run a bit. Balancing the tomatoes on both palms, he made a herky-jerky rotation around the yard, swooping in under the porch awning to avoid stepping in the pebble garden. He completed about two and a half laps, then stopped. His wrists and forearms ached from carrying the five tomato slices at such a pace and in such a posture.

Tony stood and caught his breath, taking a moment to consider his next move. It soon became clear that all the tomatoes had to go. Making a brisk circumference of the yard, he flung one slice over each of the three sides of the brick wall.

Two slices left now. Tony set the napkin on the grass and picked up one of the pieces. He curled his hand around it and joggled his wrist, measuring its slimy heft.

He looked at the now-fading wet spot on the brick wall which marked his first toss. Tony eyed the spot carefully, calibrating the distance. Finally he was ready. With an arching of his back and a high kick, he hurled the slice. It smashed into the brick well below the original spot, then dropped, somewhat mangled and torn, to the dirt.

Tony stared. He wasn't impressed. He had wanted to see the slice shatter into dozens of slimy, gooey pieces. As if it had exploded. He had envisioned a spectacular explosion, in fact.

He gathered up the last slice and flipped it casually in his right hand. One last shot, he thought.

Tony imagined himself a baseball pitcher, playing in a big league championship game on TV. He assumed a stretch position, poising his torso over his left knee. He waved off a few imaginary signals from the catcher, flexed his neck several times, then rose into the starter's position. He tightened and loosened his grip on the tomato slice. At last he brought the tomato to his glove hand.

He paused. No, it didn't feel right.

He crouched back down, taking in more signals. Okay – so the catcher advised the heater. Sounded good. Tony nodded, rose again to the starter's position. He stared at the wall, inhaling and exhaling methodically. He brought the tomato to his glove hand. He waited five beats. He looked over his left shoulder and then the right – one last check to make sure the base runners were not too presumptuous in their leads.

Then, in a spasm, Tony coiled himself and reached back. With a wild twist of his hips and a furious swing of his arm, he let fly the tomato.

It soared over the wall, slapping and clattering in the neighbor's yard.

Tony let himself fall to the ground, landing on his rump. He rolled and stretched out on his back, rubbing his tomato-moist hand into the grass. Dried sprigs of grass jabbed against his skin, attacking his legs and poking through his peach-colored knit shirt.

He rolled onto his stomach, setting his chin on the lawn. The stiff grass rankled his chin and neck, forcing him to lift his head back up. His arms and legs began to itch. He rubbed them in the grass. Dust and flakes of dead grass wafted into the air. Tony felt some of the flakes settle onto his eyelids and cheeks.

The sun baking his neck, back and legs was nice. Tony felt his body rhythms slacken. He was starting to get drowsy. He laid his head on a side.

From this perspective he saw the dog Poof, digging at the young tree. The dog's paws slashed around the exposed roots, rapidly expelling dirt into small piles. Poof worked vigorously, hips high, head and neck taut, forelegs a blur. The tree shook with each of his thrusts, leaves flapping.

Tony tensed. His breath shortened. His tongue touched the ridge of his upper lip.

He lifted himself slowly from the grass, rising on his palms and toes. He began an awkward creep.

The dog, intent on his project, did not notice until the boy was within about five feet.

Poof came to a stop in his diggings. He looked at Tony, gave a little lick of his chops, then sneezed dust from his snout. He blinked.

Tony lunged.

The boy flew through the air. Poof seemed momentarily frozen at the sight of the child. Then, after it was already too late, the dog decided to bolt out of the way. Tony came crashing down. He reached out, his forearm landing on Poof's rear half, forcing the dog to the ground. The momentum of the act sent the boy's hips careening into the tree. Stripped of most of its ground support, the slender trunk gave way with a snapping.

Poof squirmed and wriggled, surging for escape. Tony's writhing left hand clamped around the dog's right hind leg.

Poof squirmed and wriggled and pulled. But it was no use.

Tony had him.

The boy watched the dog struggle for a time, enjoying the sensation of Poof's squirming, straining leg vibrating his arm. When that was no longer of interest, Tony moved forward and brought both hands under the dog's belly. He rolled on to his back and lifted Poof into the air, bringing he and the dog face to face. Poof's dangling front paws sent grounds of dirt onto Tony's face.

Irritated, Tony lowered the dog to his chest. He curled into a fetal position and rolled himself and Poof onto the grass, making several complete rotations. Tony grinned, comparing the deftness of the maneuver to that of a Special Forces soldier or police officer.

The feeling dissipated, however, as Tony's position on the grass afforded him a clear view of the tree's devastation. It was flattened – torn and bent woundedly against the trough Poof had dug.

Tony clutched Poof to his breast. The dog exhaled loudly through his nose, surprised by Tony's pressure.

Tony looked at the dying tree.

Poof started to squirm again. His back legs clawed at Tony's midsection. But the boy held firm. In fact, he increased his pressure.

Poof began to whine.

Tony, annoyed, sat up on his knees. He released Poof from his arms, but held on to the dog's forelegs as it scrambled upright on the grass. Poof stood unsurely, looking at Tony. The dog's head bobbed up and down in unison with its now heavy breaths.

Poof made another desperate surge for freedom, whining and rebelling against the boy's hold, throwing himself low to the ground, hind legs churning against the brittle grass.

But Tony's grip was absolute. After a few moments Poof calmed, seeming to surrender. He glanced at Tony and lowered his head.

"Now whatcha gonna do?" said Tony gruffly. He grinned and stared at the dog.

"Now what?" said Tony.

The dog's only movements were twitches of his small head. The movements fascinated Tony. The boy felt a rush of excitement. Those twitches of Poof's – he was drawn to them. They were delicate and denuded in a way Tony had never before observed in animals.

Tony again asked the dog what he was going to do. But Poof only continued to stand and twitch, his head bowed.

With a wild expenditure of energy, Tony flung the dog up into the air. Poof, legs flailing, flipped on to his back.

Tony crashed down on top. Poof issued a cry that was half scream, half bark, and was then silent. Tony hung his head over the dog, feeling Poof's warm, slightly sour breath on his face.

He stared at Poof's shiny black eyes. The dog looked away nervously. But Tony continued to stare. Indeed, he grew frustrated when the animal refused to return his gaze. It was suddenly highly important that the dog look at him.

Tony found Poof's eyes extremely intriguing. They were different – not at all like those of humans. They lacked the clear delineation of pupil and sclera, the subtleties of color found in the eyes of people. Poof's eyes were like wet black marbles, and Tony wanted to inspect them closely.

Tony lifted off the dog and slid onto his knees, putting one leg on each side of Poof's head. He clamped both his hands around Poof's neck – his fingers laced at the back of the dog's head, his thumbs under its dirty blue collar.

Poof gulped. He took in several quick breaths. He blinked his eyes rapidly.

Tony increased the pressure of his hands.

Poof began to panic, kicking his legs ineffectually against Tony's behind. With great effort Poof sought to move his head up and beyond Tony's grip.

Tony applied more pressure.

Poof's eyes rolled up in their sockets. The dog kicked and squirmed, straining its neck upwards. It was as if, Tony thought, Poof was somehow trying to separate his head from the rest of his body.

Tony added more pressure around the dog's throat.

The boy studied Poof's tongue. It was appearing frequently now, exiting the dog's mouth in slow, almost meditative strokes. Tony could hear the spooned-oatmeal sound of the tongue against the dog's black lips.

The sight and sound captured Tony: The strange, black lips themselves, and the look of the tongue – the tiny grooves, like tiny cuts, in unexpected patterns on the bed of the tongue. The tongue itself seemed a suddenly bizarre thing to Tony – so very small it was, of a bright pink, almost orange color.

Tony tightened his grip yet again.

Poof gulped strenuously. Tony could feel the dog's Adam's apple against his thumbs, struggling to rise and fall.

Tony tightened, just a fraction more.

Poof's tongue came out, trembling and slow. It was the noise a person makes when their mouth is dry, concluded Tony. He watched the slow heave and collapse of the dog's pointy rib cage.

Poof rasped. It started as a low, guttural scratching noise, but moved along the octaves to finally resemble a kind of dull whistle. After another increment of pressure from Tony, Poof began to make a hacking, cough-like sound.

Tony could feel the texture of Poof's trachea against his thumbs. It was almost as if he could feel the air itself as it squeezed down into the dog's lungs.

Tony felt a warm, pulsing sensation flood his hips and the base of his spine, oozing up toward his shoulders.

Again he increased the pressure.

Poof's eyes were glassy, unmoving. The dog was no longer making a sound.

Tony marveled at his hands, at his grip so uniformly tight around the dog's throat. It was though an incredible ball of humming power had attached itself to the ends of his arms.

As Tony almost imperceptibly tightened his hold, an angry sharp rapping shattered the moment.

Tony jerked around, his heart slamming.

Tony saw Grandma Lorraine through the big bay window. She raked the window again with a key, before turning and disappearing.

In another second Tony heard the back door wheeze open. Grandma Lorraine came at him like a bee swarm.

"*Oh, you!*" she shrieked. She walked toward Tony with long, furious strides.

Tony released Poof's throat and hopped off the dog, falling to the grass. He felt a wave of hotness in his cheeks, the beginnings of tears in his eyes.

"*Ouhhh!*" Grandma Lorraine warbled.

She knelt to the grass over the dog. She came forward so quickly she nicked Tony in the face with her sharp, bony shoulder. The boy scooted away, his right cheek smarting.

Grandma Lorraine curled her arms around Poof and brought him to her chest. The dog licked feebly at Grandma Lorraine's chin and neck.

"He's crying!" Grandma Lorraine wailed.

She looked at Tony with an anguished, burgundy-colored expression. "What did you do to him, my poor baby!"

Tony said nothing. He watched Grandma Lorraine cradle the dog.

Grandma Lorraine moved Poof to her right arm and swung at Tony with her left.

"What – you – !"

Tony leaned out of the path of her attack. The momentum of her lunge carried Grandma Lorraine to the grass in a heap.

"*Ouhh,*" she ululated. "Oh, you kid."

Grandma Lorraine sat, patting Poof's head.

"He's shaking, look at him." She wiped moisture from her face with the collar of her blouse, then lowered her head to nuzzle the dog.

"And look at my tree! Ouhhh…"

Tony walked to the porch and sat in the chair. He picked up his book and rested it on his lap. He wiped dots of tears from the corners of his eyes. He inhaled and sighed. His nose was stuffy. His stomach was quaking.

Grandma Lorraine kissed Poof once more and rose. Poof shook himself, collar jingling, and began a tender-footed walk.

"Look at him, my poor baby," said Grandma Lorraine.

She turned toward Tony, walked a few steps, then stopped in the lengthening shade of the porch awning. She wagged a finger at him.

"Boy, oh boy, this is the last straw, mister. Wait till I tell your mother. Boy, have you got it coming."

Grandma Lorraine walked away, then circled back. She wagged her finger again.

"I'm going to go get Poof some water and don't you touch him!"

Grandma Lorraine walked to the back door and went inside.

Poof, still shaking, limped up to the porch. He saw Tony and halted. The boy looked away.

Grandma Lorraine came back out. "C'mere, baby," she said, setting a green plastic bowl on the ground. Poof stepped timidly over and began to drink. "That's a good baby boy. Yes, that's my good baby boy, aren't you, aren't you, yes you are…"

Grandma Lorraine stood watching a moment, then said, "My beer." She went back into the house, returning seconds later with a fresh can of cold Hamm's. She sat down, only to rise again to administer to Poof. She picked up the dog and carried him to the swing.

She pointed her finger at Tony and yelled once more about what she would tell his mother.

Tony's head felt itchy. He began to scratch his scalp ferociously, all over, at the temples and the crown and at the point where the skull curved into the spine, until he felt the skin break. He tore up his face as he scratched, squinching his nose and scrambling his eyes.

"Stop it!" Grandma Lorraine screeched. "Stop it! Stop scratching! Ow, stop it!"

Tony stopped.

Grandma Lorraine sighed, popped the tab on her beer. She offered the first drink to Poof, and he lapped from the can.

DAGGER

1

The sun fell down on California. Inside a large beach villa, lights flared. The place belonged to Pete Dagger, all-star American writer.

Dagger was among the biggest of the writers, perhaps the largest of the era. He was a top multi-millionaire popular artist who was loved by the critics. He was huge with the academics, who sucked from his marrow, and also with the cynics in the underground, who were hot and bothered by his slashing, ripping style and bottomless defiance.

Like many of the greats, Dagger was no genius-come-lately. He had been recognized only after years and years of surviving on ketchup soup and kool-aid, after years and years of struggle up mountains of scorn and indifference. He had survived the painful years of short-story writing; the dabbling in "journalism"; the job stints as dishwasher, data-input man, and motel clerk. He had overcome the harrowing years of hostility and suspicion from friends, colleagues and family. He had prevailed despite his stabbing bouts of doubt; his frightening drunk sprees; a general case of self-loathing.

Few critics had initially discerned Dagger's particular epochalness. His first book, *Copper's Gold*, had received vague, if somewhat polite, notices in the small number of journals that chose to review it (many a career was in fact badly tarnished by the early failure of critics and editors to identify the breadth of Dagger and his achievement). The public response to this sterling volume was similarly rather sluggish, and initial hardback sales of *Copper's Gold* petered out at about 910,000 copies.

However, Dagger's second book, the cutting, bittersweet masterpiece *The Sun, Hey, Strawberries*, was an instant global paperback best-seller, prompting a renewed wave of interest in *Copper's Gold*. The first book had then mounted a keen comeback, soon overtaking the second on the sales charts – and to the amazement of Dagger and many others, Pete Dagger had become the proverbial worldwide rage. With critics from Maine to Madagascar suddenly struggling to say enough good things about these two textual jewels, Dagger was inexorably propelled to the summit of literary regard, a position he maintained to the present day.

In the years since its publication, *Copper's Gold* had lost none of its legendary luster, remaining among the most preeminent of Dagger's classic texts. The 329-page standard American paperback version was now in its twenty-eighth printing. At last count, it had been translated into 71 languages (in editions of varying page-lengths). It was taught in all but the very most pious high school districts of the U.S.A., as well as in most of the modern-leaning universities of Europe, Canada, Asia and the former Soviet Union. And it had made Dagger millions and millions of dollars, with no sign of slowing down.

Dagger's latest, the glam-stained sci-fi satire *Is He In Pain, Queenie?*, was his ninth book. The most recent figures, fresh from the conglomerate head-office, showed it had sold 41 million copies so far worldwide. And it was still on the upcline. The rights had been sold in Malaysia, and a publisher in Santiago, Chile had just put in what was believed to be a record bid for Latin America.

The book, indeed, was quite universally loved, and had added another coating of shine to Dagger's literary reputation (which was already glisteningly formidable, save for his mostly forgotten fourth book, the semi-autobiographical *Dromedary*, which had initially been published in a limited, premium-priced first edition of seven damask-covered octavo volumes) as the most ruthlessly brilliant author of his generation. Indeed, the consensus was starting to move beyond even that: Dagger's name had started to crop up now and then among the ranks of some of the more major Russian, French and Portuguese giants.

History, of course, would be the ultimate judge. Yet there could be no denying that Pete Dagger had the essential vitals – the question was simply no longer open to dispute by serious people. Because Pete Dagger was the actual thing itself – the real, the pure, the absolute, no-bars item. He was a visionary, a shaman, a revolutionary, a humanist, a misanthrope, a true pro, and pretty tough stuff. He just had it. He God to earnest had it. His books were treasures, straight and unbidden.

There was, of course, next to no competition. Dagger had seen to that. His singing, stamping excavations, his drench-filled revelations, his crushingly excellent stories, death-defying prose gambits, witheringly incisive dissection of the political situation – his lightness, his darkness – his faith, humor and melancholy – hope, despair, joy – dread and wit – the scathing opprobrium – his allusions to the Biblical Christ, his enraged assault on the organized Church – his meditations re: man v. machine – that little bit of unnamable insatiable – had basically killed off and rendered unusable all challengers. By that we refer to: The pallid sardonics waving their flags; the clever card-sellers; the panting word-women; the thriller tripemeisters and the horror turds; the university-learned phlegmatists; the technophile doughboys; the cruddy computer crumbs; zhivagoing doctors; panoramic pie-pushers; moody revanchists; dullardly ethnicians; foolish and mistaken A-students; pea-brained peace prize candidates; the tired Jews; gin-slapped country-club stemwinders; bungling zeitgeist-sniffers; the hordes of goshing girls; provincial dreck-kings; sports dopes; media-mooing mindtwerps; science-loving schlong-necks; Godly gabbling goonies; flatulizing financial finnanegans; ironicizing trash-truckers; crime-crazed schtickmen; screenplay-flogging schlock-jacks; plastic-fingered sex-phonies; the corporate-vetted dingbat dimwits; the shoddily fallaciously shabbily drearily – Dagger had shot and smashed them all down, to the cheers of a delighted, word-wary world.

As night fell down on California in early spring, Pete Dagger sat before his electric typewriter and crafted, with his bare hands, another masterpiece. He looked like a normal man of fifty-seven, about six feet tall, 195 pounds, except for his face, which was creased like a De Kooning, and his eyes, which looked like a pair of little blue fish freshly plucked from the Pacific. As Dagger typed, passages of stunning luminosity took shape. It was as though his fingers themselves were wired to the hot, burbling, frothing cone of humanity – or anti-humanity, as the case would have it. The words spilled forth, providing another piercing, rending glimpse at the secret whispered soul of existence. The new book had the working title *Too Many Vikings*. Well, perhaps the title would need a little work, come to think of it.

Dagger's beachside villa was a conventional-enough looking place, as such places go. Of multiple split-level design, it featured a pool-Jacuzzi-sauna complex, with direct beach access and special fog lights; an expansive French-Italian kitchen; a collection of functional Finnish-Dutch furniture, representative of several design moments; five bedrooms, six bathrooms, two studies, three dinettes, and one library; artworks, among them several pieces by Chinese, Arabian and Salvadoran dissidents; a combined billiards room/satellite theatre/bar-disco/championship-regulation Scrabble sanctum; a six-car garage, filled with six cars, two bicycles and three motorcycles; and detached servant's hut (unoccupied for several years now). Dagger didn't care so much for all the stuff, but it had just piled up over the years. After all, one had to do something with one's money; one couldn't just let it sit there.

Perhaps Dagger's only "unusual" possession was a handmade stone pornographic chess set, which occupied a place of prominence in the main sitting room. This had been sent to him by a fan from Scotland.

The phone rang. Dagger's hand snapped at the black receiver, seizing it in mid-jangle.

"Hello?... Well hello, Jack," Dagger said with a thin chuckle. "Hello to you, too... Well of course, of course... Absolutely, why not... send her right over... Oh, fine... Yep, another one, you got it... Two hundred thou or so? Sure, shouldn't be a problem. I'll have it sent over first thing... Twenties and fifties only? You betcha, buddy... Okay, be seeing you... You bet, we certainly, certainly should... Toodle-oo to you too."

Dagger hung up. He sat there, calmly, and stroked his brief beard. Then Pete Dagger began to softly cry. His heart almost seemed to crack open.

Yes, it was that time again. Another girl was coming.

It was as basic as that, yet also more. So, so much, much more. It was the most beautiful thing he could think of, in fact. A pretty girl. Well, now – a pretty young woman. A pretty woman-girl. Dagger shut off his typewriter and sat in his chair, drowning inside.

2

Dagger never knew where, exactly, the girls came from nor, exactly, why. He only knew his friend Jack would send them, by car or by bus, and they would stay until they left. It might be a few hours, a day, a week, but rarely much longer than a month. Dagger gathered that the girls were employees of Jack's – or if not outright employees, most certainly "associates" of some kind. Something. It was all very unclear to Dagger. Yet he never inquired of the details. It seemed he never quite wanted to know all that much.

Well, Dagger knew Jack was involved in what loosely could be called "entertainment" – principally films and modeling and so forth, and also the dancing industry perhaps, and perhaps also what might be called the courier business. Dagger had gathered that – indeed, he was well aware of it. He had, after all, bankrolled a goodly number of Jack's projects over the years. These had been far from profitable, at least financially, at least from Dagger's perspective – Dagger had never seen a single return off any of his investments. But as I say, Dagger never properly inquired. He never missed the money, and he just never inquired.

Dagger didn't mind. Hardly. Pete Dagger had more money than he rightly knew what to do with. Indeed, small armies of men and women toiled around the globe to ensure that his money was being constantly turned into more. Because the system worked to Pete Dagger's benefit now. He had crossed a certain fiduciary threshold, and there would be no turning back. There could not be any turning back – not the way the system worked today, so long as you had crossed the threshold. And Dagger had crossed that threshold – lord, but he had.

He therefore donated to Jack whatever the other man requested, and whenever he requested it. Gladly. In fact, joyously.

It was the least Dagger could do. He liked to think of it as his little unique role in the necessary redistribution of wealth. Because Dagger was of the belief that the money he gave Jack eventually, somehow, wound up in the hands of people who could really use it – working people, struggling people. An utterly indistinct conclave of poor souls, doomed dreamers and generally irresponsible laggards – in any case, people to whom it might somehow make a difference.

Well, maybe it wasn't exactly like that, all things considered – perhaps it was a bit more complicated. Perhaps indeed. But Dagger chose not to dwell on it, at least not for very long. One couldn't worry about everything, after all. One couldn't avoid one's responsibility, certainly, but one couldn't worry about everything – though one did, of course, have to draw a line somewhere. Yes – at about murder and torture and nuclear war, Dagger supposed. Terrorism, too.

Pete Dagger had met Jack several years ago – around the time of Dagger's now legendary Hollywood spree that had followed the premiere of *Sasquatch Plutarch*, his seventh book for which he'd written the screenplay in four days. The country music had been playing rather loudly the one night, and Jack had rather astutely meshed himself into Dagger's circle of a groggy midnight, weaving in with deep pockets of good cheer, jokes – and, as it happened, a sultry passel of airy young beauties.

Now, years later, the beauties had not stopped coming – the cavalcade had not ceased. Certainly *not*.

Dagger trembled, just thinking about it. Gosh, it was horrible – yet he could think of nothing better.

These girls – what in silky blue heaven were they doing? Well, okay – they were modeling and dancing and starring in film projects – this Dagger had gathered. And he'd gathered that the films and other projects were not being produced by the major

Hollywood studios – at least not the ones that churned out the movies and television programs based on his books. But that was about all Dagger knew.

Well, Dagger knew – he was almost positively certain – that other men, perhaps many other men, were involved. On some level, Dagger knew they most certainly were.

He cringed and trembled anew at the notion, at the idea of what might be happening. Gosh, these were girls gone bad! Bad, bad, filthy little cheapies! But so wonderful, too. Wonderful! So young and good smelling. So pretty. So delightful. So quivering with life. So to be cherished. But so bad! Bad! So very bad!

The doorbell rang. Dagger shuddered. She was there, she had come. Dagger's heart swished like an eyeball in solution. Thank God he'd already gotten everything ready. Her room was prepared, he'd double-checked it just seconds ago. The kitchen was fully stocked, he'd checked. The bathrooms were spotless. The boy had come earlier that afternoon to clean the pools.

Dagger jogged to the entryway and put his hand on the console. Would he use the surveillance video monitor? No. Dear no! The first look-see was always best in the flesh.

Dagger bent himself and peered through the front door fisheye. *There she was!* Standing under the bright and glimmery porch bulbs. Ah, and pretty as could be. Blue backpack over a shoulder. Auburn-colored hair, rolled up in front, wavy on the sides. Snapping gum. Hooped earrings, the size of half-dollars. A cute little – what was that? – yes, a little glittery stud, stuck there in the nose, above the right nostril. The eyes – approximately turquoise, it appeared. And those full lips, he was looking at them now – so hideously full! Well, she may have been a bit on the short side, legwise, considered Dagger – oh, but it didn't matter, not that much.

Dagger's heart raced and flipped. It somersaulted, darted, backstroked, butterflied and chicken-winged.

He drew open the door, a curious, expectant beam across his bearded visage.

"Well hello there," he said in a fell swoop.

"Hi."

Her head cocked to a side. A hand raised itself in a tentative signal of greeting.

"Yes," said Dagger, "Jack said you would be here, and here you are." He laughed lightly. "It's Sandra, isn't it, yes? Sandra?"

She smiled. "That's me."

"Well come in, come in," Dagger said, showing her the way.

After Dagger had hung her coat, he disappeared into the kitchen. He called out, "May I get you something? A ginger ale, perhaps?"

"Okay."

"With ice?"

"Okay."

Dagger's shaking hands fumbled. A block of ice pitched to the imported pink stones of the kitchen floor, shattering in a crack of sliding crystal.

"Just another minute," he called out. "I'm afraid I've spilled."

Dagger at last returned to the sitting room. On his right palm he balanced a chrome tray with two small bottles of ginger ale, glass tumblers, one bowl of broken ice and another of macadamia nuts.

Sandra was seated on the white velvet couch, her legs crossed.

"That's a interesting chess set," she said, pointing. "Never seen one like that before."

Dagger's knees buckled. Ice clinked. He set the tray on the coffee table and slumped next to her, heart beating, air fluttering about his nostrils.

"Yes," he said weakly, "I suppose it is rather somewhat rare."

"Can I smoke in here?" she said, leaning forward suddenly. "Do you mind?"

"Oh, please do," Dagger said. "I'll run and get you an ashtray."

He sprang up and walked briskly to the hallway closet.

"Wow, *Time* magazine," he heard Sandra say.

She rose from the couch to inspect the framed object on the wall. It was a layout of Dagger from several years ago. He was on his strip of beach, hair whipping in the breeze, staring straight into the camera. He was wearing a black and red silk samurai costume. In his hands he held a huge, decorative, curving sword, of the kind one might possibly find in a movie about pirates. "He Writes The Books," text said in large yellow type. Below that, in somewhat smaller type, it said: "Pete Dagger Cuts to the Bone."

"Wow, that's you on the cover of *Time!*"

Dagger was returning with the ashtray.

"Yes," he said, grinning and setting down the ashtray.

There was a soft clunking noise.

3

It was morning, a little before five a.m. Pete Dagger rose in his bed chamber, electrically awake. He went to the toilet, had a rub of his beard and a drink of water from the sink. He walked blinkingly down the hall to his study, hesitated a moment in the doorway, and finally set the lights a-burning. He sat before his computer/typewriter and inhaled. He flipped on the machine and began to labor once more upon the latest masterpiece.

Pete Dagger trained his concentration and worked. A diamond of a word was quickly followed by a sapphire. Next came a ruby of a verb, a platinum participle, a perfect pearl of punctuation. The resulting combination was pure Peter K. Dagger – pure radiance.

And so the day began.

The clock was a strike or two past eight when Dagger paused. Was that a noise? Indeed, it appeared to have been. Dagger froze, poised over his keyboard. Now another noise. Noises. A door opening. A toilet's muffled groan. And now the muted spraying splay of shower jets.

Fingers stuttering, Dagger shut down his machine. Knees jerking, the back of his neck squirming, he scuttled past the bathroom in question and descended the stairs to the kitchen.

When Sandra at last appeared, Dagger had the table miraculously set. It contained a small silver decanter of steaming coffee; tea in a sturdy porcelain crock; a pitcher of chilled grapefruit juice; lightly toasted bagels, still warm; cream cheese, lox, margarine and apricot jam; muesli, in tandem with fresh goat's milk; ham slices and honey; and basketed fruit, still water-splendored from Dagger's focused rinsing the moment before.

Sandra damply crossed the ingress of the breakfast dinette, a candy-striped towel about her head.

"Well good morning, Sandra," Dagger said.

"Hello."

The young woman was barefoot. In addition to the towel, she wore a large mint-green T-shirt, torn in one spot at the collar, with the large inscription VISUALIZE WHIRLED PEAS emblazoned in blue on the front. Sandra glanced at Dagger, smiled from one side of her mouth, and sat down at the table.

Dagger heard the tweet of birds, flutting and scruffing in the trees beyond the window. Golden sunshine poured between the venetian window slats. Dagger observed that Sandra did not appear to be wearing anything beneath her T-shirt.

"Wow, thank you for breakfast," she said. "You didn't have to, you know."

"Oh, come now," said Dagger. "It's my pleasure. Sleep well, did you?"

"Yes, very well," she said, offering a smile. "Really, thanks a lot for letting me stay here."

"Oh, no problem. Quite seriously, it's not a problem at all. That's a funny T-shirt, by the way."

Dagger grinned.

"Yeah," Sandra said. A glint of blue-gold jumped from her nose bauble, surprising Dagger as it veered. "It's a joke on world peace. Get it? Whirled peas?"

"I do, I do."

Sandra lifted a toasted bagel-half to her plate and picked up a knife. With her other hand she lifted the pot of honey. Dagger poured himself a steaming black dash of coffee. He gazed at Sandra and felt his blood racing. His heart galloped, churned, leaped, and broke into thousands and thousands of individually bruised and crumpled pieces. In his ears, an inconcise roaring mixed with bird tweets.

"So you're a writer, huh?" Sandra said. "Mmm, this is good honey."

"Thank you," Dagger said. "Yes, that's quite right, I do write. Or type, rather. It's just a lot of typing, to be honest."

He shrugged, smiled and brought a hand to his beard. "It's a job, I guess. And I'm lucky to have it." He shrugged again. "Anyway. The honey's from Oregon, if you're wondering. A friend sent it."

Sandra ingested another bite and swallowed. "Did you ever write anything for Jack? I mean, for the things he does?"

"Ho, dear no," said Dagger, tacking on a light laugh. "But maybe that's not a bad idea, though, now that you mention it."

He chuckled, smiled, then swept his hand once more to his chin. He plunged into a swirl of brief thoughtfulness.

Sandra grinned. "I didn't think so. I mean, because you're kind of famous, right? Cover of *Time* magazine, right? I think I remember them talking about you once in school. I don't remember what they said, but – well, they were talking about you." She smiled for a moment before biting her lower lip. "I'm sorry. I guess I should have paid more attention." She hunched her shoulders and shrugged.

"Oh, no," said Dagger, "dear no. It's quite all right, Sandra. I don't know what they say myself, and would probably frankly rather not hear it, to be honest. Some fool foolishness, I would imagine, neither quite here nor there, as they say. Most likely. Where did you go to school, by the way?"

"Well, I went to high school in Tucson." Her face and neck pinkening, Sandra's eyes darted to a colorful, prison-flavored Salvadoran wall print. "I haven't started college yet, if that's what you mean. But I want to. As soon as I'm ready – I mean, when I have my money saved and stuff."

"Tucson," said Dagger, "in Arizona?"

"Yes."

"That's a pretty place, isn't it? Deserts and everything. All those empty skies. Cacti."

"Are you kidding?" said Sandra, her eyes widening. "It's super-shitty to the max. Excuse my French, but it is. Jesus Christ. Why do you think I came all the way out here?"

"Okay, okay, point taken," said Dagger, raising his hands in an "I surrender" posture. "I was just there once. It did seem very pleasant, I must say – but you're far more of an expert than I could ever be. More tea?"

"Yes, please."

The both of them ate their fill, or close to it. At which point Sandra announced Jack was sending a car to pick her up in the early afternoon.

Pete Dagger and Sandra together cleared the dishes to the kitchen and set them inside the dishwasher.

Dagger suggested a swim on the beach.

"Oh, really?" said Sandra. "Let me just run up and get my swimsuit."

Dagger, sitting down, brought up his beard hand.

"Well," he said, gazing up at her, "only if you want to, Sandra. It's a private beach access, you know. You can do whatever you want down there. No one's going to be spying or anything."

"Oh."

Sandra lowered her eyes. Her nose and lips tremored infinitesimally.

"Okay, I guess."

"Fine, then," said Dagger, gesturing at the sliding glass which led to the beach. "By all means, do as you please. Feel free, as they say."

Sandra quickly turned. As she did, Dagger caught a glimpse of a tattoo on the outer flank of her right thigh. What the – was that a flower? motorcycle? Sheesh. Some kind of *death's head?*

Dagger wasn't sure. Darn it, so many of these girls had tattoos. Between seventy and eighty percent, at least, all with at least one tattoo, somewhere. All kinds of tattoos. Navel rings, too. Nipple rings.

Dagger and Sandra strode over the warm expanse of redwood planking that led to the ocean. Hot sunlight dabbled upon their heads, the heat however made deceptive by the cool sea winds which ruffled the adjoining arrangement of palm trees and bougainvillea Birds tweeted.

Surf could be heard, pounding muffledly.

Sandra suddenly said, "You're probably going to want me to suck you off, yeah?"

Dagger gulped. His breath caught. His heart skipped, tripped, shattered, came together, fell and splintered once more. He lowered his head and walked, one step after the other. He looked up and sniffed the breeze.

"No, actually," he said, looking at her and scowling somewhat. "It hadn't crossed my mind. What makes you say that? Jack didn't say anything, did he? God, I hope not. He better not have. What a terrible thing to say to a woman."

Dagger cast a grim, beardful look at Sandra. He lowered his head and shook it.

"No, he didn't," Sandra said. "But I just figured. A girl learns a few things pretty quick out here in California."

Dagger walked. His bare toes pushed the sand. He was hearing her voice, but the words were disappearing, disappearing in the thickening salt-haze. Dagger's toes twinged against the scalding sand, the sun pestered his long, lightly-haired brown arms. The air throbbed with the ancient incense of rotting seaweed, tar and foaming froth.

These girls. Oh, these girls! Nothing but little casseroles of sugar and water, dirt and mucous, proteins and pulpy things. Little squiggly things.

Pete Dagger walked, but slowly now, vaguely, drowsy from the heat. He stood and stared at the sun-struck waves, at the geyser of brilliant white on the horizon. Sandra had flipped off her sleeper and was jogging with dancing steps toward the ocean.

4

Well, Pete Dagger thought, things were pretty much squared away. The New York trip was all arranged. There would be the awards ceremony and poultry-fish banquet, followed by any number of parties. The usual routine. It wouldn't be so bad. New York was still a hell of a town, after all, plenty of people were still promoting it. And Dagger guessed he had to see those people, sooner or later. Business was business, after all. The system was still intact. Yep – the same old unjust system, corrupt to the core, rigged to help "the rich" and enslave the rest, or a lot of them. Yes, and it probably wouldn't be changing any time soon.

Well – and so what was to be done? The answer, reflected Dagger, was not much. Unless, you mean, maybe blow it up? Burn it down? How about a new revolution of some sort? Or – perhaps a quantity of strategic tinkering, and a tiny spot of heavy lifting, to make things, uh, a little more humane and equitable, locally and globally? Dagger chuckled. Bring it on, baby, yeah yeah, mix it up if you've got the juice. Two steps forward and one step back, and vice versa, and so on, depending of course on which side ended up with more key ideological booty after what war, and how disruptive were the technologies during which political hegemonic blah-blah, and whose scales of economy were more terrific at what big moment of convergence. And importantly, who did the analysis at which particular time, after everyone was dead and no longer bothered… let the historians sort it out later. Fine, just fine. Because about the only thing Pete Dagger was certain of was that some people kept dirty asses, while others worked to stay clean. And quite a large number, in fact the majority, tended to fluctuate. And therefore, i.e., human beings were born to suffer, and art was the only thing one could or should have any confidence in, tee-hee…

Dagger did not necessarily believe in "throwing away" one's money, as such. But one was, after all, obligated to do something with one's funds. It was a basic obligation, in Dagger's view – or did you have something else in mind? Dagger chuckled. It was good, for example, to be able to hand out checks, such as the one he'd given Sandra when she finally left – for $50,000. If it didn't buy her all the way into college, thought Dagger, well, maybe it would keep her in cigarettes and pantyhose and bus tickets for a few months. Lord – well, and he'd taken her at her word about that crystal meth problem that had revealed itself. But what else could he have done? He wasn't about to have another woman around the house full-time. Dear no – how could he ever get to work with something like that going on?

Well, Dagger didn't care too much – but he did, he did. He actually did care. He sincerely loved to write those checks. And he'd keep writing them until – well, he supposed, until, for whatever reason, he no longer could.

Dagger was in the kitchen preparing a tray of drinks and nuts when the phone rang. He snapped the hand-held unit out of its cradle on the wall.

"Hello?"

Silence.

"Hello?" Dagger said again.

Nothing.

"I said, Hello? Who is this?... Hello? Is anybody there?... I said, Hello?"

Silence. Perhaps a slight hissing.

"Well," he said, "if that's the way you feel, fine." His face drew itself into a tight grin. "Hello-hello, yoo-hoo... Okay, whatever... Nice talking to you, whoop-de-whoo. No, serious, really nice, heck of a darn time. Oh yeah, sure, sure, pleasure's mine, all mine, forget it..."

Dagger suddenly grew angry. "I hope this isn't some damn game."

He slammed down the receiver. He exhaled, blinked, and turned to face his drinks.

The phone rang. He whisked the receiver off its hook.

"Hello?"

Silence. Then a voice, grainy, but unmistakable: *"Hello? Hello? I said, Hello? Who is this?…"*

Dagger's neck went erect. His eyelids flapped. The hand holding the phone lost some of its power.

"… serious, really nice, heck of a darn time… Oh yeah, sure, sure, pleasure's mine, all mine forget it… I hope this isn't some damn game."

The line clicked. Dagger stood there. The phone was beeping. Well, he thought.

He returned the receiver to its hook.

Well, so they were after him. They were coming for him. It was pretty clear now. If it wasn't clear before, it was now. Okay, so – they were coming.

What did they want? What did they already have? What did they know? What was their program?

Well, Dagger thought, he didn't care. Let them come. If that was the way they wanted it, let them come. Let them take him down. Whatever the hell they pleased. If it was going to happen, then let it. Just let it. The hell with it. Let them come. Whatever they wanted. Let them take it. Let them have it, if they wanted it so bad. What did he have to hide? Nothing. Just nothing. Everything was in the open. It was there for the taking. Let them *have it* if they wanted it so bad. *Let them have it.* They couldn't take anything from Pete Dagger. He was giving it to them for free. They couldn't take what he was already giving them, could they? So let them come. All of them, each and every one. Damn it, let them come. Come!

Dagger inhaled purposely and clapped himself on the chest. He positioned his lips in a composed posture. He walked into the sitting room. He placed the chrome tray on the coffee table and sat himself on the couch.

"That's some chess set," said his guest.

Dagger grinned. "Why thank you, Robyn, thank you very much. Yes, you're quite right about that, it is a bit unique. You're not going to find something like that down at the mall, I suppose. Certainly not every day you won't."

5

New York lazed across the horizon like a dominoes game gone berserk. On the 25th floor penthouse of a West 53d Street high-rise, Pete Dagger laughed.

It was the evening post-awards party, one of several. The room shined goldenly, smelling of professionally aged cheese, toothpicks and leather. It tinkled with the sound of jazz piano and softly clashing crystal. Pete Dagger's face was dark, a touch swollen.

A woman in her latterly thirties joined the circle, grabbing for Dagger's hand. Dagger gave it over. She spoke in a rush for perhaps 30 seconds, introducing herself and so on. She was a literary editor, as it turned out, employed by the conglomerate that ultimately owned Dagger's works, but at a slightly different imprint. Shortly it was discovered she was in possession of a question she'd always wanted to ask Pete Dagger. It concerned a character in one of his early mid-period books, the buoyant, effervescent, yet oddly elusive *Picabo Street*, which had sold 39 million at latest count.

"I'm really frankly much more interested in what you think," Dagger told the woman. "That's really what counts, you know. I just wrote the darn thing. The damn thing, excuse me."

The woman laughed, taking Dagger's remark as an invitation to elucidate her position.

"Yes, yes, perhaps so," Dagger said, nodding his head. He hoisted his wine bottle and ingested a swallow. "Yes," he went on, "now I see what you're getting at. I'd never thought about it quite that way, to be honest, but I can see you do have a point. Quite a point, actually."

Dagger rocked his head vigorously, taking in more of the wine, wiping his mouth with his sleeve.

The woman nodded, smiled, retreated a step, and studied her toes on the carpet of creamed corn.

Dagger gazed about, lazily. Quite a crowd of luminaries had shown up for the reception, he'd shaken most of their hands: Tina O'Weishaupt and L.M. Narda, Sandy Chuck and her husband Rolf, Clarence Dumanouga, Jean-Pierre Pochon, Kris Scarver and Feuilleton Hospoda, Bennett Mor-Morgentaler and Jasmine Hovnova. Not far away stood Koch Sauerlander, Edie Guillermostein, Mondrian Finefrock, Tacoma Hopps-DeGoey and Youssef Prout.

Aha, and yes, there: Robert Benko, Paula Wild, Abdelaziz Herrera, Geoff Raynoch; and Peter Fnolegh, Uragan C. Smerch, Anna Blantag, Dieter Johns, Alice Sheets Boyne, Jane Hutfless, Lester Tunbs, Claude-Ellen Robbins and her notable son, Niall. Oh yes, and to the left: Padraig Solana, Tim Tuttle, Thom Twyford, Ashtone Steavens, Vivian Rottnier, Lars Halford, certainly. And over there, oh yes, in a row – Danny O. Hulka, Pietrefesa Tillinghast, Laurence Bonaqua, Megan Pinckney-Gund, Nicola Shandybin, Tuck and Randall Potes. And Porzo Vlak, James Shamkhani, Plaxico Sachs, Appolonia Freund, Jean-Francois

Silliere, Edgar Rabbani, Carlos Hongwu. Ah, lord – the redoubtable Goerner Majlis himself, chatting with none the other than Wellmax Knippers.

Dagger, gently rubbing his wine bottle, took a long look at Giga Meist, whose red and white dress tonight was quite remarkable, as many had remarked. And indeed, yes – Otak Omarska, Bryan Bergfriedhof, Joe Bocker, Theresa Maria Aasenlich, Shigeru G. Schliem, Yoshi "Jay" Graham, T.P. Ajax, Alec Scandalios, Ferden Vell, Richard Lee Ben Jackson Burton, Maxine Hurtado y Baker, Danielle Piraino, Kirby Shelby, Bruno Hamenyakataa, Egon Lansky, Scott Rondale, Vladimir Gonzalez, Andi Pugach…

To say nothing of the assembled assorted etcetera who always attended, the faceless clutches of tenured professors, apprentice critics, Oxford-educated athletes, actors, hosts, models, promoters of Internet sites, the industry operators and the other various other lit-liking people, so many of whom had been so kind to Dagger over the years, though not always, and certainly not always on time, and with little risk to their career or whatever damn fool thing…

Dagger swiveled his head, drank from his wine. They were all periodically glancing at him, weren't they – their lips crumbly from crackers and dried fish – glasses refilling, nostrils flaring, lips writhing, fingers twisting. Lord, Dagger thought – and so many of them from Harvard or Yale, Princeton and what have you. Quite a number of them, here in this room – gone on from Yale and Brown and Princeton and so on, to make quite an impact on the world – just as the universities themselves had advertised they would.

Dagger chuckled, suckling from his wine. He was removing the bottle from his mouth when he observed his agent, Frick, darting into the hallway that he understood to contain the bathroom.

Well, he considered – now was a good time. Dagger set down the bottle of wine. It was almost finished anyway.

"You'll have to excuse me, folks," Dagger announced, none too loudly. He shrugged, grinned, and began walking.

He strode purposefully past the host and hostess, waving jovially. He breached the double door of the suite, ambled down to the elevator and hit the button. The lift doors swept open at street level. He exited and maneuvered through the revolving building entrance.

He was on the street, the lights of the New York night whirling and whipping past him. Streetlamps and neon, traffic signals and headlights, satellites and star glow bathed Dagger, disclosing and re-cosseting him in multifarious shades of darkness. He stood there, inhaling mightily.

6

Dagger wandered, roughly in the direction of Wall Street. He loosened his tie and began unbuttoning his shirt. Whew, holy. It was time to relax.

He'd almost completed the unbuttoning job, and was at the midway point of jaywalking across a boulevard, when he saw a woman – a woman who appeared to be his ex-wife. She was walking arm in arm with a tall, black-haired, thick and rather Mediterranean-seeming man.

Was it his wife? Dagger couldn't precisely say. It was quite possible she would be in New York, perhaps vacationing, perhaps even living here now. Why not? Dagger had made certain she'd received a generous settlement – 51 percent of everything. He had demanded it of his attorneys – insisted.

Gosh but Pete Dagger hoped it was her. He watched the couple, shuffling up the street, pausing to inspect the wares in a window. God, did he hope it was Maggie. Indeed – and he hoped her date was a Greek or a Turk. Why not? A strapping Greek or Turk, even an Italian, who was kind and told funny stories and happened to know a great deal about cheese-making and wine and gardening and so on, who knew about stained glass and Buddhism and great places to go in Canada. A fellow like that. Why not? God to hell – Dagger hoped it was. She deserved it. Damn it, but she did.

Dagger swooned, watching them amble down the sidewalk. He'd made it to the other side of the street but found it difficult to stand suddenly. His eyes scanned for a bench or something, somewhere to sit, but none appeared. He cringed all over. His heart gurgled and writhed and choked and squirmed. What he'd done to the poor woman – what he'd made her do.

Pete Dagger stood there, crying.

Things had just happened. Everything had been so confusing, so difficult, and then it had happened. He didn't know, he still couldn't explain – it wasn't what he'd meant, what he meant to do. No, he hadn't understood properly what it was really all about. He'd been so wrapped up in his "plan" – believing there were such things as plans and that his was good. And it had happened. He had done it, it had happened, it couldn't be reversed.

He and his wife had gone on, they'd had children. But it had happened.

He watched the woman and her companion go, disappearing down the avenue. No, he supposed. It wasn't her after all. He sighed.

Dagger continued in the direction of Wall Street. He finished unbuttoning his shirt, then took off his black tux jacket and set it atop an overflowing wire metal trashcan. A pair of nearby bums noticed, but did not immediately rush over, being otherwise occupied.

It was just so horrible. Dagger was going to rot in hell for what happened. And he deserved to. His wife didn't share in the blame – he had made it happen. Him alone. He'd been the bully, anyone would say so. Lord, it was true. God, it was so long ago, but as near to him as last minute.

And he would burn for it. There was no justice in this world or universe, not a chance of it, but if there ever were, Pete Dagger would fry forever, deep in the bowels of the nethermost craters of hell. It was that simple – it was not at all complex. The rest of it be damned. The hell with all of it. All fucking all of it.

Dagger was not far from Wall Street now. It was still humid out, but the warm breeze was soothing against his chest. He felt his sparse nest of chest hairs, the sensation of some of the hairs wiggling individually.

Things were very bad. The breeze could not make up for the fact that things were not right.

Dagger couldn't walk any longer. He came to a small public park. It was dark there, many lamps broken, one slowly blinking. He sat hunched on a bench and sobbed, wiping the tears from his cheeks and eyes with the back of a hand.

Some time passed. Dagger got up and began to walk once more. He didn't have an idea where he was going, what time it was…

He came to an underground subway entrance and stood, gazing at the dim yellow light seeping out.

7

The doorbell sounded. Pete Dagger was in his massive California villa. *Not Nearly Enough Vikings* was complete. He'd shipped it off to the publisher two days ago. The advance "buzz" was already starting to hit the newspapers and the chat shows, while the internet nuts had been foaming with speculation and anticipation for months. The movie-people were howling at his agent's door; Frick had been stoking the price for nearly a year, dangling a carrot here and there in the snouts of the top two or three music video directors. Several so-called "A-list" actresses were said to be spitefully cat-fighting it out for the lead and supporting roles – to say nothing of the scads of script bumblers scrambling for a shot at the scripture. Over at the conglomerate, meanwhile, design and marketing plans had been launched for *The Alligator Chalice and Other Typings*, a five-volume compilation of Dagger's early stories, novellas, poetry, college and community newspaper articles, as well as a recently discovered cache of hundreds of guest registration carbons he'd personally filled out during the motel clerk days.

But now night had come again, and the front doorbell was ringing. Dagger closed down his computer, shut off the light in his office and sprinted down the stairs. He poked into the eye-peep. He nodded and grinned.

There they were, as promised.

"Well hello, Jack," Dagger said warmly, throwing open the door.

"Shakespeare!" said the other man.

Jack, bare chest framed in a blue jean vest, strode in. He wore a blond straw cowboy hat with a rainbow band, swimming shorts and tan cowboy boots. No less than five chirping, clean-looking girl-women were trailing him.

"So happy you all could come," Dagger said, stepping back to avoid Jack's oncoming cowboy brim. "Everything's all ready, I hope."

And somewhere a baseball whizzed. A monkey jumped. A Japanese ate, a wounded teen sat alone. A bunny rabbit sneezed. A tyrant traduced and a document yellowed. A presentiment was occluded. Waves lapped at Antarctica. Someone appreciated another's concern. There was a no-show at the landslide. Pollution rights were traded, missile launchers were lubricated, the sounds of seals were sequenced. The pontiff expressed shame, a porcupine screamed, Van Gogh was exonerated. A manual was consulted, an elbow lay on a tabletop. Cobblestones frothed in the rain. Extremists rallied, a paperclip dropped –

The moon seemed to cover everything with its bright breath.

Pete Dagger sat in the warm, track-lit woodenness of one of the Jacuzzis out back. The enclosure flexed and shimmied, reflecting the innumerable refracting illuminations of pool splash. The chamber echoed with laughter, girlish laughter and the heartiness of men. Dagger brought a bottle to his lips and listened to the other man. It was hot in there, getting hotter now. Sweat slid from Pete Dagger, all-star writer, mixing with the chemicals and water and bodies. He sucked from the bottle, excess dribbling down his beard.

"It's bean curd, Shakes, that's all," said Jack. "You and I both know it is. It's nice and all, we can enjoy it, but we got to call it what it is. Bean curd. Maybe somebody thinks it's special. No, I don't think you do. You know it's just *bean curd*, right Pete?"

Dagger nodded.

"Yeah," Jack went on. "Beans. Beans and curd. Think about it. So why not, you know? If it ain't you, Shakespeare, it's me – right? Or some other guy. And vice versa – some other time, some other place, depending. Know what I'm saying? You don't think so?"

Dagger looked up at the man in the cowboy hat. "Yes, I do. I do, Jack."

Jack laughed. "Of course you do, Shakes, of course you do. See, it's hard, but at the same time, it's easy. It's like, it's only hard if you let it be like that – if you think too much, which I can see you doing, no offense intended. It's easier just to think of it as bean curd. You see something – bean curd. You hear something – bean curd. You hear something else – another stripe of bean curd. Know what I mean? Don't mean nothing. Just what it is. Got to keep it simple. Don't get carried away. Keep all your furniture in all the right rooms. No mix-ups. Don't let yourself get confused. Hear me, Pete?"

"Yes. Of course."

"Good." Jack nodded. "All right then. Fine. That's what I like about you, Shakespeare. You can dig it, you can relate. You're a natural, you got the natural-built star power. It'll look like you, it'll seem like you, but no one will ever believe it. Never in a million, billion years. Not you, Shakespeare. That's the fun, see? Everyone'll think it's a joke, special effects, digital hooey-gooey and whatever. Except it won't be. Me and her and her and her and her, and her, we'll know. And you'll know, of course. Hell, you'll never forget it the rest of your life. And if you do forget, we can just show you the tape."

Jack roared out a laugh, from deep in his belly, ending in a cough.

"Yes," said Dagger.

"Oh, jeez," said Jack, holding his side. "Oh, jeez. Okay, we're ready then, I guess. Ready. Aim. Action."

The blue-green waters churned. Slippery legs and arms entwined. There was laughter, moaning, a grunt, a giggle.

"Can I do the dog now, Uncle Jack?" said Dagger. His voice was husky, somewhat breathless.

"I don't care a damn what you do," said the other man. "God damn it, I don't care."

He trained the camera at Dagger's face. Dagger's eyes were wide and unblinking, his mouth wet, slightly open.

I BELIEVED

I

There were a lot of problems, I didn't know what was going on. I'd gone to college and was living in the dorms. My roommate was a red-faced guy with short arms, Chris, who always looked like he was squinting into the sun. He had a girlfriend, Leilani, from his hometown. She would drive down to the campus on weekends, and sometimes in the middle of the week, to stay for a few days. They would get drunk. I would be lying on the bed, never quite asleep. They would come in smelling like the pete-Jesus, then start in with the groaning and sucking. It was right over there on the other bed. In the morning Leilani would smoke a cigarette and Chris would ask her for the aspirin bottle.

Chris: "Aw, man, I feel like total crap. Shit, I didn't even remember coming back here last night. I hope we didn't wake you up or nothing."

Me: "No, you didn't. It's cool."

Leilani (punching Chris): "Didn't even remember, huh?"

It happened like that, it kept happening like that. I let it happen, I thought it should be okay. But it wasn't, it was terrible, I could barely take it.

Some of the dorm guys were all right. There was Bart, a Jew from L.A. We got along good from the start. We would have these discussions lasting long into the night. Bart was skeptical about almost everything, while at the same time holding highly conventional views on most subjects. He was deeply concerned about things like personal hygiene, he would hustle away to brush his teeth after every meal.

Often we would wind up discussing whether his sperm count was getting too low. He was very troubled by the possibility. He claimed it had to do with his jeans, they were too tight, they were pressing his testicles too close to his body. He feared the body heat was burning away his sperm, perhaps even affecting his natural male aggression." But the jeans felt so good, he believed they made his ass look small and his legs longer – women dug it, they were into that look. "I should just wear shorts more, that's it," he would say. I was never sure what to tell him. Despite nearly constant innuendoes and claims, Bart avoided all women and girls strenuously. He was always quick to offer up a condemnation of the female species.

Seth was also pretty good, a tall lanky kid with nearly pure blond hair. He was originally from Sweden or Norway or somewhere like that, where his family had been from one of the noble classes – or so he'd mentioned once or twice, without going into much detail. Seth was a gawky type and clumsy on his feet, but he was a very good drunk, his face would go completely red and cheery, like a glowing hot apple. He'd be shouting and bouncing off the walls, the ceiling, but he was never violent. He had an off-kilter humor and told some good stories. He liked to tell this one about how his dad had "hung out" with the Rolling

Stones in the Bahamas. Every night the hotel staff had to throw Mick and Keith over their shoulders and carry them back to their hotel rooms. They had passed out cold from all the non-stop drinking and drugs. It was a pretty good story the way Seth would tell it. But Seth was strange, too, there was a melancholy lurking. Something had happened, I was nearly sure of it. I would wonder how he'd wound up at our average no-name school. The Swedish nobility and tall blond looks, the Bahamas dad and so forth – it seemed like it should have gotten him more. Well, but maybe not.

Jay and Mark were the rocker guys on our floor. They had long hair and Mark had a little beard. They would sit in their room with the door open, tuning and strumming their guitars. They'd put some music on the stereo and invite you in for a beer from their mini-fridge. They were trying to get a band together. They were good guys, but sometimes their attitude might get you wrong. They couldn't believe you'd never heard of some band, for example. If you had heard of them, they'd start quizzing you about albums and song titles, start naming drummers. They did finally get a group of their own together, Torchcandy it was called. After graduation they moved to L.A. and started playing the clubs. I went to see them a couple times. It was all right, but the best part was always their bass player, Alex. He was a rolling around king drunk of a great guy, constantly in and out of jail for this and that, drunk driving and drunk in public. He would complain about the thousands of dollars of fines he owed the court, then scratch out a laugh and order another whiskey-beer, order one for you too. Torchcandy never became famous or put out an album, though they kept at it for years.

One Friday I had a whole load of classes and I got up to go to them. I hadn't learned yet. It was still early at the start of the year, they still had me believing in going to class and getting good grades. But this was fading fast – nearly everything I believed in was crumbling like the smelliest, most unreliable block of roquefort it was. The hardcore Republicanism, the wanting to be a "businessman," the thinking John Updike was a "great writer," etc. – it was all of it going fast. I tried to deny it for a while, I had to. I put up great resistance, doing flips and thinking myself in circles, until finally it was just too much anymore and the whole crud sack crapped out.

Matters were compounded by the sheer booze and alleged sex of college life, the one-two combo. I could drink all the beer I wanted, just about any time, and that was fine, it was real fine. But the sex aspect was preying on me, it was gobbling me up. I had a real lack of sex going, an astonishing lack of sex carrying on from the barren high school days, and it was starting to have a real impact. It seemed like all kinds of uglier, stupider guys than me couldn't seem to move three feet without catching their end in some. But I was dry. I was so very dry, I'd come up completely empty. It was rubbing me raw, torture and shame. I wasn't running it right, there was a kink in my can and I couldn't kick it straight. There was nothing, almost totally nothing for me during that first year in the dorms.

There was one guy on my floor, Phil, who had a beautiful 16-year-old girlfriend from his high school. She was there almost every weekend – this knockout babe still in high school, nice developed legs and ass but still highly girlish, boyish, whichever way you want it. She would have her hair up at the back of her head, earrings dangling above her shoulders – and this pouty, sulky, dirty, absolutely filthy look on her face – this dirty, flirty, dark-eyed naughty look that seemed permanently built into her. She didn't smile much, certainly not to the other dorm guys, but she didn't have to, you didn't want her to, she was doing completely fine.

Sometimes you could hear Phil and her having sex in his room. It would be happening all weekend, at all hours. You would be in your own room, grappling on the bed with Skinner, with Sterne, knowing it was going on just doors away, unable to take much more. You'd roll over and step out to the toilet. On your way back Phil would suddenly walk out into the hall, sweaty in just his pajama bottoms. He'd say, "Jeez, she's really got the pussy farts tonight. You guys hear it out here?" Then he would make a kind of sucking noise with his mouth – *chthlup, chthlup, chthlu-u-u-p.*

Phil was already 19 at the time, and it killed me, it destroyed me, that he would be there in his dorm room, doing whatever he wanted with a 16-year-old. Despite this, I have to say, Phil was a pretty good guy, funny and with an ear for the one-liner. He had a real charismatic energy, he could entertain you for hours with his antics. He was a heavy drugs man, though, and more often than not they would get the best of him. He would rush around in these paranoid fits, slamming doors and howling, his face twisted and sweaty, eyes boiling over. No one was much surprised when later in the year he got busted by the police for drug-selling and was kicked out of the school. Psychedelics were his game. Bart, appearing quite happy, said he had told me so.

As I say, there were problems, things weren't going very smoothly. I had been pining to get to college for years, and now here it was – no idea what to do. I was negotiating for basic wherewithal, the concepts were being juggled without my consent. You'd be walking along and someone would rush up, "Please sign this, please sign this, Kashmir must be saved!" I'd sign it. Trash and chip wrappers would swirl around the long majestic Library steps. I'd be sitting there and a mass of girls would appear, shouting and parading with their tops off and tits flopping out, protesting rape.

I remember I had to do an essay for an English composition class, the first paper of my college career. I sat in the Library and tried to write it out by hand. I had been a genius at these things in high school, but this was not going well, it was hardly going at all. I sat for several hours, coming up with only a few sentences. Most of the time was spent in despair over word choices in the first sentence. I had to make this paper absolutely perfect – everything had to be utterly brilliant, nothing less, no other option. But I didn't know anything, couldn't hope to, my head was full of crap and water. My ideas collapsed, my theories shattered, everything seemed to stop. My hand wouldn't move the pen any more. I got up and started wandering around, peering at girls, fingering the shelves of books at random. I got hot, uncomfortable, my head started to spin. I was bewildered, I didn't know what was supposed to happen. I found myself in the war section, gathering up an armful of large picture books on the Vietnam War.

There were these big puffy orange couches in one of the large main rooms of the Library. I sat down on one of them and started flipping through the Vietnam books. I was soon distracted by a large group of black students sitting at one of the wooden tables not far away. There was no studying going on there – just a bunch of laughing and throwing wads of paper at each other. It was very interesting, very absorbing. Each of the blacks was remarkably well dressed and groomed, far better than any of the whites or Asians (I didn't see any Mexicans). I watched the action for at least half an hour, then came back to the desk where I'd left my backpack and stuff. Part of me was hoping it all had been stolen. It was still there. I loaded it up and went back to the dorm. A few difficult days later, I finally got the paper done and typed it out on Chris' computer. The grade: C-plus. There were so many things wrong with that.

■■

The classes were hard for me, it took me years to catch on. I remember in the Friday class on Chaucer, the professor suddenly yelled at me, "And you, young man, what is a myth!" He was a large stocky man with a white beard and thick eyeglasses, who would sometimes brag about all the different varieties of wine he'd drunk over the weekend. He would stalk around the stage as though in a little rage, every so often blasting a question at the unsuspecting. "What is a myth!" I floundered and stuttered. It hit me that we were supposed to have looked this up somewhere or other, but I hadn't done it, I was totally unprepared. I stammered and said something about how a myth was perhaps a kind of fictional story, often designed to reveal a greater truth – for example, I said, "like Paul Bunyan."

A stunned silence seemed to suck the air out of the room. Oh dear, I remember thinking, what would happen now? I was terrified. I looked around. None of the other students were looking at me. They were scribbling in their notebooks, staring at their texts. Somebody behind me breathed loudly through their nose. "NO!" the professor screamed. He paced back and forth, muttering and wringing his hands. Some girl in the front chirped up and answered correctly, I have no idea what she said.

The class was over. I walked out into the late morning autumn sun. My arms and knees were trembling, it seemed like I was about to fall apart. College was ruining me, it was crushing me into a flat, pitiful thing. It had taken only a matter of weeks.

There was a little stand and I went over and bought a hot dog for a dollar. Before I could say anything, the guy slapped on mustard and pickle relish and handed it over. I hate relish, always have, but I didn't say anything. I sat on a bench, took a bite of the hot dog, and started crying. Tears gathered in my eyelashes. Then a little line of tears started to slide down one of my cheeks. I smeared it away. I could hardly chew the hot dog. I was swallowing it down in big hunks. Bits of it caught in my throat. The sweet relish was awful, cold and bad-tasting. I started to gag. People were walking by, I felt them looking at me. I sat very still and tried to act like everything was perfectly fine, like I was just another friendly young college man eating a hot dog in the sun. Across the way I saw a group of fraternity guys sitting at a table giving away free condoms from a fishbowl. Bunches of girls walked up and took away handfuls. I could hear them giggling as the fraternity men told terrible jokes, awful jokes, the worst jokes of all time, and invited them to parties.

I was supposed to be in another class in about ten minutes. I finished the hot dog and sat until my tears dried. It was nearly noon now. I got up and started walking, not sure where I was headed. It seemed like I would have to miss the rest of my classes for that day. I passed the Psychology building, Biology, several temporary huts housing an overflow of humanities professors. I moved very slowly, no one bothered me. It was very peaceful out there, the students quiet and gathered in their classes. The sun was hot on my back but a breeze kept things cool.

For a time I felt anxious about missing my classes. It was the first time I'd intentionally done that. It could hurt me in some way, cost me, the price could be steep. I figured maybe I would have to drop out now, the way I was botching things. It would be shameful. My people would be upset, my mother would be. What the hell had happened? How did I wind up like this? I figured I might have to just run away, go and join the Army. Work my way up, hurtle out of helicopters, become a big general. Wage covert wars on behalf of shadowy interests for vague purposes; assassinate political dissidents, newspaper reporters and others who knew too much; blunder, destroy documents, be forced to deny all knowledge in the Congressional hearings. It would be a foolish move, true – but everything was a foolish move, no matter what you did, the destination was foolishness and vice versa. No doubt I would wind up distorted and driveling, horribly deceived – but most do. Shit, I thought, what the hell was happening to me? I passed the Communications building, The Administration, Anthropology, Film Studies, two new Engineering buildings, Engineering I and Engineering II they were called. Both were done up in bright white stucco and looked like Spanish palaces.

I walked across some grass fields, came to the tennis and basketball courts complex. I sat down. The sun continued to work me over. The air was warm and dry, the smell of dead leaves and dying grass. The anxiety had passed and now I was very listless, very dull.

I watched some of the action on the tennis courts. A nice-looking girl in a ponytail was hitting it back and forth with a very hairy young man dressed in white. He had short wavy black hair, long sideburns, thick swatches of black hair on his arms and legs. He went easy on her, smiling, lobbing easy shots. She giggled, wound her arm, and knocked the ball directly into the net. I watched her nice muscled ass churn under her skirt as she ran and fetched it. She tossed it up and slapped it right back into the net. The guy smiled some more, his little unshaven jaw bobbing and bobbing, little tongue hanging unmoving in the center of his little mouth. I hated that guy, he made me sick. Just the look of him, everything was wrong. I felt like running out there and mashing his face in the grass, grinding his teeth into the dirt for a while.

My vision blurred and I stared off, nothing taking shape. I felt drool sliding out the corner of my mouth. I let it happen, a drop of drool fell on to my shirt. I put a finger in my mouth and tore off a long curving slice of fingernail. I used it to clean between my teeth, pulling out little bits of hot dog bun. I sucked off the little bits and swallowed them.

Somebody was yelling at me. I looked around, eyes trying to focus. It was guys on the basketball court. Did I want to play? They needed one more guy. A tall tan shirtless guy was motioning me over. I stood. Okay, okay. I lumbered over, wiping the drool off my face with my hand.

The tall tan guy said his name was Mitch. He grabbed me by the bicep and whispered in my ear. The sweat smell was coming off him something powerful, but his breath was sweet and minty, like from a great gum. He spoke to me in that way certain guys can to strangers, like he'd known me for years. I immediately started to feel a little better. "Take this guy," Mitch said, pointing at a guy on the other team. "All right," I said.

The guys were big, nearly all of them were big with muscles. They seemed to be juniors or seniors, their bodies looked that way, full adult-type bodies. There were two or three black guys, one on our team. My blood started to unfreeze, I ran up and down the pavement with them. I darted across the key, jumped into the fray, crashed the boards for the rebound. I got off a couple of important passes but badly muffed an easy lay-up early on. The guy I was supposed to take was quick, oh he was quick, not so tall but quick. He left me standing and put in two jumpers in a row.

I hung my head and burned red, the guys were thinking I didn't belong out there. I knew they were. Mitch came over and told me to get low on my guy, to keep my legs wide and low, deny him the ball, get in the way and tangle up his legs every time he tried to run. I went ahead and did it. Knocked the guy down a couple times, nothing too serious. He got a little steamed and glared at me, but he barely touched the ball the rest of the game, I was on to his tricks. It was a tight game too, fast, motion, ball control – I was struggling for air, it'd been months since I'd run it out like that.

Mitch was the star for our team, he was putting in about every other hoop it seemed like. He was six-three, six-four, I figured he'd probably been a great high school superstar. I could see him out there under the gym lights, sparkling white and green uniform, hair shining, teeth perfect, light-haired thighs bulging. He would have fucked half the cheerleading squad and dumped them right after. They'd be bitter and fighting each other, writing him long letters stained with their lipstick and aromatic pens. The guy on Mitch was big and tough, a big black guy with a golden earring in the shape of a sledgehammer. Mitch and him were going at it, banging bodies, grunting, falling on their asses. Shaking hands after a particularly good battle.

It was coming down to the wire, we were neck and neck with them. Mitch threw up a hook from the top of the key. I clawed past two guys, raced in for the rebound. The ball came down. It bounced off my hand, there was a scramble. A big oafy pasty red-haired guy on the other team grabbed for it. An elbow flew, there was a whap, a clunk. I saw white dots, a purple flash, a whirl of black twirlies. I fell to the ground. The ball was in my hands. I heard footsteps madly all around, guys screaming for me to dish it off. I lay there. Nothing doing.

"Hold up, hold up, he's bleedin'," said one of the black guys.

The terrible oafy guy had bashed my lips, split the inside of my upper lip against my teeth. I got to my feet. A layer of tears was over my eyes. I did what I could to keep them from falling out.

The oafy guy came over to apologize. I shook his hand. A tear rolled out. "You okay?" said Mitch. "You think you can make it?" "You okay, man?" said the black guy. I wiped the tear, brought my shirt up and wiped it away quick. My whole face hurt. My nose was running, I was tasting blood. I spat and spat, pulled up

my shirt again and spat into that. I wanted to sit down but didn't.
I couldn't have.

I spat again, wiped again, and spat once more, this time from
between my teeth. "I'm okay, I'm okay," I said. I clapped the ball
between my hands. "C'mon, let's go!" I shouted. "Let's go!"

I dished it in and we ran. It was very tight, close to the end of
the game now. It went back and forth a few times, then they
pinned us deep in our end, threatening to do us in. They kept
shooting, shooting, getting their own rebounds and shooting, but
nothing fell for them. Suddenly, Mitch pulled free in the center of
the throng. He launched himself skyward, hung there, kicked –
and came down with it.

I turned and exploded into the clear. I was alone and streaking
towards the open basket. Mitch reached back and tossed it. I ran, I
flew, I went off like a gun. The ball was coming. It was coming,
coming, going, it was too far. I was too weak, too slow, not fast. It
came down and bounced. I made a wild leap. I grabbed the thing
and threw it blindly over my shoulder.

I came down, rolled, crashed in to the chainlink fence. I heard a
struggle, the ball against the backboard, the ball against the metal.
Then shouts, cheers, curses. I turned and looked. Our guy had got
it and put it in. Game over.

Some of the guys came over to help me up and pat me on the
back. I stood unsurely. The sun was dropping, beginning to drop
behind the trees. A touch of the fall coolness touched suddenly
against the back of my legs.

Mitch invited me to join them for beers. "Come and have a few
pitchers with us," he said, shaking my hand. I was still a long
ways from twenty-one, but it didn't matter in the college town. It
was the last thing that mattered. You could hardly walk into the
town without drinking some beer, no matter how old you were. I
didn't answer. I was trembling, I ached all over. My lip had

swollen. My arms hurt, my elbows, my nose, my knee. Beer sounded good, it really did. Cold beer, sitting around with Mitch and the guys.

I told him no. I wanted to go, but at the same time, I couldn't. I'm still not sure why. All I knew was that I couldn't. Maybe no reason. Maybe it sounds funny, but there it was. I couldn't go. It was decided. I said thanks and told Mitch no. "You sure you don't want to?" he said. I nodded. "All right then, see you around."

They walked off and I stood there.

▌▌▌

The air and light were turning from orange and purple to purple and blue, the breeze was scraping together the leaves of the palm trees like pieces of sandpaper. I picked up my backpack and moved gingerly down to the dorm place for food, making it with about 20 minutes before closing. The food in this place was no good, it wasn't helping, but there was no alternative. The food came with the dorm fee, there was no getting out of it.

The place was nearly empty. Everyone tended to come early on Fridays so as to get an early start on the drinking and so forth. It was quiet, just a few small groups. Some were huddled over textbooks, others grab-assed, played funny with rows of leftover desserts. Two options tonight: Meatloaf, peas, corn and diced carrots with cornbread; breaded chicken breasts with salad and fries. I took the chicken, along with a big plastic cup of coke with ice. Coffee.

I sat down and took a long drink off the soda. It felt good to finally sit on my ass. With my tongue I rubbed some coke ice against my swollen lip, then crunched down. My mind was blank, eyelids heavy.

A copy of the college newspaper had been left sitting on the table. I took bites and flipped through the gray dusty thing. One of the main articles had a lot of rowdy talk from the student government leaders, the school Administration, the various deans. They were all staking out turf, taking all-or-nothing stands, squabbling over the high ground. The issue concerned pennies' worth of new fees the school was imposing for some purpose or other, it was never made quite clear. Most of the op-ed letters focused on Reagan, the U.S.A. president. Various crimes and massacres he had committed in Central America, his rape and pillage of the Constitution, his foolish antagonism of the good people of the Soviet Union.

I closed the paper and sent it sliding down the empty table. I took another drink off the coke and looked around.

I saw her one table over, sitting by herself at the end of the row – the girl known around the dorms as "Spoogeface."

I'm fairly confident only a very few number of girls, no matter how ambitious or dexterous, have ever been able to earn a moniker like "Spoogeface" – let alone within the first six weeks or so of freshman year. Yet there she was. Indeed, as I sat there this girl was already legendary, already an icon – the concept of "Spoogeface" had already wormed itself deep into the dorm male lexicon, a codeword and point of constant, frequently multi-layer reference.

There she was now, at the end of the row – resting up, laying in a few groceries. Alone. She was always alone, in sober public places you almost always saw her alone. It was her fate, the way the world wanted it – alone, the signal confirmation of her particular triumph.

I watched her fork it in. Bleach blond hair, straight-cut bangs low to the eyes. Squishy-soft thighs spreading out over the plastic chair, feet barely touching the ground – she wasn't one of the tall ones. Not looking at anything in particular. In went another forkful – a nibble of chicken breast, a bite of salad, ranch dressing, quick napkin follow-up. It was always sort of amazing to see, even at a distance – the lazy-eyed, torpid aura of wonderful sleaze that projected from that pudgy brown face. The baked-in sultriness that glowed out, that radiated beyond the heavy daubs of makeup that she laid over her still acne-flavored cheeks.

I've heard it said it was all in my mind – in all our minds. Sure it was. It was even in her walk – a slightly forward lean, high-heeled small steps. The ass seeming to convulse and jounce to a slightly different, slightly slower tempo from the rest of it. My best image always had her laying on a pool deck in the sun. Her hair would be wet but drying; mirror sunglasses; rainbow-stripe bikini, most of it crammed up her ass; a surrounding stench of chlorine and suntan lotion.

I felt a sudden pang of pity and sympathy, a desire to befriend and help her – somehow. But no, nothing doing, not a chance. Something like that would take nerve, guts, vision, genius. I sat there and picked at my chicken, dipped my fries in barbeque sauce, got up and went for a refill of coke. It could not have been easy to have found oneself the object of endless tales/jokes/tributes from legions of leering and farty 18-year-old men. And the diligent, alert young college freshwomen – Spoogeface got the tribute of polite, refined obliviousness from most of these. That, or it would be an overly kind and smiling response, one that seemed to indicate an extremely high interest in the things Spoogeface might have to say. All the clear-eyed young women of college, they who stalked the dorm complex, hot on the lookout for any injustice and all possible threats to their clout as reasonable, responsible, sex-loving women of the future.

My sweet Spoogeface, my dear, my princess – she persevered with nary a whimper. Never once, in all the times I observed her, did she appear unnerved in the slightest by the visceral ruckus she inspired among the dormfolk. Never once did I discern her crawling into some self-conscious prison, some shell, never did I witness her donning the sackcloth the gregarious college youths had so readily set out for her. There was always a hazy cheerfulness to her being, a certain smoggy sort of sunniness, to complement the golden rich aura of magnificent sottedness that clung all over her.

It should be noted that justice was, I think, in due time delivered unto Spoogeface. Dorm life had deteriorated the young men of college to the extent that, toward the end of the year, a bodily encounter with "The Spooge" had become a prized plum – a treasured rite conferred only on the lucky or the truly, unremorsefully manly. You might witness or hear tale of them, the young college males jousting for her affections across the span of many a drunken evening. Jockeying, lurking in her midst, trailing her into parties, venturing near with banter at the ready, hoping against hope that they might claim membership among the unique minority of many. Mostly, it must be said, they failed – mostly.

A frenzy occurred on my floor the Sunday afternoon that Jason proudly announced he'd had an exchange with Spoogeface. A real for goodness bodily exchange. Jason was a tedious sort, but it seemed unlikely he would lie – he was tall, dark and well-manicured, after all, the more or less slow-witted and status quo-confirming sort of chap that many a woman might find agreeable for a one-off kind of affair. It had happened the evening before, Jason said. He and she had come into contact "completely by accident," during a drinking session with some friends who happened to live in her dorm building.

What happened, how was it, how was it? the young dorm men of my floor clamored.

"The greatest ever," Jason stated. Better than we could imagine – indeed, better than we could hope to imagine. The young men of dorm wailed at this news, there was a great gnashing. Jason flashed his clean white teeth, grinning like the newly crowned Olympic skeet-shooting champion. "Right between the eyes," he informed. "Direct hit – a bullseye." He held his hands like pistols, pointed them, blew the tops of his fingers. He danced a little jig.

The young men of dorm howled and demanded corroborating evidence, of which Jason had little. Few of the fellows wanted to believe him, and some, I'm sure, never did.

I believed.

IV

I came back to the dorm. Chris and Leilani were gone, already out for the night, I hoped. Likewise for the rest of the floor, hardly anyone was around. I went in for a shower, then lay on the bed sucking from a bottle of water. It would probably be an early night. Shoot, I was exhausted, what a day. It looked like Chris and Leilani would have to go it alone tonight, I would be out.

I flipped open one of my textbooks. It was something by Richelieu, perhaps Montesquieu. Quite badly written, it seemed, it was hard to see what they were getting at. If it was what I thought it was, it was too obvious. That's funny. I put the book down on my chest and lay there. I must have dozed off for a while. Then there was a knock on the door.

Bart walked in. Let's go out, he said, go see what's going on in the town. What time is it, I wondered. Almost nine. All right, I said. I got dressed and we went out there.

We walked among the dorm towers, heading for the college town. The people were partying in the dorms, a big Friday night bash on every other floor. Music blasted out from every fourth or fifth window, different tunes but the same three ideas, as loud as they could make it. The air was fresh and the wind blew, not cold but something less than warm.

We passed out of the dorm area, went through acres of empty parking lots, crossed over into the town. The great majority of the students lived out here, stuffed cheek to jowl in block after block of slapped-up stucco and wood apartments. The place was laid out like grid of dirty cardboard boxes, intercut by lines of palm trees and rows of automatic teller machines.

Drunk mobs, slobbering and cheering, roamed about. They migrated among the apartment buildings, pushed themselves into loud yellow cafes, into slick-floored beerhalls, sticky-walled pizza joints, humid places which served chicken burritos. Cars squealed and jumped curbs, skidded to stops on front lawns. Horns bleep-bleeped, people shouted down from balconies. Packs of girls screamed and ran from door to door. The air squirmed with shouts and hoots, laughs and shrieks. You might catch whiffs of marijuana, people ran crazy on pills, but mostly it was beer – beer in puddles, beer on shirtfronts, beer misting in the wind.

Let's go get a beer, Bart said, at least one beer. We came down an asphalt driveway into a backyard. A band was going at it at the mouth of the garage. The singer screeched hysterically, a beard pasted on his chin and a rubber chicken on the top of his head. The drummer twirled and smashed away, grimacing. A guy was playing a toilet plunger into a microphone.

A lengthy line had formed behind a keg of beer. Someone was laying in the grass to the left, passed out, a regalia of vomit on his collar. Possible pea involvement. A girl was crying, sobbing, people were gathered around her, speaking urgently, kindly. A sweating pile of guys grasped at each other laughing and collapsed to the ground. They got up, veered into us, knocked against us. I sagged and took it. Bart scowled and pushed against them, cursing softly, checking his windbreaker for stains.

Girls passed by smiling, mouths wide, the smell of fruit punch, vodka, schnapps leaping off them. Another assemblage of joshing guys in red faces trailed, some of these carrying plastic gallon milk cartons of beer. I let them go, all of them, I didn't care. I took a deep breath, felt my body shimmer in its aching. I flicked my tongue in and out of the gash in my upper lip. Let them have at it. I didn't care just then, I didn't have enough to get into it. Start in with the jokes and pleading, the jacking up the red-rooster noise, all with the express aim of vaulting into the circle of pussy possibility. The other guys would get them anyway, they always had. I didn't have the banter. There was no use any more in pretending that girls didn't exist, like in high school, but I still didn't have it. Bart and I finished our beers, crushing the cups underfoot.

We moved back into the streets. Red lights were flashing at the end of the block, red lights touching over everything. We came down and saw the police sitting on some guy's back, a hippie of some kind. Ten cops, three or four police cars. The hippie moaned, his beard knocked against the ground, a cop was pushing his head down. A crowd was gathering. A guy shouted, "Police brutality! Police brutality!" He laughed, a bunch of people laughed. Close by, another girl was crying, sniffling. A police officer led her away, sat her down in the police car, closed the door. On the other side of the park, a siren wailed, an ambulance maneuvered, turning finally to head deeper into town.

We kept moving, Bart and I, mouths motoring. We covered the gamut – war, peace, sex, death, money, homosexuality, Hitler, the films of Robert De Niro. Bart said he'd made a mistake to major in history, already he knew it was a mistake. His dad had told him he would make a mistake and sure enough he had. This got him started on some stories about his grandfather. Then quickly on to another tale about the girlfriend he claimed to have had for two years in high school. She'd dumped him near the end of senior year, right before the prom. Turned into a "different girl" overnight, started going out with every other guy, even with a couple of his "friends." Then older men, he'd heard she was dating "older men" now, back in his home town.

A picture of this girl reared itself in my mind – a slutty little smirk on her face, dark hair carefully snipped above the shoulders, medium tits pushing out beneath a fuzzy sweater, high heels and tights doing most of the real work.

The thought of her excited me for a moment, but not much longer. I laughed, made a remark, tried to ease Bart out of it. I didn't care to hear too much more. There were so many old girlfriend stories out there, it seemed like almost every other guy had one. If not that, it was somebody's suicide. I'd heard so many girlfriend and suicide stories already since coming to college – somebody from their home town, somebody they maybe knew, somebody their friend had known or heard about. Each of them so dramatic, so horrifying and special and so sad, in their own unique way. People didn't seem to care how many times they told it or to who. It was such a sad, sad world, plenty of suffering, everyone could have some. Just made you want to cry and cry.

Bart and I walked over to a little store. We came out with tall plastic bottles of soda, bags of chips and pretzels, a package of sour apple gum. We went down to the ocean and sat on the cliffs with the wind and ate the chips and drank the sodas, wallowing our shoes in the sand and looking up at the moon. We stayed out there until past two.

Bart and I dropped away from each other after that first year. Things got swept along, the speeds shifted. I got tied up in this and that and Bart went his own way, whatever it was, I was never able to get a handle on it. We would run into each other now and again, unexpectedly at some event, usually a party. It was always a nice, friendly chat we would have, full of jokes, funny stuff, nonsense. But I don't know, it never lasted very long, always just a few minutes. We never took it from there.

I don't know where Bart is now. It does not make me sad, it only is what happened. We could not talk for very long any more. There was always something pulling me away. I let it pull me without a thought. I was happy for it, there always seemed by then something which could not wait much longer, something which seemed far more important – a drink, a revolution, a cunt, a song, a hoax.

THE UNTUNING
OF THE SKY

1

had my motorbike, there was that. It wasn't much, but I had it – wheels that went. Piece of junk, yeah, typical oil can – but it rode me around the town.

I was on it this one afternoon, basically just tooling, when basically out of nowhere this big rig came whacking through the intersection.

It was coming straight at me. No time to think. Not nearly enough.

I clicked through the odds. Putting a full crush on the brakes seemed the obvious monkey, though none too smart. Fat chance of trying to swerve or beat the big boy at the pass. No other way – to hell with the odds – I had to lay it down.

So down I went – smack into some lady's dirty white hatch job.

Let me elucidate: This whole thing happened so fast. Not really a chance in the slightest to think any of it through right.

Well, but the chick must have caught me peripheral-wise, and that was good, at least there was that. Her tires screeched. There was an impact, but it wasn't what you would call a bang. I threw out a little thank-you for that, to whoever. Then there was a squeal, I heard the rig roar. This was followed by a honk, another clunk, and a big whir that was almost – almost – way too close. Like forever almost too close. For the slightest edge of a second I saw myself like down from above. I was sitting in the middle of the road, things flying all around me.

I staggered up. I figured my head had probably banged the lady's door, at a fairly rapid velocity – but I didn't see any extreme emergency, the skullwork seemed pretty much intact, just a throb and some standard dizziness. I felt for feeling below the waist and got an affirmative – no major damage, just your standard burning and scraping, the boots and leathers had helped there – but my hand had got clipped, stung against the ground. Not so bad necessarily, but a couple fingers worth, fingernails sheared away, a big hurt on the fingers in question and like that. There was a bunch of blood – looking like more on the way.

I know, I know, *I know* – the freaks and do-gooders had said to always wear a helmet and gloves. And I'd remembered and hadn't forgot that bit of reasonably sane advice – but sometimes the smallest thing is capable of doing a decoy and ditching your mind. You might find yourself in a hurry and so forth. And I agree, it's probably something close to a miracle that I can be here smacking down these letters right now. When I look at it, I mean – all things considered. Yeah, the things you learn to learn in this life – yeah, sometimes they pretty much amaze and strain your notions.

The chick in the hatch got out. She was a lady, late middle ages, gray hair going blue, face going orange to red, probably on to lime or some such, real soon. She was that kind, I could tell, I could see it on her. She looked over at me. Yeah, sure – she'd want to talk – I.D.'s, names, every kind of number, this sort of scene. She started to walk over.

On the other side, I saw a guy. Short hair, humped shoulders, a certain "engineering" look about him. He got out of a dark green jeep situation and started over – dull gimmicky eyes roaming about, his mouth all too tight. In any case, he must have seen the whole scenario, or part of it, and now his every expression was telling me he wanted in on it. Like it or not, he wanted a good gander at everything, at the minimum. This was what he did, what he lived his life for. Analysis, solutions, "helping out" and "do-gooding" – at the least. Also, interfering, interjecting, trying to put toothpaste back in a cylindrical tube – things of this nature. I could just tell.

So suddenly everything was falling apart. It'll happen like that. You know, things slipping right by you in one big flux – and there you are, trying to make sense of it. This was me. Things began to waver a bit. I think for a while I just went on instinct, not really sure how it was going to play out.

I gave the bike a quick look. Axle twisted, number one. Two, block cracked, probably leaking. Three – well, I didn't even want to speculate about the head gasket and chip-nut. Four, it was laying at an angle I didn't particularly like. Five, maybe it hadn't been riding so great lately. Never really had, truth told. To top it, the thing was lying half under the old bag's hatch. Even more technically, it wasn't in my name.

I backed up, very slowly at first, one inch before the next, no rush. Hands at my waist, this kind of look, nothing unusual – but watching them all the while. It was okay – nobody reached, nobody dared. But as always, the top concern was dust – dust that supposedly transmitted all day every day to whoever was subscribing – and was supposed to be actual hell to get out of your hair. But nothing, nobody. *All right.* So then I turned, casual-like, and just sort of ambled off. With everyone sort of just standing there, mouths half-open, in sort of slow-motion disbelief that I was actually doing it. But they generally always snap out of it, and it doesn't take too long for them to do so. It took this particular grouping about six-and-a-half seconds I'd say. And then they shouted, the hatch lady and the guy.

I ran, boots on pavement, rubber-tip steel toes clanging.

Well, so I figured they could try to I.D. me from the leather jacket or the "long hair" – if the cop that showed was half good, if he even bothered to take down a report. If cops were even showing up anymore for this sort of "gig." Well, but one or two would probably turn up sooner or later, I just somehow assumed so. Okay – and given that, they could probably stamp out a composite if they really wanted one. No reason for them to want such – and that was probably the exact reason why they would want it. But even if they did, it would still be a little while yet – hours – before they would be able to tag and collate the video-relay, isolate, graph and do their scan of the quad-cube cams – separate out the signifiers on their odor-sniff trackers, if they went in that direction. Hours, at least. Just hours, I didn't know how many. Simple logistics – S.O.P.

Unless – well, I figured they might try to put a trace on the bike. It might cost them some extra time and effort, but I couldn't totally exclude them from going through all the rigatoni and doing it. Actually, when I thought about it more, it was a probable. The bike would be laying in the street; the officers would scratch their heads, think and decide: Seize, sequester, and investigate it. As I say, it was nearly 100 percent a trace wouldn't come back to me directly, but you could never totally tell what they might come up with, who they might "talk to by chance" – what bit of data might come "drifting in" over the restricted channels, what a little itty of crumb of "dust" might be telling them. There's always an unattached bit or piece, or a rumor or a maybe, that a cop would say he'd heard from "a bird" or some other "public domain" source, and then that bit would end up as the basis of the frame-up. There were some cops who just had that sense, you know – just from looking at a particular scene or artifact or stream, and then they would take it from there. But just some cops.

Well, so I was out of there. I flew past a row of take-out stalls, whipped left at a plastic lawn furniture store, then slowed it down, walked, tried to take my time a little bit. I took care to keep my head ducked, but not like to overdo it.

I took a good look at my ripped hand. It was the right hand. Three of the fingers were tore pretty good, nails lifted and flayed to splinters, blood flowing all right. It was a valuable hand, the right, to be sure – but I've been known to do tricks with both gizmos. I took a bandanna from my back pocket and wrapped it tight as it would go. That helped a little, took some of the bite off. But it didn't change that the whole hand was still stung pretty good. But it was nothing I couldn't deal with.

The thing was to walk – always you got to walk, keep moving, slip yourself into a seamless mesh with the general panorama. I calmed after a bit, glad to hear no siren, no shouting, no kid gesturing and pointing. "There he is! There he is!" It can happen like that. It's always a kid, isn't it. A lot of the time it is. Typically a boy, between nine and fourteen years old.

2

Soon enough, and pretty much to my surprise, I found myself in a neighborhood I sort of recognized. Strange how it works out that way sometimes.

It was some people I'd known through an old girlfriend, folks by the name of Darryl and Carole. The two of them'd been shacked up for a few years, and I didn't know, maybe they had even gotten married by now. Not my style of individuals per se. I wasn't sure what it was – probably about everything. The two of them had always seemed somewhat too neat and tucked in and whatall, like they were too readily smiling and above-board, too over-obviously in love, too overhandedly clued-in and "evolved," too super-darn pleased with how fully they had swallowed the consensus view – hook, line and sinker, that would be – and been completely absorbed by the general overweening mush of madness and mediocrity – apparently thinking it was somehow going to benefit their sense of sanity and "security" – this type of a scene. What you can never understand about such folks is why they bother with this type of jingle, you know, like everyone can see through it without even trying. Like, if everything is so super swell grand, why didn't they already have a couple kids on the way, you know? What was holding them back from the ultimate pinnacle of happiness and existence? Or maybe it wasn't even like that, it was just that I thought it was. But who can say what people will do for appearances, you know? You hear about people doing almost anything. And sometimes you see it.

I came to the entryway and hit the button that said Darryl and Carole's name on it. The vid flickered just a twitch, then the main door buzzed. Just buzzed – *beep*. Not a single intercom peep – fine, swell. They'd just flashed on me and buzzed me right in. Fine. Or – well, maybe not fine – sure, okay. You know, it was only later that I thought about that. Thought about it *a lot*. Not then – not even a blinker of a thought about it then. I just heard the buzz and grabbed the door and started my way up there, not thinking much about something like that.

I took the elevator to the ninth floor, walked the hall, hit the doorbell. Carole answered within seconds. I tossed her a few nice to see yas, smiled real big, shook her arm with my good hand –

the left one. It was the wrong hand to be shaking with, but you can do that with a lot of girls, they don't mind, maybe they don't even notice. I stepped in and past her and kicked off some dust on their welcome mat.

Well, then I showed her some of the blood, and gave her another good laugh – hey, you know how it goes, Carole, don't you, what have you, this kind of a rap. Oddly, she seemed totally unimpressed – completely unmoved, really. No exclaiming, no cringing, no gagging, nothing like this that you might have expected from a girl. She didn't even ask how it happened. She just told me to sit down at the white formica dining room table, cool as could be. Then she walked into the kitchen and came back with a damp towel. Then she went to the bathroom and came back with a disinfectant pack, a thing of analgesic gelweb, tweezers, snippers, boxes of foam and stick-patches.

One thing right off the top, I noticed she was walking a little too slow – or – again, I guess I probably noticed it in retrospect – you know, thinking back on everything that happened. There was a bit of a slowness, a certain deliberateness, to all her movements – or there seemed to be. But as I say, it was nothing the average person would normally think twice about – at least not if it was the first time you saw it happen, or the first time you'd been over at their place in a while. The truth is, people get awkward from time to time, but it's not a completely accurate picture of how they really are.

Yeah – but sometimes it is.

Well, in any case, I didn't think it was any big deal the way she was, not then. And to tell you the whole truth, I was so much more frankly interested in her fixing up my hand. The blood had soaked completely through the bandanna wrap. The thing was really nipping at me – trembling and like that – and I wanted it gone, post-hence. She worked on it, my hand resting on the table, saying very little. We just did the usual kind of small chatter, you know – this and that. The rain and the sleet the week before, somebody she knew who bought an aardvark, somebody I knew who'd taken an ocean cruise down south (I made this up). Things of this persuasion.

With the snippers she scissored away a good portion of ragged fingernails, while with the tweezers she removed a total of what looked to be five very, very tiny bone chips. She wiped away some of the blood, and then, without much of a warning, hit the whole place with the disinfect. I howled when she did that, I couldn't help it, and this finally triggered a little tiny smile on her face – first one I'd seen on her since I'd shown up. She squeezed the hand hard in the towel folds, grinning at me.

Well, so it seemed the hand was cleaned and on the way to recovery at last. I was starting to feel a little better, and to celebrate, I really needed a smoke, I didn't care what anybody said. I reached my good hand into my jacket, extracted a butt and stuck it in my mouth. Carole saw me do it, and when she didn't say anything, I took out my lighter and lighted, puffed, and exhaled. She still didn't say anything – in fact, again, she didn't seem to notice. She just sat there doing the gel-weld and bandage work on each of the fingers individually. I puffed away and let her work.

There wasn't an ashtray around, so I dumped what was hanging in a little potted plant sitting there on the kitchen table. Carole still didn't say anything. I smoked the rest of the smoke, then butted it right there, in the little plant soil. No comment from Carole at all.

If you had asked me in the morning if this is what I'd be doing by the afternoon, I'd've said it was YOU who needed his head examined. This whole thing was like that.

3

Before too much longer, Darryl came home. As I say, he wasn't really my kind of fellow, never really had been. And in the time that had passed since I'd last seen him, he hadn't done much to improve his standing. He still stood in that kind of half-stooped way he had, and his face, if it was possible, seemed to be even more sort of brownly pale than I remembered. It also looked as if he'd put on a few pounds, most of them around the middle. You can't blame a guy for getting older, I guess, but you can sure nail him for those pounds. It was no secret anymore, the word had been out for years: Mix out the chili-dogs and fiddle-faddle, mix in a salad. I mean, it wasn't underground literature or nothing, there was no hidden taboo. Or, okay, I guess it really could have been some kind of glandular condition, now that you mention it – maybe something deep in his gene pool, something built right into his bones that he was helpless against. Yeah sure, you know, I could take the concept under consideration. Sure I would. Why the hell wouldn't I?

Anyway – and there was his hair. I didn't care for it much. It was in one of the old-fangled new styles, taking care to sculpt the sideburns so they ran really longish and thin down the sides of the face. I couldn't see that it would have been Darryl's idea, had to have been the hairstyler's or somebody's – something somebody got out of a magazine. Even though I really didn't give a damn, you still hated to see Darryl taken in like that.

Well, in any event, we exchanged greetings, Darryl and I – this and that and the other, the usual stuff all over again. I told him what a real thrill it was to see him, especially after all that time that had gone past without us seeing each other. He agreed without really saying anything, and then, without so much as word about it, walked over to the fridge and pulled out a bottle of wine. White it was. It's funny, but more people than you may realize will do this. You know, somebody they haven't seen in a while shows up – bing, it's drinks all around, no questions, regular celebration time. *Gee, sure is nice to see you ol' buddy – gulp, glurgle glurgle – 'nother refill, champ – hey, whatchyou been doing, man?* I haven't studied it or nothing, but it's something that happens.

Darryl poured three glasses and all of us sat at the kitchen table. I was thankful there was no instant mention of this old girlfriend I had. I had, I must say, sort of been anticipating something like that. Because, you know, there's folks who'll bring up something like that right from the start – just to check your reflexes, your reactions. I've seen them, I think we've all seen them somewhere or other – these people who talk up some innocent-seeming "parenthetical" aside, which ends up "by accident" drawing in the particular subject-X. You know – and there you are all of a sudden, having to deal with it. Well, but as I say, Darryl and Carole didn't, and I appreciated it, for what it was worth.

"Wow, tough break," Darryl said, when he finally got around to noticing my hand. At that point I began to tell a confusing and nonsensical story about what had happened – but something made me hesitate. I had the sudden overarching sense that it maybe wouldn't be entirely necessary to go into it all, so I just switched up in the middle with a long story about what an incredible champion princess Carole had been for fixing me up so good. And then, as a diversionary tactic, I raised my glass. We clinked them, drinking with much gusto to Carole's skill with a rag and disinfectant kit. And then I laughed – I felt like laughing for some reason – and of course they joined in. People always like to join in with someone who's laughing, they just can't help it.

After that – quick, bang – it was on to some new conversational topic. I forget what it was, some garbage crap, but we talked about it. The result: End of story on the hand issue. Darryl and Carole had grabbed the bait – or at least they seemed to. And it was totally, totally fine by me if they didn't really want to know what had happened to my hand and what had brought me to their place. I took long sips off the wine.

Well, so it didn't take long for Darryl to begin spewing on about his work. It turned out he'd recently got on with the courts system, in one of the administrative areas it was, I think. I kind of dropped my jaw when he said that, but I'm pretty sure I covered it over pretty good and none of my surprise leaked out. In any case, it seemed unlikely that I would have to worry too much, because Darryl's area of expertise was "in computers." And sure enough, that's what he was doing for the courts, something or other with their computer system – transposing files or such, setting up something or other poo-scratch. I didn't really give a damn, but it was damn obvious that whatever Darryl was doing, I was pretty damn sure it was at a probably not-cheap expense to the taxpayers.

Well, but the fact remains I didn't pay much attention to what he was saying. It sounded like just any old day job, typical thing, not connected to anything and what 99 percent of people end up doing. And anyway, it seemed more like he was talking to the walls and the windows than to any of us. He just talked on and on like that, his glasses shining, in a kind of tired-out monotone. He would perk up now and again to give me a special for-me-only look, mostly when he mentioned some particular word of jargon he must've thought I probably knew about. But I didn't know, I had zero idea. I just went ahead and winked my eyebrows back at him whenever he requested it. It was all I could do to keep looking at him and nodding my head, making like I was interested. Because mostly I was interested in staying at their place, at least for a few days, until the hand could rebound a bit.

As it happened, I didn't need to discuss or ask about whether I could crash at their place. Because after a while, Darryl and Carole got up and walked off into the kitchen to cook dinner, the two of them together. This was part of their system, I guess, the two of them making dinner like that. And I don't know, I just figured they'd probably be cooking for three. As I say, I didn't know, I just figured it. There are a lot of folks who'll do that, just bring you into what's going on simply because you're around. Set you out blankets, let you play with the kids, let you talk to the old uncle if he's there, slice you out a piece of pie along with everyone else. You know, courteous people – polite, class acts, a real credit to the species and the nation. Sure, oh sure. And well, it was really fine by me.

I sat there and reflected on the truth that sometimes it's best just to let things go at their own momentum; that sometimes, you know, things are working in your direction without you even knowing it. This wasn't always true, of course, but sometimes it was. The key was to be able to discern the exact moment when the categories shifted – when things stopped moving your way and started going against you, even if only slightly. But it has to be the *exact* moment, the exact moment in time, and sometimes you can't catch it, sometimes you haven't a prayer. Like out there at the wreck scene. But now things had almost just as quickly closed back together. Indeed, seemingly, they had.

In any event, as I was thinking these things I noticed that Darryl and Carole had barely touched their wine glasses. They were about half-empty, and it was a shame, too, because the stuff wasn't half bad. My second glass was already gone, though, and without asking – because "asking" would only have been a formality anyway, with this bunch – I poured myself another glass and looked out the window.

The city stretched out in every direction, flat and barely moving, like a particularly ugly tablecloth. The sun was going down, it was really going down now. It was a beautiful red whirl, fabulating yellows and pinks and purples splaying out to all sides, smearing themselves into the skyline blue. I heard Darryl and Carole shuffling in the kitchen. They weren't saying a word. I heard the fizz of water boiling, the weak, "deadish" steps of their feet on the linoleum. Another night at home, I guess. Some guy pops in with a bloody hand. Fix him up and feed him some chow.

4

Dinner was a pasta dish, a spaghetti-type deal. It was pretty half-rate, truth told, and I felt kind of bad for Darryl and Carole. I mean, it was exactly the sort of spaghetti dish you'd get, say, from college girls, on those special nights when they kicked out their roommates and wanted to play the single woman having her man-friend over for supper and a little "dessert." You know, it was maybe a type of delicate pasta you'd never quite seen before, or had an odd green sauce, like blended lettuce leaves; but she'd been a ham-handed amateur, she'd lacked the touch, her mother hadn't trained her right – there was too much of the wrong spices, too much salt or something. And the pasta pieces like rubber, the vegetables cut too big, too much oregano, too little artichoke. The thing tasting more like a recipe looks than a meal is supposed to taste. Also, there was never enough sauce, you were always gagging by the end, but you don't want to be untoward by asking if there's any more of the stuff. The kind of dish, you know, where all the parmesan flakes and tabasco you can shake only takes you so far. You know?

Darryl and Carole's pasta wasn't much different. Maybe I had a bite or two. Or none, actually. Guess I just wasn't that hungry – nor, I had to admit, had I been there to see exactly what ingredients they had chosen during the cooking adventure. Not that I didn't *trust* or whatever – it was just that I didn't see the positive aspect of potentially making things more complicated. I moved the stringy bits around the plate, made a few slicing maneuvers, lifted a forkful or two, set it back down, spread the bits around the plate a little more. After about five minutes, I rushed the plate into the kitchen and dumped the goop in the garbage, covering it over with the empty bag from the pasta and a couple pounds of paper towels.

"Wow, it was really great," I told them. "Thank you so much, both of you. It was really special. Thanks again. I mean, really…"

They nodded, kept forking it in, double and triple portions. I stuck with the wine – a fresh bottle of something red, which I brought out and opened myself with extra fanfare.

There wasn't much dinner talk. I mean, Darryl talked about something or other, about his work computers or colleagues, I think. But that was that. And I can't remember that Carole said anything at all until we were almost finished. Her cue was that it was almost time for some television programs they watched. She got up and started to clear away the dishes, then slid past us into the living room.

Well, so I poured the last of the wine and trooped out with Darryl to the couches to watch the programs. They were your typical shows, yeah, various comedies, "buddy" and "friends" shows, goofy but good solid-citizen types trying to figure out their love life or their job or both or whatever, but the "laffs" keep getting in the way, nothing resolved in the end. We watched one of those (I didn't laugh once), and then a show about made-up aliens causing this and that mystery, this kind of thing, and the people trying to hunt them down but never quite getting a clue. This one was a total joke designed by and for idiots, but Darryl and Carole watched in complete silence, drinking in every second. They sighed when it was time for the commercials. And they watched these too, the commercials, all the way through. And they laughed and laughed at the unfunny jokes that were in them.

Then boom, abruptly the news came on. I hadn't expected this, but here it was, nothing to do about it. We sat there as the chick read off the stories, nobody saying anything. The one about the wreck caught me big by surprise – because it was high up on the list, like the second or third one she read off. I didn't think it would be that big of a case. But then I saw, or rather heard, why: They'd gone ahead and thrown in a "shootout" with the cops... and, wouldn't you know it, one of the "boys" had taken a few titanium tips in a couple of the wrong fleshy soft places. Now, apparently, I was a Class-A fugitive.

I sat there mesmerized as the news chick read it off. I could hardly believe my own ears. This was a new low, even for them! The depths they had sunk in their desperation! A bike wreck was a bike wreck, but a cop shooting rap was the purest gangway to the bigs. The very purest. Something had clearly snapped out there, and now they were starting to get serious. *Facts be damned!*

I figured they would absolutely no doubt have the bike down at the lab by now – tinkering with it, hoisting it under their cephalo-tubes and essence-scopes, maybe even doing a full echo-skeletal in hopes of re-locking a print or two. Then comparing/contrasting the apparent data against whatever the computers might be kicking out vis a vis bio-meter imagery/hatch-lady and the engineer. Then putting out the trace – installation of composite-trigger alarms at all theoretical transit points was the strongest bet. I thought over the probabilities. Yeah, it was all pretty possible. Likely, in fact, given the circumstances.

Then again, maybe not. Maybe it was possible I didn't leave them skedaddle behind – maybe they were woofing under the entirely wrong rosebush. Those lab guys weren't always so smart, despite what they said in TV and on the movies. They weren't always something to worry about. I mean, sometimes they were, but you could never know. It was that way all over the place. It was true that some of the cops could match two with two more and come up with whatever that gave you. But there were a lot of the guys, and maybe a majority, who tended to subtract or multiply, depending on what they might have had for their second lunch. This was how they earned their living, and it didn't bother hardly anybody. They let anyone on the police force these days. The more the merrier.

Well, so the item passed and the news went on to the hate and the dogs, the cakes and the basketball, the stuff that keeps the crowds after all the blood's done. They both watched pretty much without expression during the obligatory "Freedom Update," consisting of your basic smug, context-free hate toward the freedom-haters and "bombers," whomever they happened to be at the moment. Yeah, groovy. When those two minutes were up, Carole laughed slightly at the dogs, and Darryl hit the remote to turn up the volume for the basketball, and they both watched with basically complete total interest about the young girl who baked the big long cake for the starving and stupid. I began to calm down a bit. Darryl and Carole didn't seem to be thinking about taking two and then another two or three, and trying to put them together. I was pretty relieved, really.

I lit up a smoke during the bit about the cakes. Darryl and Carole didn't seem to notice. As I say, this was strange, because the last time I'd been to their place was for a party, and they the both of them had been pretty uptight and had pushed all the smokers out to the balcony. Them – and a few other do-gooders who had appeared excessively concerned about the "health" of people other than themselves. *Oh no! Smoking is bad! It's so so so so bad for you! It'll kill you! Please! Think about your health!* Yeah, I remembered thinking – thanks sooooo *much* for your concern.

Besides, smoking was only an *alleged* killer. *No* – the facts were *not* in. Still not. Oh dearie. How about – serious head trauma, combined with castration via hand-axe? Head slammed into a television, stabbed multiple times with a corkscrew, stomped on and choked? Also castrated, just to make sure. Happened to a poor fella at a downtown hotel just last week – I'd read all about it about in the "news" myself. Now something like that was *guaranteed* to kill. You know? And no – they hadn't yet caught the "killer" – a left-hander, they claimed, as based on their detailed forensic analysis of the "castration-stroke angle."

In any case, neither of them made a move to get an ashtray or anything. So, what the hay – I dropped the ash right there on the carpet. When the smoke was over, I dropped the butt on the floor and mashed it out with my boot. Not so much as a word from either of them. I guess it was possible – they just didn't notice. Tired or whatever, wanting to relax after work.

Soon after the news, Darryl announced he was thirsty and went to the kitchen. Perhaps seeking a simple change of pace, I got up and followed him out there. Dishes from the spaghetti meal were everywhere. I figured that after Darryl had quenched his thirst, he would roll up his sleeves and get down to work. He was that kind of guy, I thought – the kind who, in fact, would insist on doing the dishes. But he didn't do that. Instead, he poured himself a glass of orange juice from a carton in the fridge, and stood there with his hand on his hip. I guess I was trying to talk him up a little, you know, get some goodwill going, since I didn't know how long I would have to be staying at his pad.

I watched him take little mouse sips from the orange juice. He was holding the glass with the ends of his fingers, not in the palm – a quirk, I guess. I was talking, this and that, when to my amazement, Darryl emptied the juice into the sink. Just like that, like it was tap water or something. About half a glass had been left. I craned my neck and watched the juice swirl down and away. I had to make sure I'd seen it.

Darryl motioned to something on the countertop.

"Look at this new thing we got for our blender," he said, picking up a piece of metal and twisting it around under the kitchen light.

I looked at it with him, but I can't say I followed much of what he was saying.

5

Carole threw a blanket on the couch, a big puffy number, red and yellow with blurry strips of whiteness. My fingers were still throbbing pretty good, but I could feel the repair work underway, the fibers relinking and redrawing themselves. I turned off the television and lay there, trying to think up the next moves. But there must have been a jigger in the works, nothing was laying out very clearly. I got up and drank down two more bottles of wine, red and white flavors, smoked another half a pack. Things settled into a kind of easy peaceful quease. I resolved to just let things *ride* hour to hour, you know, while also remaining fully prepared to do whatever it took – to *act* – to confront challenges and change the *facts* of a given situation – if *necessary*. Yes – *as always*. I don't know what time it was when I passed out.

In the dream, there was a light bulb burning in the distance behind me. But I was going the other way, trying to leave. It wasn't clear why. I moved through the dimness, found the light switch on the wall. I hit it, kept hitting it, but the light wouldn't go on. Lost there in the darkness, I couldn't find the door. I kept hitting the switch, but the light never appeared. I kept moving along the wall, straining and fumbling in vain for a door handle. It did not appear. Then they attacked.

They seemed like *hands*... but no bodies were attached. There were no bodies anywhere in that whole place. All I felt were these hands – or maybe they weren't even hands, now that I look back on it... maybe, you know, they were more like *objects* – hands and *objects*. They reached toward my pockets, knocking into me, grasping at my legs. They were insistent, demanding. Their attacks did not inflict pain... yet their mad, unyielding persistence was wounding all the same. They felt hard and cold, with a sharp "poking" quality to them... yet I could not discern shape. I pushed and pushed, kept pushing –

I started to panic. The dirty devils! A feeling of helplessness fell over me, I was losing my grasp, it was excruciating. I was sliding, sliding... yet never quite moving, never getting anywhere...

Darryl was already gone when I opened my eyes in the bright bitterness of morning. I didn't like that, him slipping out without me hearing him. But I could hear Carole getting ready. I watched her in the doorway, slipping on her shoes. She swept her looping brown hair out of her eyes and looked over at me. Or maybe she was just staring off. Well, it didn't matter, the blankets were over my head. I was peeking through an opening, so I don't think she saw I was awake. But I saw her.

Her earrings hung big and low and were shaped like Sri Lanka. She was wearing a grey pants-suit, the top vest part without any sleeves. I guessed you could wear a long-sleeved shirt underneath. Carole didn't, though, it was just her bare arms streaming out of there. Her arms were more white than tan, but they were fine, fine arms, with a few freckled spots here and there. They looked to still have a layer of soft girl's fat on them, which tended to dull the contours of the biceps and whatnot. But that was just fine.

And then I saw Carole's breasts billowing out into the vest, pressing up against it, making it curve just so. I mean, I tell you, the mounds were really filling up that deal, fleshing out the vest in a way that was really making me look, hunkered down there on the couch. I'd never noticed that kind of thing on Carole before. What the hell, I was thinking. But then before I could think it all the way through, she threw on this huge fake brown fur coat, opened the door, shut it, and was gone. Her heels clacked down the hall a ways, then faded. The apartment was completely silent.

I leaked myself in the bathroom, then wandered into the kitchen to look for a cup of coffee. I espied a nice friendly red maker – the jug underneath was already about half full. I put my good hand to it. Like I figured – still warm, probably from Darryl or Carole this morning. I flicked the ON switch to hot it back up.

I sat back and took a look around the kitchen. A lot of fancy stuff in there, really, no shortage of it. Sets of shiny pans on the walls, a butcher's collection of shining long knives with black handles, a fleet of tiny English teacups with matching saucers. The pea green tile-work looked to be a fairly recent addition, as did the white lino floor. The counters held blenders, toasters, juicers, a coffee grinder, and a blocky something that looked like it might be a gourmet electric bread maker. Nice stuff, for what it was worth.

Then I got pissed. I mean, I got *pissed*. The kitchen was a total mess – a sty. All the dirty spaghetti dishes from the night before. The stuff was untouched, resting in heaps and jumbles on both sides of the sink. What – did Darryl and Carole expect me to do them? I guessed that was possibly maybe the idea, me being an unannounced guest and all – you know, having an obligation to do my part to keep the household up and running.

I went out to the kitchen table to look for a note or something that would explain this in so many words. There was a note all right – in reference to a spare set of keys to the place. Signed – DARRYL.

Nice, very nice. *Very fucking nice.* They'd left keys so I could lock up should I need to step out for a jiffy, but not so much as a word about the dirty dog-sty kitchen they'd left behind. I sat at the table and lit up a smoke.

I got up after a while and poured a cup of the coffee. It was okay, a little heavy for my tastes, like they overdid it with too much coffee poured in the filter and not enough water. In any case, I drank, then headed back to the kitchen for a stab at the dishes.

First, there was the matter of unloading the dishwasher, which was already stuffed with clean dry dishes. I didn't like that. At least they could have unloaded this for me, yeah, even if it made them a few minutes late getting to work. I slammed the dishwasher door shut, not at all happy. I picked up last night's sauce pan. They hadn't even bothered to run this under water. The sauce was beginning to harden and crust. The worst, the worst. I tossed the pan into the sink and hit it with a blast of hot water. Then I noticed all the dishes were like this – everything smeared over with hardened pasta leavings – plus leftover goop that had not been eaten or refrigerated but had been allowed to sit out all night. The goop smelled, too, it *stank,* a pile of old spaghetti left out all night. A fly, or what seemed to be a fly, buzzed in from somewhere and landed on a fork covered with little bits of red-brown meat – buzzing, buzzing.

This was not good at all. What did they think I was? Did they forget to notice that one of my hands was all banged up and bloodied? That I was in no position to be scrubbing their dishware all day? And so on?

Well, so I ended up making quick work of the dishes. There was a rubber trash can in one of the corners, and into it everything went. I mean everything – plates, forks, knives, glasses, pans, stirring spoons, bowls, everything. I could hear it all smashing up in there as I tossed – *boom boom boom crack*. After everything was cleared away, I grabbed a sponge and wiped down the countertops and table to a sparkling shine. I scrubbed and scrubbed until I could scrub no more, then tossed the sponge into the trash as well.

Everything was ship-shape at last.

Then that "bird" buzzed by again – otherwise known as a "fly." I'd had about rather enough of him. I seized one of the long kitchen pitchfork-style things and stabbed him as he zipped by on another sortie. Either I was super-quick, or he was unusually slow. I tossed him to the counter and, using one of the small kitchen knives, picked the dirty little turd-lover apart under the bright kitchen bar bulb – wing by wing, leg by leg, antennae by antennae, haltere by haltere, "compound eye" by "compound eye," – piece by piece – mandible, maxilla, thorax, anthrax, asshole, butthole and the rest of it.

The creepy turd-licker tore to bits like the worst cheap toy, spilling like dirt on to the counter, vanishing before my eyes.

Yes, this was how they *designed* them: To crumble into "dust."

6

Well, so the hours crawled by. It wasn't even noon, and I'd already gone through most of Darryl and Carole's place. Very little was of interest. There was the big "entertainment" dingus, containing thousands of "favorite" shows and films and various extravaganzas; music tune files, three or nine years past the expiration date; pie and pizza recipes; along with "games" galore and an overdose of baseball / basketball player clips / statistical data / game strategoes. There was the kitchen stuff, clothes, shoes, electric razors, electric nose hair slicers, etc. Not much else. No cargo of old family jewelry or stock certificates stashed away that I could find. I did come across one manila envelope, containing ten twenties – emergency standby cash, one would figure – and about seventeen other dollars of this and that that was laying around.

Well, so I was sort of screaming my hair out. It was the silence in that place, in that whole neighborhood. I didn't get it, didn't understand. Every so often you could hear a clunk or rattle of some kind in the building. But there was no one walking by with keys, no chattering or humming, not even a single kid yelling or crying. In the middle of the morning a garbage truck trawled by, so at least there'd been some grinding and clanking. But it lasted only a minute or two. After that, nothing.

I watched out the windows. A few people slunk by now and then, a mysterious-like air about them as they gawked this way and that over their shoulders, before melting around a building or into one of the towers. There were few cars.

In one of the kitchen cabinets I found a couple more bottles of wine. I popped one of the reds, a fancy label burgundy, went back out to the living room and lit a few butts. I was just ashing wherever at this point, hardly caring about anything, and lipping freely from the bottle, gargling it down in giant swallows. If

Darryl and Carole said a word about anything when they got home, well, okay, I would just have a good laugh and try to paper it over somehow, take a broom to the place if I had to.

I scanned through the tunes, picked out a classical piece, swung over the volume till it was pretty much blasting. It was a Stravinsky. I wasn't so familiar with his work or anything, but I'd seen the name, it was something you ran across. It was okay tunes, yeah, a bit flutey in parts, for my tastes, but it wasn't like a lot of the overly flowery tunes you might hear. It mostly roared, came at you unexpected. Soft twirling noises suddenly blending into these chug-chug-chuggery-style bleats and booms and blats. Elements of the suspensefully sinister and wicked, but no, not quite cynical. Seemed like at least a million suckers had stolen parts of it for their movies. Anyway, it was okay, fine, went well with the wine.

Well, so it was at this point that I noticed a shelf of books and what have you, there in the living room, that I hadn't yet gone through. In fact, it looked like photo albums up there, family treasures, and I didn't suddenly like the look of that. I didn't give a flying care in hell about the books of ancient artwork and the stacks of fat-ass computer manuals and the rest of it. But the photo albums, now, that was not at all what I wanted to see. I bolted from the couch and pulled them down, there must have been three or four of these photo books. I tore them open and scanned the pages.

It was just as I'd expected, I'd seen it coming even as I'd been sitting there. And I was in absolutely no mood for it.

It was my ex, my ex-girlfriend. Shots of her all over the stupid place. I sat there flipping the pages – all the while getting more and more completely furious. There was no need for this, absolutely NONE. I could hardly believe my eyes were seeing it. The nerve of Darryl and Carole, to do something like this.

I scanned the pages. There was even a picture of me with Susan. The two of us together, smiling like the whole world went around only for our pleasure. Two geeks with golden beer cans in their hands. Olden days, man, old stuff! A bunch of bologna pictures like this.

I set the photo albums on fire. I flung the burning carcasses into the kitchen sink when they got too hot to hold.

I threw open the sliding glass and walked on to the balcony. I stood there and lit a smoke. Frigid winds and breezes smacked me in the head, ruffled me on all sides. I looked around and saw the sun already on its slow dive down again. I saw clouds, some of them pink from the sun, some of them red from the same source. The clouds moved, they were moving – swirling up and smashing down against each other. Up and down they went, back and forth. Wave upon wave of the clouds, piles of perfectly white clouds. And red ones and pink ones and orange, this way and that – and darker clouds behind them, piling up in big purple stacks. The wind whacked away at me.

The cool fresh crispness washed over my bare arms and neck – the crispness zooming in at my ankles and flowing up my pants legs. It felt good and relaxing, went a long way toward steadying the nerves. You know, just smelling that nice cold air, having it swirl around my face and leak up into my nose and lungs – a fresh jolt of chemicals and minerals.

The wind hardened my nipples – caused my arms to pimple, the hair on my arms to stick up and jig.

Very serious weather.

Before too long, though, it hit me that it was only some coldness – and I wasn't sure I liked it any more. I was suddenly asking myself, What are you doing, standing there in the cold? What are you *doing* – to have come all this way since day one, boxing and contorting through it all, kicking past all and everything else, to just stand there in the cold? Past mommy the moonbat and daddy the dipshit, past Wanda the wonder-whore and Susan the slinky-slut – and the rest of the cast of mucky-mucks?

Now – in the cold and this silence?

I turned around and stormed back in – half-expecting to find someone with a metallic clipboard in their hands, taking notes. But there wasn't.

In one of the kitchen cupboards I found a bottle of tequila, three-quarters full. I powered down a couple gulps to steady myself, and then I powered down a few more. I grabbed the bottle and went walking around, looking, noticing things. Odd, it seemed.

Different places on the kitchen table. All over the lamp in the living room. On the patch of lino by the front door. On the glass leading to the balcony. Everywhere.

Dust.

7

In any event, I realized I was out of smokes. I'd found a little cedar stash box of Darryl and Carole's during my searches, but that was not what you did, you did not smoke dope. There was an obligation to stay fit and healthy, and the way I looked at it, you did not do dope according to this equation. Marijuana was in that category, and funny pills, and anything you shoved in your arm, or up your nose, or up your ass, that was not under doctor's orders. There were no issues about it, as far as I was concerned, no arguments. It was just not done.

Typically, Darryl and Carole had dope. And typically, they had rolling papers. And they had a little stone turquoise dope pipe in their little stash case – but they did not have smokes. Just dope, streetcorner dope, and not even the merest swag of tobacco to mix it with. Low class, no class, nothing class. It was just too *typical*. I agree – it's a big problem – people are just too *unoriginal*… most of them… Eating, grabbing, clawing, stinking, crying, gagging, puking, mess-creating… Not much more. Oh sure, your standard "variations" will pop up from time to time, here and there – I know, fuck you, it's part of the species, "evolutionarily" – just keep slugging away at it – at *anything* – long enough and you're bound to come up with *something*… But no one would ever, ever lose money betting on people doing the typical or unoriginal thing. The years had learned me that the soft and greedy thing was a particular favorite with most folks – especially if they had the illusion that they could *get away with it,* or that it would somehow benefit their vaguely-defined and contradictory sense of "security." Sure, funny stuff, hilarious, keep you snorting and giggling all day. Ha-HA! Ah, people. Yes of course, it was their *natural* condition, and there was nothing nobody could or should do about it…

I thought of them sitting there with their little pile, the blinds closed behind them, Darryl rolling it out, careful not to drop, leaning over the newspaper-draped coffee table. Carole sitting there thinking she was blitzed out on real super-excellent drain-your-brains stuff, her eyes all sleepy and dumb and not worth a thing, weird bullshit twangy music floating all out everywhere, just the right volume but hardly loud enough. I'd seen that kind of scene, probably too many times. Anyhow, I realized I would have to go out to get smokes.

I found what looked like a brand new cowboy hat sitting in one of the closets. I shoved it on, grabbed the keys and hurtled the stairs through that box of a building.

Still not a noise in there. Only my footsteps, echoing.

8

The streets were cold, windy and wispy. I planted the cowboy brim low over my eyes, wrapped tight the leather jacket, tucked my bandaged hand underneath – a precaution, to keep the profile low.

I had zero idea where the nearest certified dealer might be, I hadn't taken the time to notice the day before, coming in there as fast as I had. I picked a street at random and started to hike. Not a good move. Nothing in sight – no stores, no quik-marts, not a burger stand. Just the streets and the blocks of the towers. Not a single car was even moving.

Then I saw one – espied it over my shoulder behind me as it crested down along the ridge. A low navy sedan, somewhere in the top of the midline models. Shiny-shiny, dual-antenna, probably not long off the lot. I could hear it purring along, but it didn't seem to be in any particular hurry. I didn't like this – what was with these cars?

I couldn't be sure, but it seemed as though maybe the car paused slightly as it came to the intersection.

LIKE TO CHECK ME OUT?

I wasn't sure. Maybe not, probably not – but how to know? I slowed my step and listened to the soft whir-whir of the engine behind me. Whirring and whirring.

I waited and kept waiting. My skin started to crawl. The whirring, me standing there, whirring – that damn stupid *whir-whir-whirring* behind me. And then I couldn't – my nerves jerked out of control, kicking up against my skin like saw teeth.

I whipped around – I had to know who was in there!

I wasn't quick enough. By the time I turned and was able to focus, the car rocketed and was gone. I caught nothing but fumes and grinding gravel.

Bastard! The cheap bastard!

I sprinted to the corner as the vehicle cowardly fled. I had to pick up a license plate number or something – anything.

But I was too late. I couldn't really tell anything. Nothing 100 percent definite.

This was the worst, the absolute worst. I stood there, enraged and totally panicking at the same time.

Time trawled, my mind giving the slo-mo treatment to what had happened, to what I'd seen – to what I THOUGHT I'd seen.

After far too long, I realized how exposed I was. I was just standing there! I sprinted off blindly to the left, making for some hedges along one of the near towers. I got there, ducked in, and began sucking in big mouthfuls of air.

After a while I was able to think. And I didn't like in the slightest what I was telling myself.

9

Well, so I finally got some smokes. A three-hour operation, all told. Picked the pack at this joint deep off the avenues. They had everything you could possibly want – smokes, candy, soda-pop, dog food, canned nuts, batteries, sunflower seeds, fully decked-out Network Security apparatus down all aisles. For eats and for safety, to keep up the weight and to cut down on all the "crime." A big, big rip-off on the price, but I hardly, hardly cared. All I was thinking was, the borrowed Dr. Larry Chamish official bonded magnetized Tobacco-I.D. had better still scan clean on the OK-Tobacco machine. All I was thinking was that I had to get back on the streets. All I was thinking was that I had to get back to Darryl and Carole's and get back off the streets.

This I knew: Things had clearly shifted – or were now *shifting*. Or seemed to be. But if they were, it wasn't at all clear yet which way they were angling. Which made it, at least at this juncture, impossible to accurately assess/evaluate my position – let alone determine what might be required to correct it – if adjustments were in fact needed.

I didn't like it. I couldn't say anything for absolute certain – but there was no margin for juggling the chances to find out. Juggling was simply not an option now. I couldn't afford to flirt with anything like that.

In any case, all I was thinking was that I had to make myself like a *blur*.

I don't think I'd ever seen it so bad. The heat that was coming down. It felt like they had dispatched half the unmarked cars in the fleet. I doubt I was wrong – I mean, it was just *reeking* out there of "special-op." The silence, the silence – and then the cars, the cars, followed by the silence. I mean, sometimes you really wonder what they're thinking, you wonder what they're saying to each other when they plot their strategies down at police headquarters. You wonder what they teach them down at the fuzz-academy, and whether they do it with a straight face.

I zigged and zagged my way across the city grid, doubling back several times, crawling into bushes and dumpsters when necessary. Early on I ditched the cowboy hat, taking care to wipe it clean of hair, other DNA material and any little leavings of "dust" that might have agglomerated. At another point I removed my leather jacket and tied my blood-stained bandanna around my head, gang-style. Back behind some bushes, the jacket came back on, and then I set out in the opposite direction, arcing on a rough southwesterly route back to Darryl and Carole's. After that initial car sighting, I don't think they ever got but a whiff of me.

No doubt my image – or my succession of images – had been captured by the intersection and commerce cubes. But it would probably be a little while yet before the facial bone-structure analysis kicked out a match and they were able to properly synch the graph. Or actually, not much time at all – the computers and satellites would do it *bingo*. But then the he-cop or she-cop down at cop-central would have to look at it and decide to do something. And to do that, first they'd have to put down the hot mutton-and-cheese. And those can be some good sandwiches.

Even so – it should have taken, charitably speaking, just half a day – max – to fully articulate the data, collate with their other sources, map the flight trajectory and trigger the tangent cogs. And then on to the Fabrication Staff, as it was known at the pig-pen. That would have involved hitting a button, plugging the "data-gaps," and hitting another button to notify the media and corporate "partners." And then, per regulation, at least four hours more, at the ultra-latest, to launch the hit squad – get it briefed, get clearance from the chiefs and ombudstaff, distribute the armor, muster the support units and trucks – and start scouting the plot coordinates.

Which meant: Sooner or later I would be descended upon, with untold fury and a great whaling sound. Probably sooner.

Which meant: Why hadn't it happened yet?

Which meant: What was their program?

There was an extremely intense 10 minutes or so that I spent huddled under some cardboard boxes behind a bakery. That was when the copter came. It caught me unawares as I was belly-crawling through an alley, but I'd heard it in time, hovering in from the southeast, the barely audible *whup-whup*. Never saw any of the rotor blades or even a direct shadow – but I heard, I heard. The masking technology they use only goes so far. Despite all the billions and billions thrown at it, they haven't yet come up with a workable nano-machine that makes negative noise, or that can completely reflect, refract and dissemble over the skies of an urban tactical situation – not to my knowledge, at least. And so I was quick enough to clamber under the pile of boxes and wait it out. I was also pretty lucky. It was almost 1000 percent they had deployed thermo-radex sensors. I pulled myself snug to the outside wall of the bakery, made myself as flat and straight as could be. On their readout screens, I must have looked just like another pan of sweetbread, fresh from the oven.

10

Darryl was the first to come in. He opened the door with a gentle jingling of keys. I swung down on him from the attic opening. I whacked the biggest of the kitchen butcher machetes into his left arm. Right above the elbow or so.

He staggered and collapsed to a knee. The arm fell to the ground with a thud and a roll.

To my astonishment, there was no blood – only a few driblets of a white substance. Darryl didn't scream or howl or anything. Instead, he tried to scuttle away in the direction of the living room.

I stuck out a leg. He stumbled, tripped along the rug, and came to a rest with his back to the base of the couch. He was moving awkwardly – trying to get away, I guess.

I threw the kitchen ax. It caught him at an angle slightly above the nose, the blade going about an inch into his forehead.

Darryl stopped moving.

There was still no blood, only the dribbly white substance. It ran down Darryl's face, pooling around his collar and tie. I came over and put a finger in it. Sort of warm and waxy.

I didn't like it. I tried not to let my mind gallop.

I succeeded. I took deep, steadying breaths.

I decided to wait it out a little more. No rash action, I had to hold tight. You can never really tell how clever they can sometimes suddenly become. You have to expect the unexpected – and then look back at what seemed obvious in the first place.

And expect both things to happen simultaneously.

Carole came in not long after that. I took off her clothes and cut her into a bunch of little pieces. She more or less felt like flesh, but she too had only the white stuff inside her.

I waited to see what would happen. A few hours went by. No one else showed up. I waited and kept waiting. I started to tire. I needed some food, some grub, some rest. Blood was running from my bandaged hand, down my arm, rolling off my elbow, landing in droplets on the carpet. My heart was really going. I could hear it – booming and banging, flipping and flopping, flouncing around in the damn silence of that place.

I walked out around midnight, not really caring if five or six platoons of foaming at the mouth cops were waiting outside.

No. They weren't.

I lit a smoke, and walked.

OH, BALLS!

ey man, I think I'm gonna go take a break," said Marty, rising and reaching for a towel. "I think I might start to ralph."

"Oh, shut up," said Bill. "You're gonna go jackoff. Siddown. You're not going anywhere."

"Yeh dude, mellow out," said Hub. "This is just the good part now anyway. The ladies are coming down any minute, so don't be a flake, dude. Don't flake out, okay?"

Marty sat back down on the sauna seat.

"Dude, just let me get you another beer," said Bill, getting up. "That's what you need. You'll feel better."

"Okay," said Marty. "All right."

Marty and Hub sat as Bill stumbled up the stairs toward the others. They heard the door open and then happy laughing. The group had been playing strip Twister or something, and the game had quickly disintegrated under a reliable alcoholic escort. Marty and Bill and Hub were the first to have been banished to the sauna.

"You all right?" asked Hub.

"Yeh," said Marty. "I told you. I'm just... fucking wasted, man."

"Right on," said Hub, clapping his bare chest with both hands and flexing his wide neck. "Good work if you can get it."

"Yeh," said Marty, slapping Hub five. "You got that right, cuz."

"Hey – what do you think of Laura, dude," Hub said.

Marty had begun to stare off. He didn't respond immediately.

Hub, slightly a-fluster, said: "Hey man, dude – I said, What do you think of Laura, man?"

"Oh yeh, man," Marty said. He brought to his mind the image of the tall, seemingly plain brunette who had come to the party. He'd chatted with her a bit, for about a minute, but he didn't really know what to think, considering she was a newcomer to the group, someone from someone's school or work. She had freckles. Ah well, he supposed he wouldn't mind being with her for a night, if it came to that.

But jeez – it probably wouldn't.

"Oh yeh, she's a good one, real hot, man," Marty told Hub. "But there's the problem that, you know, you're a fag."

Hub cussed.

"Oh, fuck you, you fuckin' cocknut!" he rejoindered, his lips smearing together then widening apart. "You're the fuckin' jerkoff fruit!"

Laughing, the young man Hub rose and rushed Marty, knocking into him and jostling about. Marty adeptly rolled with the attack, regained his balance and quickly achieved a strategic position on the larger fellow. After further jockeying, Marty succeeded in repelling Hub to the ground. Hub tumbled and then sat with a laughing, breathless look, his hair mussed.

Marty half-observed Hub's flaccid penis and heat-engorged scrotal sac, resting on the tiled slick floor.

"No, serious," Marty said, watching as Hub got up and walked back to his seat. "You like her or something? You think so? Really?"

Hub paused for a moment, considering how to gauge Marty's play. "I dunno if I like her," he said at last, with a somewhat greasy, embarrassed grin, "but you know, well, you know, maybe, yeh, somethin' like that. Maybe, you know, yeah."

Marty sat there, nodding.

"Shit," said Hub, "where's Bill with the beer? I'm thirsty as a shit-fuck."

"Yeh," said Marty.

Suddenly they heard the unlatching of the door up top. It was the others.

"Oh crap, here they come," said Marty. *"Hub, quit raping me!"* he yelled loudly so the others would hear.

"Shut yer trap!" cried Hub.

The two young men laughed at great volume.

Bill came ambling nudely down the stairs with a torn 12-pak box of light beer. Elaine, Jack, Milly, Laura, Flan, Nick, Rick and Walt followed with their own shiny faces and naked bodies. Some were tall and pale, others thin. One was quite fat and had dark creases.

They sat and passed around beer cans and bottles of spirits, consciously yet nonchalantly covering their genitals with careful placings of thighs and hands – save, of course, for the up-front Hub, who had staked much of his reputation on his apparent willingness to let things "hang." There was a brief struggle over a grey-blue pipe containing a very small quantity of inexpensive marijuana. Marty saw Hub wrestle it away from Walt, wrap his thick hands about it, and take a big inhale.

"Hey, Rick has an erection!" the doughy blond Milly exclaimed with evident whimsy. The stocky, nominally intense Rick feigned embarrassment and twisted his legs atop his weenie.

After a time, Elaine, who was one of the group's main leaders – along with Hub – withdrew her purple lips from a bottle of tequila and announced another game for the assembly.

"Hey," she said, "let's tell about our most shocking and embarrassing dreams, like ones we really had."

The room grew silent with pain.

"Oh, come on."

"Yeah, fuck off."

"Come off it, man."

"Come off what?" said Jack, adding a great peal of laughter.

"No, I'm serious," insisted Elaine forwardly. "Here, I'll start," she said, grabbing again for the bottle of tequila. "It was when I was about 14 and I was dreaming that I was laying naked, strapped down on this big huge steel table, and it was really cold! And I didn't know where I was, but I was looking around and there were these super bright lights and this high green ceiling, like it was an operating room or something…"

Marty took his eyes from her and began to wander them around the room. He thought it all so regrettable suddenly, everything. His eyes grazed over the bodies of his friends. The sight of their flesh, much of it now becoming oily in the sauna heat, began to make him sick. Such awful bodies they were, twisted into bizarre configurations, some of them snowy, wet and pasty, others dark as though recently barbecued. He lingered his eyes over knobs of breast and tried to squeeze his vision under mushy thighs of flab. He then went around the room focusing on mouths, and they were disturbing open things, grubby and obvious but of strange shapes.

He flipped the mouths upside-down and imagined the chins as noses, and it was funny in some way, but not for long. Because then he thought of fingernails, fingernails translucently white and hard and clipped off, lying in warm water, intermingling with hair near a drain on the floor. And then it was hair – he was overcome by the specter of all the hair pouring out of the heads in that room, stinking unclean hot hair flowing from the heads and bodies, hair of miserable scratchiness and brittleness and length, tumbling out uncontrollably and becoming tangled in a suddenly appearing flood of blood which emerged from the spaces between the sauna-room tiles. And the hair rose on the wave of blood and became sopped, drippy and black. Marty was neck-deep in the hair and blood, and when he breathed the hair moved with slimy, silky ease and slipped down his throat, and he couldn't breathe.

He looked at the flesh, the flesh vaguely glistening in the low-watted light. Ugly flesh casting invisible rays, nipples casting shadows, deep crevasses in the fat like expired sausages bundled in twine. He concentrated on shriveled ghostly penises, saw gaping, dripping vaginas – layer upon layer of them, piled on one another, hairy and shaven, blurring into a single folding, receding, bifurcating, suffocating pink-red sludge, and scabs and little holes, dozens of them, woven into the red-pink walls themselves. And next noises came to him, the crunching and cracking and grinding of bones, and scalps tearing from heads, skulls smashing against stone, faces grimacing in howl.

He smelled the sweat and marijuana and alcohol, chemical-toxic residues seeping from the skins. The scent was heavy and darkly sweet, like rotting vegetables or certain types of vomit. He looked around the room and thought of all the food going into the open mouths, so many thousands of pounds of food, powering the misshapen legs and sharp elbows and proud eyes and active sphincters. Marty sat there and contemplated the fact of ten active, and potentially wet at this very moment, anuses.

He felt a shove on his left arm. It was Walt.

"C'mon man, Marty," someone said. "Your turn, dude. Craziest dream, man."

"Aw man," said Marty. "Oh, wow."

"C'mon, you sleeping?" someone said to a few laughs.

"All right, all right," said Marty. He licked his lips and began.

"Yeah, I guess I was about 16 and, um, in this dream I was watching myself sleep, like I was above myself watching myself sleep in this dark purple room. And the window curtains were open above the bed, and this silver-white moonlight was sparkling over everything. And then this beautiful woman in a white nightgown came in and walked over to the bed. The gown somehow fell away to the floor, and these huge, big, full breasts came swinging out. And she had all this long, flowing dark hair coming down over her shoulders and everything. And then she climbed into the bed and rolled next to me under the sheets. And she had this incredible white skin, you know, so soft and smooth, perfect. And she started kissing me. And then she climbed on top of me, and we were doing it, you know, fucking up and down. And – this is where, I don't know, it gets crazy. I could feel my penis, my cock, you know, it began to swell and swell. I mean, and I couldn't stop it or nothin'. It kept getting bigger and bigger until it felt like it was about two feet long or something. And then, because it was so big, it seemed like I was starting to hurt her. She made this little squeaky noise and got off me. And then when she leaned over to kiss me, I saw for the first time that she was my mother. It was my own mom."

Marty looked around the room, not quite seeing anything. "And," he went on, "she kissed me really deeply then, this kind of wet, warm kiss – and it was really true, it was my mom, I mean it smelled like her and everything. And that was when I started to get scared, this really real feeling of being scared that you get in dreams. And then my mom, she stopped kissing me and grabbed on to my huge penis that was still there. And with this little flick of her wrist, she just snapped it right off from my body. Click, like that. Snapped my dick off, like it was some kind of toy or something."

Marty paused to swallow saliva. "And she brought it up and held it out for me to touch. And I didn't know what to do, so I just ran my hands over it a few times. It was hard and big and incredibly smooth and nice. And I remember feeling glad, because I thought it was great that I had a penis that was so big. I felt happy about it, really happy. And then my mom set the penis down on the bed next to me, then she laid her head on my shoulder and went to sleep. And the last thing I remember was that the sheets were really cool to the touch, and peaceful. Everything in the room was this kind of beautiful purplish-white, and silver… And that's it, I guess. That's all."

"Okay, your turn, Hub," someone said, perhaps Flan.

THE CABBAGE

I was up relatively early. The apartment was warm, cooler in the corners; the light still tentative, gray. I fell to the ground and pressed out twenty-five sit-ups. I flipped onto my back and squeezed in twenty-five stomach crunches.

I went into the kitchen and lighted a cigarette at the stove. I made instant coffee, poured cereal into a bowl with milk, and had a look at yesterday's newspaper. The economic indicators were open to differing interpretations, but some of the executives were quoted as saying the cycle could be near an end. The Semites were haggling over land. In athletics, one of the teams had won.

I dressed and went in. I put a skinny green cloth tie over a white knit shirt. I put on navy blue slacks, then the old black wing-tips, the ones with the new hard plastic soles.

*

I got into the building. It seemed fine enough. The office was well-lit, the waste baskets empty. Everyone was there, no one seemed out.

The morning man came by with the coffee and moist rolls. I got one of each. I chewed down the roll while standing at my work area, then took the coffee into the hallway for a smoke.

Dolphy Mandess was out there. He was in his fifties, burly but tall, a clean shave and a slight wheeze. Dolph smoked at least a pack-plus per day, letting the ashes fall indifferently against his belly.

Dolph wasn't a particularly good worker, everybody knew it. He tended to have a consistent level of sloppiness in what he did, his ideas always seemed slightly off. A few people found his manner inconsiderate, at times verging outright rude. He was nobody's favorite. But he was, in my view, basically harmless, maybe even pretty good. Things seemed to wash right off him, he would let things pass. I never saw him pack a grudge, or try to carry beefs to the bosses.

We chatted a few minutes. Dolph told me about the dinner he had last night. It had involved beef with a cream sauce, potatoes, a salad, white wine. He'd finished up with strawberry ice cream, coffee, then a "nice cigar with cognac." This had happened at a little restaurant next to his apartment. Then he'd gone to his neighborhood shop and picked up two videos, both geopolitical action dramas.

We walked back in and got to work.

*

We were busy for a good stretch of the morning. Then it calmed, not a lot to do. Most of us were just sitting there, waiting for the bosses to make the next move. I walked over to the Staff Area, selected a magazine, and came back to my desk.

Katha Cane, a thick girl with long white hands, worked a few desks over. She was always on the phone, different people, but a lot of times her husband, Alan. They seemed to have troubles, a crisis every couple days. From what I understood, they had been married only a few years. But I had never spoken to her about it.

I heard Katha sigh deeply, followed by what was probably the start of some sobbing. Her voice was crackly and choked. Then she was definitely sobbing.

"I think I am obsessed," I heard her say. She was almost whispering. "I don't know what to do."

I looked at the back of her brown head, at the tousles of medium-length hair, probably freshly washed that morning. I visualized the tears sliding down her cheeks.

Katha hung up the phone, got up and headed off in the direction of the Ladies'. I'd seen this before, this kind of routine. She returned with a clump of tissues and sat at her desk.

Maya, the department secretary, was Katha's good office friend. Maya was probably twenty years older than Katha, but they seemed to have a somewhat close relationship, at least on the surface. Maya came over to share in Katha's misery. It was part of the routine. They talked for a few moments, Katha telling what had happened. I wasn't able to hear everything.

"Oh, you can't tell men all these details," Maya said. I saw the top of Maya's gray mound of hair weaving on the other side of the divider. "I always told my husband too much before I learned. It was like medical school over at our house. It drove him crazy."

Katha was still sobbing. It seemed like she was trying to prevent it from developing into a full-fleshed cry.

Maya said, "You can't do this to him, honey. Men just can't understand certain things. You have to control your information."

"I know," said Katha. She sobbed and sighed.

At that point Costa, our immediate supervisor, appeared, carrying sheafs of fresh work in both arms. He handed a stack each to Katha and I, nodded generically, and walked away to his area without saying a word.

Costa was thin and trim, not so tall. Generally brisk in manner. He spent most of the day inside his "office" – a roofless glass enclosure that was pushed up against one wall in our main workroom. You could see him at all hours behind the glass. He would be sorting over papers, tapping on his computer, hunched over his desk, having a sandwich and bag of chips for lunch. He seemed to leave the place only to distribute assignments, or for periodic meetings with the higher-ups. Most of the staff called this glass enclosure "The Aquarium," alternately "The Terrarium." But never when Costa was in listening distance.

I glanced over the new work. Katha sighed again. She got up and looked at me. She was wearing a black dress with gold braid on the arms and around the neck. Her eyes were red but she beamed at me. She dabbed at her eyes with a tissue, and beamed at me. I tried to keep my face as smooth and placid as possible.

Her smiling like that made me feel good. Finally I smiled back at her, but didn't say anything. Katha turned and walked back toward the Ladies. She was a big girl, taller than the average, plumpish, with wide ankles that her nylons worked hard to disguise. I felt goodwill toward her. I wanted everything to work out.

❋

I took a big inhale and turned to my work. As I did, something in my swivel chair gave way with a clank. I pitched forward. A bolt hit the carpet, rolled and came to a stop against the toe of my left wing-tip.

I stood and pulled at the seat. It came free from the rolling lower carriage with a dull clang.

"Hell," said Standrie.

Standrie was one of the veteran employees. He was thin-necked and stoop-shouldered, a fan of dark turtlenecks and tweed sportscoats with patches on the elbows, this type of look. Like

Dolphy Mandess, Standrie had been with the company for more than 20 years. But, also like Dolph, he'd never really climbed the ladder of advancement and promotion. The only difference between them and me was the word "Senior" attached to the front of their job title. And probably a little more money.

Standrie stood from his desk and walked over.

"Would you look at that," he said.

He bent down to inspect the bottom half of the chair. He fingered it roughly with his thumb and forefinger, then looked up at me.

"Just came apart on you?"

I nodded. "Yeah, it did."

"Hell. And they expect us to work like this."

Standrie shook his head, shrugged, and walked back to his area. He picked up a pencil and stared at something.

I put the seat back on the rolling carriage and wheeled the chair into one of the far corners. I walked over to Maya and handed her the bolt. She sighed and shook her head. The chair was only a few months old, she said, but now the men from Maintenance would have to be called.

I grabbed a free chair from the Staff Area, rolled it over to my desk, and got down to work.

*

Around quitting time Eddie came over. He was the fellow always trying to be the department rough boy, the one always so unique and shining exceptionally bright. He did things like: Not tucking his shirts in all the way; wearing a ball cap to the office on Fridays; putting his feet up on his desk just as one of the bosses walked by; tossing perfectly good pens into the trash; trying to trap you in a discussion about sports; volunteering brash and unconventional ideas to reorganize the entire office at staff meetings. Today he was trying to organize another office get-together, to have everyone come out for drinks at a bar he liked. The place had dozens of televisions hanging from the ceiling.

"No, thanks," I said. "Not today, Eddie."

"Oh, c'mon. You never go out with anybody. What, you think you're too good or something?"

"C'mon, gimme a break for once. I'm trying to finish something here."

"That's cool."

Eddie turned and shuffled back to his area. His pants appeared to be hanging too low on his hips – so low, in fact, that you couldn't get a glimpse of his socks between the pant cuff and the shoe top. In any case, he would be the kind who wouldn't be wearing any socks, and the kind who would try to conceal such a fact.

*

A little while later it was quitting time. A group of them filed out, Eddie at the head of the pack. I waited until they were gone, then put on my sportscoat and walked out.

It was cold and crisp, lots of people in the streets. I came to a stand, threw a coin on the counter, and grabbed one of the papers. I walked a few blocks to Russell's, a diner. I sat in a booth.

The waitress, Kim, came over. We talked for a few minutes. She was a tall girl, Kim, and good looking. She had slender, tan, muscular legs, a long neck and a straight back. Her boyfriend, Tommy, rode a motorcycle. I'd seen them together at a bar one night, standing in the corner, swaying to some beer commercial blues. Kim had had her hair out, brown and long and falling onto the shoulders of her leather jacket. Now she had it, as she always did when she was working, in a bun at the back of her head, clipped up with black metal pins. All the waitresses at Russell's wore short dark skirts with light blue collared shirts.

I said something and Kim giggled. She had big straight teeth, very straight clean white teeth, probably the work of long years of braces. I liked Kim. I figured she was the kind of girl who had worn dirty white socks to the knees. I imagined her running back and forth over neighborhood lawns, chasing after cats, looking at ants, sending paper boats down the gutter in the rain. Her mother would be inside the house, moaning about muddy clothes.

Kim brought me my food. I had a grilled cheese-with-tomato sandwich, french fries, a Coke filled halfway with crushed ice. I pulled the sandwich apart, inserted a piece of lettuce, left the onion on the side, and sprinkled some tabasco. I opened the newspaper and took a bite.

The newspaper was full of missiles and municipal sewage systems. There had been an oil spill in South America, and a massacre, six dead, in Connecticut – a military man, according to the arresting authorities. In our own town, a convention of weightlifters was under way at the ExpoCenter.

Kim came over as I was biting into the second half of the sandwich.

"Look at this," she said.

She showed me one of her shoes. They were typical white worker's utility shoes, ladies-style. The heel was peeling away from one of Kim's. The glue had failed. She played with the heel with the toe of her other shoe. It made a flap-flap sound.

"Hell, Kim," I said. "Take 'em back. Take 'em back and demand a refund."

"I will. I'm going to. They're not even that old."

She narrowed her eyes, her face completely serious.

I finished my meal. Kim brought me a cup of coffee in a heavy white mug. She leaned down, setting it before me with a little smile. I folded the newspaper and put it aside. I sat in the booth, savoring the smell of the hot coffee. Coffee tastes best when it's a shade cooler than drinkably hot. The restaurant was filling up with the supper rush. I listened to the kitchen workers banging the dishware and grilling the meat, toasting the bread, chopping the lettuce, churning the chili, whatever else they do. A radio was on somewhere, the cymbal smashes of pop songs coming through over the din. Kim scurried back and forth, her tan arms flawlessly balancing multiple plates heaped with food. She was quick on her feet, she really was.

I had two refills of coffee, paid my bill and left. Kim got a big tip.

*

Night was spreading, the blackness seeping through. People were on the way home, bundles in arms, hands gripping satchels and shopping bags. Or they were heading out – stepping from cabs, hair slicked back, eyes searching, jewelry swinging. Above me, I saw two birds land on a building and step into a pipe.
I walked toward the center square. Bursts of cold wind smacked against my cheeks, hurled trash across the pavement, re-froze puddles of water into ice. Buses and streetcars backed up in long queues before vaulting forward. A woman in a red hat and purple coat hung to a strap, lurching from side to side. Then, not far from me on the street, a child in earmuffs screamed. He or she was led away by a woman wearing yellow leather gloves and a blue scarf.
I passed through the center and came to the river. It was empty out there. I walked to the abandoned docks and descended the stairs to the river line. Along the edges of the river ran uneven

strips of ice, about ten feet wide. I heard the river flowing, but couldn't see it. Too dark now, probably.

I turned and ascended a second set of stairs leading back to the street. I headed toward the bridge. I took a cigarette from my sportscoat pocket and lighted it.

At the bridge a large red dog loped over. Her minder trailed behind, strolling along with what looked to be a stick in his hand. The dog was friendly and long-haired. I scratched behind her ears. She leaped up my legs and nipped at the bottom fringe of my sportscoat, hitting my thighs with her paws.

I took a hit from my smoke and quickly ashed. To my astonishment, the dog leaped at the clump of falling grayness – and speared it with her tongue. She just grabbed the ash right out of the air. She licked her mouth a few strokes, then looked up at me with a stare of bewilderment. She had eaten the ash. I felt like laughing, but wasn't sure if I should.

The dog sneezed. She threw her head to the ground and began to paw at her muzzle. I laughed then, and halfheartedly lunged at her. She jumped back, grinned, whined, wagged her tail, and sprinted away. She came bounding back, then raced away again.

The dog's minder came up. He was a fellow of forty or more, medium build and very short hair, office-style slacks and shoes but a blue and white ski jacket on his back. A thick black mustache sprawled in the center of his face. He nodded at me friendly, then waved his stick in the air wildly.

"C'mere, Rusty!" he shouted. The dog galloped toward him, veered, circled around and darted into the street. A man on a motorcycle beeped.

The minder murmured and swept past me, walking after his animal.

*

I headed back toward the center. The cops were out by now, trawling in their low-lying prowl cars. In front of an Italian restaurant, a couple extracted themselves from a dark, shiny compact. The restaurant's cherry neon sign lit them from behind. The woman was younger and blond, with a white stole around her shoulders. Her hair was heaped on top of her head like a small golden mountain. The man seemed severe, short and bearded, wearing a black suit and a red and blue striped tie. He checked to make sure his coat was buttoned.

I walked along, stepping carefully over the curbs. Cars pulsed around me, headlight beams bobbing over dips in the road. I came to the Luminous Dolphin. I walked in and sat at the bar. The place was empty. It was still early, not even eight.

The barkeep came over.

"Hey, Hamid," I said.

"Hey," he said, giving a small tight grin.

I ordered and he poured and brought it over. I left it sitting on the counter and took a long suck from the top. It went down smooth, with a kick on the far side, as intended. I raised it, drained it, and ordered another.

Hamid poured and brought it over. He was balding, but kept himself neat. He cupped his chin in his hands, his elbows on the bar.

"Yeah?"

"These friends of mine got in this bad car accident, man. Tim and Liz, out at Wister Bay. Liz got her spine snapped, but I guess she'll be okay. That's what they say. Tim's still unconscious. They had to airlift him to the military hospital. They say there's only a 50-50 chance he'll wake up again."

"Jesus, Hamid."

*

I headed toward the Metro. It was getting along near ten p.m. or thereabouts. Not so many people out now – mostly couples signaling for taxis, and dark solitary forms disappearing into alleyways. I figured it was maybe time to turn in for the night.

I came to Stindel Station. I stood at the top of the escalator, but didn't go in. It flashed that I should have called someone several hours ago, but had forgotten – or perhaps hadn't tried very hard to remember. Now it was late. If I called now, I would have to be apologetic. Perhaps extremely apologetic. The person would most likely be angry. Even disappointed.

She also could have called. I pulled the phone out of my inside jacket pocket. It appeared as if she had, in fact, called. And no, I hadn't heard it. Yes, maybe the ringer was still on the fritz. Maybe I'd mistakenly hit the mute button. These phones could be more complicated than they seemed.

I supposed everything would be all right. Hopefully, at least, no one would die.

I lighted a smoke and kept walking. It felt good to walk. The wind pressed in under my chin, but it was nothing intolerable. I came to Auk Hill Station. I passed that as well.

I decided to loop back towards the center. The street emptied out near The Eighth & Dime. Why not, I decided to go over there.

It was crowded and cheery, a bunch of people, chattering and clinking glasses, this sort of an atmosphere. I went up to the woodstrip bar and ordered a few, sitting there, having a few smokes. On the second drink, the fellow on the next stool asked for a cig and a light.

I gave him what he wanted. The guy was weaving a bit, struggling to keep his eyes open, but he didn't seem very menacing. He wore a blue-grey sweater, tattered jeans and a big black clock on his wrist. His hairstyle was next to nothing on the sides, but sat in a big loose pile on the top. It ran long and thin down the back of his neck. Dark brown hair.

He wanted to talk. I heard him a few minutes, a loose general speech. He told a story about his boss. The boss didn't understand what was going on. He didn't see that it was himself – the boss – who was screwing things up at the company, making it terrible for everybody. The boss said cruel and stupid things, he didn't even know how the company worked. The fellow moved on to something concerning bees, I believe, about hives he'd seen at a ranch somewhere. Then something reminded him of a movie that was out – the movie of the TV show, perhaps. And on to music something, a girl band, a blond singer. And then a bit about an internet site whose focus was another internet site.

I excused myself, leaving a fresh smoke for him on the counter. I used the Men's, ordered another round, and found an empty table by the window.

*

I was in at work the next day. I'd made it in on time, but I was buttery, it was difficult to keep a focus. I could feel myself tottering as I stood in the hall smoking. I was thankful not a lot was going on. The e-mail had messages about someone's car trapped in the lot by a white lift-back, and something about a new pay deduction the management wanted to impose for some purpose or other. It wasn't very much money.

There was a third message. It was entitled, simply, *Dick*.

well, thanks. i turned down two different offers to spend the evening with you. one of them was my friend who is leaving at the end of the month. i waited for you to call. not interested in your explanations. yes im sure it all makes perfect sense. i have given you ample opportunity to tell me to fuck off in a way that was not inconvenient for me. do not see why you had to do it like this. right, ciao. L.

I deleted the three messages.

We had a full crew, and that helped. Costa did a pretty fair job of spreading around what work there was. When it was time for a break, I smoked two cigarettes instead of the usual one. When I wasn't smoking or working, I sat at my desk and read. One of the magazines had a lengthy article about how the world's oceans were running out of fish. The piece had several graphs and flowcharts to explain it. But it seemed simple enough: The fishermen were fishing too much. They were even using lasers and computer radars designed for missile systems.

I went straight home, didn't even bother to check the mailbox. I sat at the table, opened a bag of peanuts. I was still a bit wobbly, but I felt better than I had at work.

I walked into my annex room and looked out the window. The sun was going down, throwing a pink ribbon across the horizon. There was a smear of yellow at the bottom, a blur of blue up top. The downtown towers stuck up, heavy and black and sharply angled. Some had lights in their windows.

I took a few tubes and spread out some paint. I took a brush to a piece of cut cardboard. I ended up using four brushes to slash on the colors. I ran short of green, and realized I would need to open a fresh tube of yellow. I broke the seal but no paint came out. It looked like the top of the tube was plugged with a knot of oil. I went ahead and squeezed anyway. The rear part of the tube split apart, globbing wet yellow onto my hand. I spread it onto the board with my fingers.

I hit the cardboard until it was filled. By then the sun was mostly gone.

I came back into the kitchen and washed up. I took off my shirt and threw it on the pile. I took the knife and made myself three toasted cheese sandwiches. I lit a smoke, then walked back into the annex.

The room stank with the paint. I examined what I'd done. There were a few things I wasn't very happy with, but it seemed fruitless to fool with it any more. I finished the smoke and walked out of the annex. I went to the stereo, flipped on the news radio, and lay down on the couch.

It was past four a.m. when I awoke. My arms, fingers, face and ears were freezing cold, but my groin felt lathered in sweat. My heart was beating fast. I felt uncertain. I took off my pants, shoes and socks, switched off the stereo, and went into the bedroom.

*

I was back at the office. People seemed all abuzz about something, but no one was talking, at least not to me. These things were usually nothing you'd end up thinking about for more than three seconds, but sometimes you were curious. Anyway, aside from a mid-morning flurry, we weren't very busy.

I looked across the room and saw Costa hunched inside his glass enclosure. He was handling some papers, shifting them around on his desk.

I figured it wouldn't be long before he came back around, and thus rejected the idea of having another quick smoke. It's no good when the boss is always finding your desk empty, even when there's nothing going on. Something always gets said to you eventually. That's a slap you never really need.

I turned back around. Standrie was standing on the other side of my work area.

"Ever seen anything like this?"

He was holding a white comb. I hoped it wasn't a game or some joke he was trying out.

"Sure, it's a toothbrush," I said.

"Funny. This is a comb. But it's made, get this, out of 100 percent bone. Bought it after work last night at that import place around the corner."

"Bone?"

"Yeah, bone – like the kind that's in your head, young fellow." He laughed.

"What kind of bone?" I reached out for the thing. "Here, let me test it."

He pulled it beyond my reach. "No you don't," he said. "No you don't."

"All right," I said. "Well, so what kind of bone?"

He lifted his eyebrows and shrugged. "I honestly don't know. All I know is the guy said it was made out of actual, real bone. He didn't say what kind. Whale bone? Dinosaur bone? I have no idea. I guess I should've asked. But it's guaranteed bone. Or so they say." He shrugged again.

"Didn't even ask? What kind of guy are you, anyway?"

Standrie frowned. "Hey there, mister. I didn't come here to be insulted."

"I'm sorry, I didn't mean to insult anybody. I was just wondering, that's all. Well, are you going to let me touch it? Your mysterious bone comb?"

He walked around the divider, sat in an empty chair, and handed it over. It felt a little heavier than your normal plastic comb, but was of the same general design, about five inches long. Its surface seemed a bit rougher than the plastic kind, but the color was off. Not white, really, but not at all yellow. Not quite a tan color.

My grip loosened. The comb hit my thigh and fell to the ground.

"Whoops."

"Hey now – "

Standrie bent to the floor and snatched it up. He eyed me woundedly, then stuck the comb in the chest pocket of his vest. He shook his head and walked back to his area.

Costa was soon wordlessly along, bearing a thick sheaf.

*

A little before noon I stepped out to Russell's for a mug of chili and a small salad. Kim wasn't in yet, she didn't start work until three.

I made quick work of the chili and did without coffee. I was wiping my mouth when the bells and chimes over at St. Darabel's started gonging away. I waited until it was over, then paid up and returned to the office.

I paused at my desk to check for messages, then headed for the Men's to urinate and wash up.

To get there, I had to pass by the Ladies'. The door was halfway open, and I peered in. Katha Cane was standing at the sink in front of the mirror. I gave her a nod and kept walking, but she called to me. I turned back around.

"Yeah?"

She said: "Can you help me with this... thing?"

Katha had her hands at the back of her neck. One of them was fiddling with something on her clothing, the other was holding up her long brown hair. Looked like a dress problem, or maybe something to do with a necklace.

"Sure. Whatcha need?"

"It's this thing here. I can't get it."

I came in and stood behind her. It was the first time I'd ever been inside the Ladies'. The atmosphere seemed different than in the Men's – thicker but also softer, maybe, and without the blanketing rotting stench. The tiles had salmon trim, whereas this was dark blue in the Men's. The design of the tiles was the same in both places.

A simple clasp at the top of Katha's dress was undone. It was in a relatively remote location, but I didn't exactly see why she couldn't have handled it herself. But it also didn't seem like that big of a deal to help her out.

I took hold of the two parts and joined them.

"There you go," I said. "All taken care of."

"Thanks a lot."

I saw her in the mirror. She was smiling super huge. Her cheeks were pink, shining. Her eyes were large and dark.

"Well," I said. I took a step backward. "Okay, I'll see you back out there, I guess. I got to use the Men's."

I dropped my eyes from the mirror and hooked a thumb over my shoulder. I walked out and went to the Men's.

*

I felt like reading something when work was over. I walked out of the office thinking of something good and substantial – maybe a modern novel, if one could be found that didn't feel like plastic. A political expose, or maybe a vindictive little history of something, also sounded pretty good. All I knew was I didn't want to be converted to anything, I didn't want to be impressed. I didn't want to hear how everything was changing. I didn't want to have the world opened up and laid at my feet.

I went over to one of the newer chain shops. It was clean and bright and cool in there, the only noise your feet against the carpet. I browsed around a while, thumbing through maybe a dozen things. But everything seemed too complicated or too expensive, or seemed to be working too hard to get my attention. I ended up in the magazines section, looking at pornography. To mix things up, I flipped through a magazine on motorcycle racing.

THE TALE OF
LANNY THE DOG

1

I met Gerd Pitta in Europe, the eastern half, not long before the end of the century. We had been hired together to work in the same department of a multinational corporation. We shook hands for the first time during the afternoon session of Orientation Day. If I remember correctly, we shared a few pleasant, and most likely very mundane, words.

Gerd was tall – an inch, maybe two, higher than me. He had large, thick pink hands, and these featured a set of scrupulously cleaned and cropped fingernails. Indeed, the same could be said generally, at least as far as his physical person went: Gerd was large, thick, and rather pink. The effect was perhaps magnified by his hair coverings. Gerd had dark orangish head hair (slightly balding), an orange goatee pasted to a broad chin, and a scrabble of reddish-orange on the tops of his hands and forearms.

He had the look of a fellow who doesn't miss many meals – not to say he was exactly fat. I wouldn't say fat, in the sense of the people who have the rolls and waves of squishy excess tumbling off them, pressing against their clothing. Gerd was more thickly solid, I suppose – or better yet, stout. His shoulders were staunch and rounded, and his legs appeared somewhat meaty, in the style of one who has spent a lot of time stationary, perhaps on a couch. He didn't seem able to move all that quickly. But even so, I must say, he really didn't appear to be in too bad a shape for someone in his early- to mid-thirties (which was about five or seven years older than I was).

Gerd actually looked a lot like a junior college football tackle, ten or fifteen years after his last game. Well, taking into account the goatee and the rest of his orange coverings, you could say he looked like a retired football tackle from some backwoods country college. But Gerd, I would come to know, was derived from private schools in upper Pennsylvania.

The Orientation was held on the third floor of the company headquarters. The building was a sleek-sided gray catacomb, which sat like an old giant car battery on a ridge near the main downtown square. The room itself was basically unremarkable – an arrangement of chairs with fold-out desk-tops, a video projector and screen, and several brightly-buffed silver tanks reeking with the sweet and sickly odor of overcooked coffee.

In any event, it was a struggle not to notice Gerd. He was continually raising his hand and blurting out questions. Often they weren't even questions – only statements indicating that he generally understood what was going on. I wasn't sitting that far from him, and after the first several outbursts, I began to feel slightly bad. What he was saying – well, it was of a long-winded and shoddy quality. It was obvious, basic things he was asking about ("So what you're saying is we have to take the compensatory time within the next year? But what if, for whatever reason, we don't? Then what?") and I don't believe I was the only one to get frustrated. Or maybe it was merely something to do with his manner – the glaringly affable, grinning and self-consciously earnest way in which he framed his utterances. I recall a feeling short of loathing, but rather more than simple irritation, descending upon me as I sat listening to Gerd's circumlocutions. The things he was asking, the way he was saying them... they seemed to amount to little more than a crude strategy to curry favor with the session leader and anyone else susceptible to such machinations.

After a time, I began to experience a kind of mental claustrophobia. Maybe it was even a kind of embarrassment. I looked over and watched Gerd's mouth as it formed and enunciated his words. His mouth was a tiny, small thing, with thin, unremarkable lips that barely revealed themselves beyond the orange cloud of his goatee. His eyes seemed dim and remote as they roamed behind the lenses of his round, gold-framed reading glasses. Someone else, perhaps, would have found him intellectual, even owlish.

Still, I was reluctant to dismiss him out of hand – or at least I felt guilty about it. I felt a strong compulsion to give Gerd the extra benefit of the doubt. It was, after all, "Orientation Day," and a surfeit of nerves – perhaps manifest in a lot of useless questions and statements – was hardly a major transgression. Indeed, all things considered, he still seemed nice enough. He seemed friendly and perhaps genuinely affable – and I could see no legitimate reason to doubt it.

I would later learn that Gerd had a wife, Debbie, and also a dog, called Lanny.

2

At the outset, Gerd and I were placed on the same shift. Our jobs required that we worked mainly autonomously, but there were occasions when teamwork was necessary. The company ground out product 24 hours a day, seven days a week, and this sometimes necessitated unusual scheduling contortions. For example, you might work a Tuesday through Saturday evening shift, for as many as six or eight weeks. Then, with little warning, they'd stick you in a 4-10-3 slot. This meant you did four days at a fairly miserable ten hours a pop, but got the next three days off. But as I say, there was generally no telling where you'd wind up in any given month. It had even been written into our job descriptions. The official policy was that the bosses needed the scheduling flexibility – no questions asked – because of the nature of the 24-hour operation. The workload was never particularly oppressive, however, no matter when you were shifted – which left plenty of time for the employees to talk among themselves when the opportunity presented itself.

Not a lot was going on one afternoon when Gerd drifted over to my area, sat at an empty work station, and began fingering through an armful of papers. Every so often he would check the papers against something on the computer screen.

He raised his head and said, "So what do you think of this place?"

"The job?"

"No, the city, I mean."

"Oh," I said. "It's fine, I guess. It's a little rough around the edges, you know, but overall I'm liking it so far. I thought that one old bridge down by the river was pretty incredible, and I've been to a couple neat pubs." I nodded. "I think it's pretty all right. Don't you think?"

Gerd shook his head gravely. "I think it's one of the filthiest places I've ever seen."

"Filthiest?"

"Yeah, filthiest."

I watched as Gerd's face started to pinken a bit more than usual. His jowls wobbled ever so slightly, while the rest of his facial flesh seemed to tighten.

"You don't think so?" he said. "I've never seen such filthy streets. Garbage all everywhere, crap everywhere. They pile it right there on the street corners, like some Third World nation. Seems like they never even empty the frigging trash cans. Out where I live, the dumpsters overflow day after day and no one does anything about it. I saw some kids playing in broken bottles and stuff the other day. Right out there in the street. I couldn't believe it."

"Sounds incredible," I said.

""And all the streets stink, too, don't they? Stink like cheddar cheese – worse than that. Literally stink. All those car fumes like that. And this is supposed to be Europe – so-called civilization. Go figure. And graffiti everywhere, on almost every possible surface. I don't know how it is where you live, but you shoulda seen – "

I interrupted him. "Look, I've seen some pretty trashy American cities, lots of them. Ever been to San Francisco, for example? What about L.A.?"

"What about it?" he said, raising his voice. "All right, okay, I hear you. But that's different, smog and stuff. Here there's just crap – piles of paper and junk, crap everywhere. Literally everywhere. Dogshit all over the sidewalks. Streets stink. Anyway, in The States the main thing is crime. I'll give them that – there's hardly any crime here, comparatively. You can feel pretty safe walking the streets at night. But still – that doesn't mean it's any safer overall. In fact, it's probably more dangerous overall."

"Huh?"

"I mean, yeah," Gerd said, a hint of exasperation noticeable. "Just take the industrial accident protection, for example. There is none here. Just walking around is a health hazard. Everywhere you have to walk under scaffolding where they're renovating some building. There's cranes up over your head every ten feet. Or holes – you must have seen them, all those huge, like, craters in the ground, where they're putting in new pipes or whatever."

He held his arms apart for a few seconds, as if cradling a large invisible cauldron or other object. Then his palms came clapping down on the tops of his thighs.

I started to say something – what, I wasn't exactly sure.

But it didn't matter – I didn't have a chance to get even the first word out.

Gerd's face suddenly lightened. He rose from the desk, smiled cheerfully and gave me a pat on the shoulder. The intense, troubled look in his eyes was gone. He scooped up his sheaf of papers.

"Well, I gotta get back. Fun's over. Nice talking to you."

"Okay, see you around," I said.

He started to walk away. I looked down at my work.

But then he turned around.

"Hey," he said, "we ought to go out some time, have dinner some place, wine and stuff. You're not a bad guy to talk to. Yeah, you know, we could get together, meet each other's wives, have some chow…"

I nodded. "Yeah, uh…"

"Give me a call, okay? Here's my number."

Gerd tore a scrap from his sheaf, scribbled on it, and tossed it in my direction. And then he walked off.

3

Dee and I adjusted, as well as we could, to Eastern Europe. The region, of course, was undergoing a tremendous change: A shift from "central planning" and "the command economy" and "the police state," to something – to something that was different. What it would end up being was not quite clear yet, but it was obvious the "transformation" would take a considerable amount of time. There were plusses and minuses, of course, but what seemed largely indisputable was that many of the countries of Eastern Europe were at long last heading toward the development of more "open," more modern, and indeed, "more Western" societies. "Historical forces" at work again, I suppose. And perhaps so. But I don't claim to be an expert, and don't want to be considered one.

It didn't take long for Dee to find work, at the local branch of a large Swiss-owned company, which was both lucky and nice. Though work monopolized most of our time, life was fairly leisurely, at least more so than it had been before we came to Europe. We idled languid, fragrant afternoons in hilly, statue-studded parks; munched flaky pastry at umbrella-shrouded pavilions along the river; stared in mute wonder at elaborate iron lamp posts and exquisite carved wooden door panels; floated across expansive sun-dashed cobblestone mezzanines; fawned over fabulously fusty friezes, frontispieces and fandulas; and roamed a seemingly endless cavalcade of crumbling castles, moss-drenched cemeteries, monstrous vaulted churches, time-encrusted bridges, dusty, decaying monasteries, graceful galleries... Yes, it was Europe – Eastern Europe, to be exact, in the time following what were popularly called revolutions.

Certainly, the local food selection wasn't always the healthiest, and indeed, the street pollution was not something that was easily overlooked. But it was the first time in years that neither of us had needed a car to get around. The tram system and underground metro were more than enough to suit our needs.

In any event, we had moved to Europe, and life was fairly interesting. Things were fine – indeed, they were even pretty good. But only, I must add, for the initial few months. Because, well – I don't know, I guess certain things had been building up again. At the start of that first winter, I began to have another problem with my drinking. Looking back, it seems that neither Dee nor I really saw it coming.

As has been well documented, European societies are far more at ease with alcohol than our American society. Europeans drink alcohol like Americans swallow aspirin – and in the vast majority of cases, with the same results. For someone with my characteristics, then, the European alcohol society presented a kind of best-possible-of-all-worst-worlds. To sit in those shadowy, smoky, golden-lit pubs and restaurants, hunkered over a thick, perfectly-pitched beer or spectral glass of well-built wine, and at a very decent price – sitting there and watching the time go so nicely and quietly and good-naturedly – well, I found it almost impossible to resist. The situation was not helped by the fact that I was not restrained by the responsibility of having to drive a car. Which left only Dee, and the necessity of having to show up at work in somewhat decent condition, as "limits."

A good many of my expeditions were undertaken with Phrom, one of the few people from my work with whom I'd formed the semblance of a social bond. He was a short man and mostly unremarkable, I suppose – but there was a certain spark between us, as there often is among guzzlers of a certain caliber. Importantly, Phrom was not adverse to a good friendly, buggering argument. We spent at least a half-dozen nights in furious discourse, arriving in the vicinity of dawn rather shouting at each other about subjects neither of us could remember with much clarity. However, as time went on, Phrom – who was a bit older and had his own wife to contend with – was not willing, or was perhaps unable, to match my considerable ambition, and began to beg off from "our programmes," as we called them. (Phrom and I stayed friendly, however, and to this day remain quite fond of one another). In any case, for much of the rest of the time, I was on my own.

Things seemed to escalate significantly around November and December. I was not prepared for the prospect of night falling before four in the afternoon, as it did; nor could I ever quite accept the fact that in parts of Eastern Europe, clouds, along with a kind of general grayness, could obscure the sun for literally weeks at a time. It was simply not something I was able to come to quick and amicable terms with.

On more than one stay-at-home evening, I recall feeling harrowingly and hopelessly trapped between the proposed brightness, warmth and quiet cheerfulness of our apartment, and the engulfing gloom and wind and ice which I knew lay just beyond the door. I found the contrast between the two extremes suffocating, harsh, maddening – and, it now seems, ultimately unbearable. (A note to the reader: I wish neither to aggrandize nor to indulge in an extended interpretation of these events and sensations; nor to suggest they were by themselves in any way directly responsible for my behavior. For it is quite clear to me that perhaps I merely felt like getting drunk, and no alternative explanation is necessary.)

"I'll be home by twelve, one at the very latest," I would tell Dee, as I bundled myself at the doorway in preparation for the night's mission. "Probably not much later than that. I'm not planning to get drunk. I've got too much to do at work tomorrow." She must have heard the speech ten times before she stopped seeing me to the door. If I wanted to say goodbye, I had to track her down in the bedroom or bathtub.

I found myself drawn to the brooding sensuality of the cobblestone streets, the hovering neon, the flickering palaces and dripping alleyways that marked the city at night. I cannot rightly say that I remember many details – the exact places I went, the acquaintances I may have made, the things that might have been said. Mostly there is only a succession of images: A collection of laughing people with shining faces, passing bottles around a hexagonal-shaped table. Heavily sweating Arab youths in squeaking leather jackets, selling hash for a dollar in a dim alehouse basement. A gravely bearded young local poet informing me, with only a half-glimmer in his eye, that Americans "never" say the word "cacti." A bleach-blond woman's half-shut eyes and lovely cheekbones, a high-pitched chattering whine exiting her mouth in a dialect I could not hope to understand.

And these: Steam wafting from my vomit at the foot of a stone angel, in a snow-drifted park whose location I've forgotten. Being roughed awake one morning by patrolmen in front of the train station, snow frozen to the fur collar of my jacket. A bitter, seemingly unending argument with an Australian, concerning the relative greatness of particular rock and roll bands. Dizzily climbing aboard a tram, falling asleep, and waking at the very same tram stop – two hours later, and with a hangover the size of Montana. At dawn, hurrying and stumbling across the frozen road, gripped with the fear that something white was following me. Dee's glowering silence, as I returned rank and shivering in the full flower of morning, unable to form the rudimentary sentences needed to beg her for a cup of cool water.

I readily admit: I treated Dee wrong during this period. Wrong, bad, and bad wrong. I've no qualms about revealing this. And I can only consider myself very lucky indeed that Dee chose not to start making threats, or undertake any other drastic action, as part of some foolhardy bid to curtail my rampage. In my view, she would have remained well within the proper boundaries to have extended her tactics beyond the level of devastating glares, screaming fits, the occasional tearful breakdown, and a steady fusillade of nasty, dead-eye comments. That she did not so extend them is testament to her perseverance, patience, and, I think, perspicacity.

The spree slowed to an end with the approach of spring. Mainly, I think, I was exhausted.

Dee and I had survived.

4

My work, meanwhile, continued to muddle along. I'd had plenty worse jobs before, some real bottom of a rat's ass situations, and thus I was grateful to have found this particular employment, no mistake about it. I even enjoyed some aspects of the work. However, there was little question that our department was not run very well – the management was simply lacking. At best, this led to irritation on my part; at worst, frustration, quickly followed by apathy. It was hard to see what the bosses were "getting right," if anything. They consistently oversaw a general massive squandering of resources and personnel; their guidance resulted in nothing so much as a plethora of missed opportunities; and armed with educations from some of the most esteemed universities in the recent history of mankind, they proved themselves adept at failing to follow-up on the most basic issues, or to take step one toward rectifying even the most glaring of the departmental shortcomings.

Again, as I say, these are clear issues of "management," as viewed from the perspective of someone near the bottom of this particular corporate totem pole. I should emphasize that I had no serious problems with the rank-and-file workers or the job itself. My colleagues were, for the most part, fine and decent, hardworking people, if, however, somewhat tiresome on an individual basis. There was Phrom, of course, and also Wimmer and Jody, Bill and Durazzo, Hagerty from Kansas and Kimi from England, Del the old codger. I also worked from time to time with Taylor, Barry, Ross, Landler and Julian. And Gerd.

Rory Symmonds, on the other hand, was one of the assistant bosses. He was immensely unpleasant to talk to, and perhaps for this reason, tended to smell deeply of deodorant and cologne. Uniquely, he also kept a bottle of mouthwash on his desk. He would go out to the hall for a cigarette, then return to his desk and swirl the mouthwash – spitting it into his cubicle trash bin when he was done. But it was far more than that – Rory was notorious for being incomplete and incorrect in his work, and for being nasty whenever he was called on it. He had an exceptional ability to claim "illness" or "meetings" whenever key projects were nearing completion, or for disappearing for hours at a time when important decisions needed to be made. He also had an ugly propensity to glad-hand, chuckle and backslap whenever the various men from senior management stopped by to see what was "going on" in the department. The staff's dislike for Rory was hardly concealed – people openly, and only slightly lowering their voices, used words like "bungler" and "ass" to describe him. But, ours being a large and ossified company, nary an effort was ever made to remove Rory or force him to account. I would daresay he's probably still there now – probably with several promotions.

Hennings, who was in his early-to-mid thirties, was the top brass in the department. A thin, carefully trimmed man who walked with a substantial loping quality, he'd been with the company for about ten years, rising up through the ranks. He moved somewhat mysteriously, wasn't much of a leader, and didn't always seem aware of what the department was doing. That said, Hennings didn't necessarily seem like such a bad guy. Some on the staff thought he was preoccupied with multiple intrigues involving the company elite, continually massaging his contacts in preparation for a leap into the senior hierarchy. Others held the view that he'd manufactured his tense, yet somehow aloof, posture only to secure long lunch hours and not be bothered with day-to-day problems, of which there were many. Still others proposed he was blithely incompetent. I myself, for whatever reason, favored the "intrigues theory" – though, I must say, I have no direct evidence, only my observations and my own personal "vibe" from working there.

But I see nothing very remarkable in any of this. Every company or group has its own peculiar way of doing things – and indeed, "quirks" and abuses and incompetence can be found under every rock, on every mountain. And in the global economy, people are of course "free" to move along from workplace to workplace at their whim. Depending, of course, on what their passport says, and what the market will bear.

5

As time went on, Gerd expounded on some of the things that concerned him. He seemed to catch me at the most vulnerable moments. For example, I would spend most of the workday in close proximity to several people. But a time would inevitably come when somehow they'd all be gone – off to the bathroom, out for coffee, just to wander around – and those would be the moments Gerd would appear. He would sit or stand with his hands in his pockets, grinning and guffawing in his way and then suddenly drawing serious. Every so often he would stroke his goatee or swing his head from side to side, cracking the bones in his neck, as he unburdened himself of another tale about the city in which we lived.

* There was no "fresh milk" to be had. All the milk was contained in "flimsy cardboard boxes," and rare was the shop that bothered to refrigerate this product. Also, the expiration date on the milk was often "literally months" in advance. Gerd couldn't seem to understand how it could be possible – or get over it.

* The food in the restaurants was bad. Expatriates at our company were paid at a "Western scale." This meant that while we weren't "rich" (far from it), we were fairly well off in a local economy that was still largely subsidized (the average "local" earned about $300 per month). Many of my colleagues, it must be said, exploited their relative wealth to dine on a regular basis at the sort of prestige, gourmet "European" establishments they could only dream about going to back home. Gerd was continually telling stories about how he and his wife had patronized this or that pricey restaurant – say, $45-50 per head – and everything had gone wrong. Slow service, "soiled" silverware, clogged bathroom sink, "canned carrots," a "long black hair" in the food, and so on. But still he kept going, particularly to places someone would recommend. The next day he would report to anyone who would listen on how unimpressed he'd been.

* The local people were "thieves and criminals." They were "corrupt," "liars," and "dominated by greed." In addition, they were often "incredibly rude," and had "never heard of deodorant." Gerd told numerous tales about store clerks returning too little change, about "price-gouging" in the downtown stores, about "criminal" police officers trying to "extort" him for offenses that didn't occur, about getting "harassed" by the packs of prostitutes which congregated nightly around some of the major

squares. He also liked to repeat stories he'd read in the English-language newspaper, mostly about "Russian mafia hits" or the many scandals and financial frauds involving the new post-Communist government.

* The compact discs were too expensive. Gerd couldn't be paying the $20 or higher import price for something that was "far cheaper" in The States. He said he had a friend who would pick him up discs for $11.99 or cheaper at the Wal-Mart back home, then ship them across the ocean. Gerd maintained it was "a lot" better to do it this way – despite the mailing costs, shipping delay, Wal-Mart's lack of good selection, and general hassle.

* This same friend also regularly sent Gerd videos of TV programs that had been shown in The States. These included sitcom episodes, police dramas, college basketball games, and news documentaries. Gerd could often be found critiquing these programs with zeal, even though no one else at work had had a chance to see them.

* Some of the local staff at our company got involved in a fairly sleazy "sex" scandal. The story got around of a young, married administrative assistant sleeping around with two or three different men on the staff. Apparently, she got pregnant, then left her husband, only to be scorned as a lying tramp, or something along those lines, by the guy she believed to be the father of the child. Finally, the story went, she ended up marrying a fifth guy, whom she'd somehow convinced was the father of the kid. Which of the guys was the actual father, however, remained unclear, at least according to the rumor mill. It did seem sort of wild, the sort of stuff you'd hear (I'm still not sure what ended up happening in the end, or even how true any of it was). In any case, where most people were maybe a little embarrassed, or thought the story funny, or sad, to Gerd it was clear evidence of dementia and backwardness. "That's totally insane," he told me in an excited

whisper, his eyes darting. "It's crazy, don't you think? I'm not one who likes to judge or anything, but you got to draw a line somewhere. That's the way diseases get spread, people not caring like that." Then he seemed to withdraw a little. "Shoot, I don't know. Maybe it's just their culture, the way they do it over here. I've heard that."

* Gerd had heard that the local health and education systems had "collapsed." The Communists had of course mismanaged everything into the ground, and tortured anybody who disagreed with them – and they had. But now, with the "free-market" economy still in its early stages, there wasn't enough money for things like new books and the latest miracle medicines and Western-standard equipment. The doctors and teachers, he added, were "poorly trained and probably incompetent." Gerd noted that he was able to travel to The States for his dental and physical checkups. But he feared "what could happen, God forbid," should he ever need emergency treatment.

* He still couldn't "stand" the pollution. On separate occasions he described the "high levels of toxins" in the air due to "inadequately filtered" incinerators; the probability of "unregulated" nuclear waste disposal; the fact that many cars were not equipped with "catalytic converters," which resulted in the streets being "filled with possibly carcinogenic fumes and poisons."

There were other things that bothered him as well, such the mysterious absence of "black people," and a shortage of elevators in many of the buildings, a circumstance that sometimes required Gerd to walk up many flights of stairs.

On the positive side, Gerd did like what he called "all the bare midriffs walking around" – a reference, I came to understand, to the city's pretty young women, who were legion – and the fact there were "hardly any" homeless people begging for money on the streets, as compared to places "like New York." The few bums that were there, he surmised, were "probably war refugees from ex-Yugoslavia or the former Soviet Union." But the bums weren't all bad. Gerd was rather charmed the day he saw one down-on-his-luck fellow in the subway trying to grub up some change by selling little turtles from a bucket.

One Tuesday, I noticed Gerd speaking excitedly on the phone. He hung up, signed out from his work station, put on his coat, stuck his head in Hennings's office, and departed.

The next day, he didn't show up. At about mid-morning, I stepped out to the hall for a cup of coffee. Hagerty, Ross and Phrom were sitting at the table, talking softly. I soon learned Gerd was amidst a crisis. It was his dog, Lanny. The dog was older, evidently. It was also diabetic – diabetic or something serious like that. The story was that all three Pittas had taken a weekend trip to Vienna or Kiev or some such place. But, in a horrible lapse, Gerd's wife, Debbie, had left the dog's medicine kit aboard the train. Now, back in our backward East European capital, they were having trouble rounding up the replacement syringes and antidotes, the special dog drugs, whatever it was that Lanny required. The dog was apparently very badly sick – on the verge of slipping into a "coma." It was unknown if the thing was going to survive.

This information came from Hagerty, who had evidently become one of Gerd's buddies. Hagerty, whose face held a kind of perpetual bird-like expression, explained that the dog was Gerd and Debbie's prized possession and "best friend." Some kind of a special poodle or something. They'd had it since just after they married, 11 or 12 years ago.

Ross and Phrom exchanged tentative looks. Hagerty sipped deliberately from his machine-drawn cappuccino. I, for one, sighed.

It was announced the next day that Lanny had been saved.

6

A few weeks later, an announcement appeared on our department's communal post-it board: Gerd was having a party Friday night. It was not something I was initially inclined toward going to. But I mentioned it to Dee, and she sort of liked the idea. Her argument was that she wanted to see who I worked with, to put some faces to the names I'd been mentioning. But I still wasn't sure.

After a few hours of tossing it over, I decided: Why not. At worse, I figured, it might be a few hours of hassle, but it probably wouldn't hurt that bad. Work-wise, our attendance could even be interpreted as a sign of goodwill. Besides, it was early summer. If, at a certain point, it became too difficult, Dee and I could take an early leave and wrap up the evening with some pastry and coffee. The riverbank cafes stayed open late this time of year.

We were in good mood as we dressed, joking, playing around. Dee put on a glittering, sheer aqua-colored dress, and added her good pair of black heels. I slicked my hair back, changed my shoelaces, and threw on a sportscoat and a red tie with pink bananas.

Gerd and Debbie and Lanny lived in a two-story place high on a hill. The place was already topped out at about half-full by the time we got there. Gerd spotted us as we hung our coats and hustled over to shake our hands. His tallness and girth made the entry hall seem very small.

"Glad you could come, glad you could come," he said, barely looking at me but letting his eyes linger carefully over Dee. "Everything you see here is genuine oak," he said as he led us into the living room. "We had it shipped over from our house in The States. Everything's almost exactly how we had it back home."

He led us around to a few other rooms. But we didn't get to see Lanny just yet.

The Pittas' apartment was a pretty nice place, I must admit – opulently appointed, and containing nearly every possible appliance. The living room windows held frankly spectacular views of the city. Also, by my estimate, the place was about three or four times bigger than two people and a sickly dog needed. But shit, why not.

We were introduced to Debbie in the living room, where she was standing next to the huge Sony satellite TV, which took up about as much space as a fireplace. Debbie was a small woman, but powerfully built and full-faced. She wore her hair in a kind of blond mini-beehive. Enormous gold seashell-type things hung from her ears. She was wearing a tan-cream skirt/sleeveless-top style outfit, knit fabric, of a style you might normally expect to find on women in their late 40s or 50s.

"It's so nice to meet you," she said to me. She spoke in a way in which each sentence sort of trailed off into the high end, as though she were asking a question. She went on: "Gerd's told me so much about you I almost feel like I know you already. Oh, gee – doesn't everybody always say that? God, I'm embarrassed. So much for first impressions." She laughed.

I drank down my bottle of beer and asked if either Dee or Debbie happened to need something from the bar. Dee shot me her look – the one that seems to refer to "my drinking." The hell with it, I thought. We'd come all the way out there.

Before heading to the bar I stopped at the toilet to kill a little time. Inside was a wooden rack, sloppily filled with dozens of magazines. I closed and locked the door and started to sort through the pile. The rack contained copies of the last three or four months of *Rolling Stone, Time, Spin, Wired, Newsweek, Talk, The New Yorker, Vanity Fair, Sports Illustrated, The Nation, Men's Health, Entertainment Weekly,* and two different magazines devoted entirely to "Apple Computers." Everything had been sent by subscription from The States.

After about ten minutes I went back out. Almost every one from the department had come, except for Rory Symmonds and the local staff. Indeed, I didn't detect a single local in attendance. I was a little surprised to see Hennings, the department chief, working behind the bar. He didn't necessarily seem to be the kind to volunteer for such duty – but what did I know? I'm sure he had his reasons, and fairly decent ones. Hennings dished me out a fresh and frosty beer. We exchanged a few unthreatening expressions and stale laughs.

Dee and I spent most of the evening on the roof-top deck, munching from a table that had been set out with shrimp, cheeses, crackers, crabcakes, a variety of creamy salads, and nuts. A red plastic tub full of ice and beer bottles had, helpfully, also been placed nearby. The night was warm, with soft wind gushes sailing over the hills and pooling upon the deck. The view, I have to admit, was actually pretty close to "priceless." The city downtown was arrayed to perfection like a child's toy set, all golden cupolas, jaunty turrets, severe towers and pompous colonnades. Behind and to the sides, quietly lit red-tile residential neighborhoods folded seamlessly into the hills. In a way, it seemed so ridiculously flawless, so fabulously picturesque, it seemed almost like a joke. It was hard to believe this was actually "Europe." It was too much like "Europe" – too much like some fairyland, some storybook version. It's always sort of a shock to find things like you imagined them.

Phrom soon made his entrance, a beer in each hand and an extra in his coat pocket. He told me a number of things I hadn't heard before – such as that Gerd and Debbie were paying nearly $2,400 a month – in good American money – to live in this place. I was astounded. This was a truly astronomical figure, even given the size and location of the apartment. Phrom said he'd heard they had decided to combine what they were paying on their mortgage back in The States with the generous housing allowance the company gave all expatriate employees. He said the Pittas also hired a housekeeper, a local girl, twice per week.

I mentioned Hennings working behind the bar. Phrom grinned dubiously in his way – and wondered that I found it surprising. After all, he said, Gerd and Hennings had been friends going back years and years, at least since college. Hadn't I heard? In fact, he said, Hennings had been Gerd's best man at his marriage to Debbie. I expressed my astonishment – while inside I felt a burgeoning quease.

This was a bit foul, wasn't it – a bit of funny smelling cheese business that wasn't the least bit humorous. At least to me it wasn't. I just don't like the game when it's played this way. I really don't. It leaves me with the feeling that you can never trust the way things seem.

I stood there and felt lousy and stupid – like a bit player in some cheap fraud, a dupe, like somebody who had been questioned by the cops but not directly implicated in the crime. I told Phrom the deal smacked of a "greasy cover-up." He allowed that it hadn't been announced or even widely discussed – but he seemed to think I should have somehow heard about it before now. But the truth was, I hadn't. No one had told me, Gerd had never mentioned it once during all our talks, and I guess I hadn't been sharp enough to pick it up on my own. Still – I really hadn't suspected such a thing was possible in this day and age. I mean, it just seemed to go that little bit too far, that little bit too *sneaky* – the hell with the "meritocracy" and all the other happy crap they rammed down your craw by way of explaining how things "really work." Hennings, of course, had been the chief job interviewer. He'd made the final executive decision to hire us all. Now, to learn he'd flipped his pal-buddy one of the spots, a full-paying job in Europe, like it was some freebie apple from a fruit box… Granted, Gerd wasn't "unqualified" for the job, in the widest sense of the word; at the same time, surely there were hundreds of people, at the least, who were just as qualified or more qualified. They, however, weren't chummy-chum-chum with Hennings.

I was almost certain Hennings and Gerd had, at least to some degree, deliberately hush-hushed the deal at the office, or at least played it down. They certainly didn't go around behaving like any special buddies. Indeed, they almost seemed to go out of their way to act like they had only the typical, distantly friendly relationship shared by many a boss and underling. I was pretty disturbed – almost angry, really – to find out it was part of some cover-up. If questioned about it, I'm sure they would have screwed serious looks on their faces and claimed it was all highly "above-board," that Gerd had met all the qualifications and then some, that the friendship really wasn't a factor, no, not at all, never…

I drank two beers in rapid succession, Phrom laughing as I used his body to conceal myself from Dee, who had been cornered by the old badger Del on the other side of the deck.

At around 11 o'clock a surge of excitement rippled through the party. It was time for Lanny's treatment – and we could all get a look at the dog if we wanted. Gerd and Debbie were giving tours of Lanny's quarters. Dee insisted we go. The dog had his own room.

"Okay now, please be quiet," Gerd said, leading us into the spacious, dark enclosure. "Lanny likes people, but he might get upset if there's too many loud voices." Debbie, meanwhile, was explaining in a soft voice that Lanny was still "in the recovery phase" from the scare that had occurred after they left the medicine kit on the train.

The way they told it, it had taken some doing to find a local vet who could both aid Lanny and provide the replacement drug elixirs the dog needed to survive. Gerd said that Lanny had also spent about a week at a special clinic they had found, at an eventual cost of some $600. It would be a few more weeks yet before Lanny would be fully mobile. They were trying to keep him as rested as possible.

The room was outfitted like a small hospital. Wall shelves held animal blood pressure-reading devices, bottles of pills and various nozzle-ended contraptions, tubing, a long row of dog-care and veterinary texts. The place smelled humidly of dog – dog mixed with a faint chemical, medical-type scent.

Lanny was curled on a pink blanket in a wicker basket against the far wall, in the center of an oval of soft white lamplight. A group of about four of us crept over. Lanny was blond-gray in color, and very skinny. He was missing patches of hair, mainly on his legs and rump. Purplish marks dotted his forelegs and back thighs. Needle-marks, I figured.

As we neared, Lanny's tail rolled slowly, once, and he raised his head. He appeared very tired. He blinked his eyes. His tail rolled again. Then he made a motion as if he were going to move – as if he were going to act on his instinct to smile and greet us. But even trying seemed to pain him. He let out a high, weak whine.

"Relax, boy, relax," Gerd said, patting him.

Gerd looked at us and smiled, the lamplight reflecting in his glasses.

I gave Lanny one last glance, turned and walked out. I fetched myself a beer.

7

Afterwards at a riverside cafe, Dee had surprisingly little to say. Judging from her comments, my colleagues seemed to her a basically "okay" bunch, the sort of people likely to be found almost anywhere Americans may gather. As for Debbie, Dee was for the most part restrained, expressing a kind of sisterly, patient sorrow as she tried to explain and come to terms with the various choices that had apparently been made.

Finally she came to Gerd.

"Ugh," she said, laughing and spooning up a morsel of peach pecan ice cream. Then she shivered. "No offense, man – but what a weird obnoxious creephead. Seriously, Pete, I got the spooks after the first two seconds. I can't even imagine that guy loose in the office at work. Poor you. How horrible."

She laughed again.

She had a certain point, I guess – but for some reason I didn't want to be a party to it just then. It just didn't feel right. Truth told, I was actually kind of offended. Gerd and Hennings may have had their little unannounced special relationship, but that was their business. I didn't want to give a damn about it. I was also thinking now and again about Lanny. The way he was laying there, with that light on him.

"Come on, be nice for once," I said. "Gerd's as okay as anybody, all right? He does a competent job at work. And however he is otherwise, it's his business. We don't have to hang out with him, and we didn't have to hang out with him tonight. No one forced us to go over there. Besides, his dog is sick."

Dee snickered.

We finished our coffees and ice cream and went home. I happened to walk by as Dee was slipping out of her dress, and caught a whiff of her body odor. Or rather, her odor, combined with the smell of her dress fabric. In any case, I was aroused. I finished removing the dress, grabbed her from behind, and rolled us both onto the bed. I started pulling at her bra with my teeth.

"Are you drunk?" she said.

Perhaps she meant it as a joke. But it made me angry. Not mad, but a little angry. I felt my blood pound. A snap of energy rose from my ankles, kicked around in my chest, pressed against my ears. But only for a moment. Because I decided to let it go. Just let it go, no further questions. I set it free without a second thought.

Dee hadn't bathed since the morning. Her smell was intoxicating. I threw her arms over her head and inhaled her, inching from her neck on down.

8

A work friend of Dee's, Ivona, had invited us to spend a few days out at her lakeside cottage. The place was about six hours away by car. The plan was to go out there, spend the next three days waterskiing and hanging around with Ivona and her "businessman" husband, then another day for the drive back. Five days total. Ivona was a local woman, and she and Dee had become rather close over the past several months. Dee really wanted to go, and it did seem like a good idea – a chance to see the countryside, and spend a few days relaxing in the sun (at least if the weather held). After all, we hadn't taken a vacation since we'd arrived. That was getting close to a year ago.

Dee was able to get the time off, no problem, but there were complications at my work. The typical procedure was to put in the formal paperwork for a vacation at least six weeks in advance – this was written in stone. But Ivona had given us just three weeks advance warning. Still, it looked possible. All I needed was for someone to switch days with me. Maybe we couldn't be gone for all five days, but maybe four days was possible. I didn't think it would be a problem. People were always filling in for one another. I'd done it myself once or twice. The bosses didn't mind, so long as the day-switching wasn't excessive, and that they were notified about it in advance.

I sat down with the month's schedule. We were lucky: I wasn't shifted on two of the days we needed. The other three days looked like trouble, however. A few folks had filed for summer vacation long ago, and some had already left the country. This meant the department was already skeleton-staffed.

The options were limited. I studied and studied the schedule. Only one name kept coming up: Gerd Pitta.

After about an hour I emerged with the solution. We would shorten the trip from five to four days. It would require us to take a bus or possibly even rent a car, since traveling with Ivona and her husband, as the original plan called for, would probably no longer be feasible. But that would be fine, possibly even fun. What was needed, however, was for Gerd to agree to a minor change in his work-week. I would substitute for him at the start of "his week," thus beginning "my week" a day early. He would then start and end his week a day later than scheduled. True, it would mean he would have to work Saturday. But he would have a free day at the start of the next week. Things would even out in the end. Plus, I would owe him one. It didn't seem like a bad trade to me. Not a great one, maybe, but certainly not the worst.

I put the plan to Gerd the next afternoon. First I let him give me an update on Lanny's condition ("Lots and lots better. Walking around quite a bit, he even jumped on the couch yesterday. We took him out for some fresh air…"), then I hit him with it.

Gerd's face seemed to close up ever so slightly. Midway through my spiel, his eyes started darting back and forth. At last I was done. It had taken maybe 40 seconds.

He inhaled noisily two or three times and said: "Well – I don't know, frankly. I'll have to think about it. We were maybe thinking of taking off or something. Give me a few days, okay?" He clapped me on the shoulder and walked away.

The same day, about four hours later, he sauntered over to my area.

"Anything going on?" he said. "I've got nothing to do except play with myself. All done until quitting time."

"Yeah," I said, gesturing at my work, "just about to finish up myself."

Gerd sat down and started typing away at one of the communal computer work stations. After a few moments he looked my way and said, "Hey, are you an internet person? You do it much?"

"No," I said, "hardly at all."

"Really? Why not?"

"I don't know. I guess I just don't care for it."

"You're kidding."

"No, serious." I shrugged. "I really don't care for it."

"Why?"

"I don't know. I guess it just makes me feel bad. I get a bad feeling from it."

"Wow," Gerd said. "Care to explain?"

I sighed. I shot a blast of air from my mouth into the flap of hair hanging over my forehead.

"Gee, I don't know if there's so much to explain," I said. "I just don't know what the big deal is. The internet – I mean, it seems like just the same crap as always, but slightly different colors maybe, a little faster on some things. Advertising and garbage, selling stuff. Stupidity, futility, uselessness… You know – new and improved, the same old garbage. And more of it. Lots more."

Gerd said nothing.

"Shit, I don't know," I went on. "It makes me tired to hear them saying over and over how it's supposed to change everything. Maybe it will, in some way, but I doubt for the better. Probably for the worse, in the end. Maybe if it really helps medical treatments or something, that would be all right. But really, what is there? Not much. Just the same old garbage. The same crap, just from a different asshole. Or maybe a slightly different shade of crap, from a slightly different asshole. Know what I mean?"

"You really think so?" he said. "Wow. Interesting."

"I don't know if it's so interesting. It's just how I see it."

"Yeah," he said. "Me, personally, I adore it, ever since it came out. It's a big bunch of fun. I can spend hours at a time, you know, just goofing off, checking things out, seeing what's new. Seems like the time goes by in a few minutes."

"That's what your wife said at your party." (This was a little lie – Debbie had said no such thing. I'm not sure why I said this; it just came out.)

"Did she?" He broke into a smile. "Yeah, I guess I do do it a lot. That's funny. Do, do. Doo-doo."

Gerd was scanning through some internet site as we talked. I couldn't tell what it was, but it seemed very energetic, many bright colors and little boxes of text. The bosses didn't mind if we used "the web" during spare moments. Or so they said. But I tended to doubt their sincerity. You had to use a personal sign-in code to access any element of the company computing system, and they could theoretically keep tabs on what you looked at. They had said as much in a lengthy document they made everyone sign at the time of hire. If shove came to kick, I doubted they would restrain themselves from using your "net-surfing" record against you in some way.

I said, "What sort of stuff do you look at, if you don't mind my asking."

"Oh, all kinds, really," Gerd said. "Dog and veterinary stuff a lot of times, you know, because of Lanny. Sports scores – there's statistics galore out there, if that's up your alley." He laughed. "And there's a lot of porn out there, of course – not that I look at any of that stuff, no way. I can do just fine without a daily dose of triple-anal, thanks," he said, chuckling and raising his hands in a gesture of refusal.

"And, uh, let's see," he went on, rubbing his beard. "My old college has a site – I check that out to see what's going on. Yeah, and every so often I check out these various chat-rooms they have out there. Such as on Hemingway, for example. I'm a big Hemingway fan, you know, I've read three biographies on him. There's a lot of Hemingway people on-line, having discussions about this and that about him, his life and stuff. It can get kind of crazy. And music – there's all kinds of stuff out there about music and bands. You like music?"

"Sure, love it."

"Yeah, you might want to check it out more, then. There's been a lot of hilarious stuff out there about the Cobain suicide, for example. Kurt Cobain, you know, from Nirvana. I was looking at some of that the other day. Somebody put out a picture they claimed was the police photo of the suicide scene. It was really amazing. No head at all. Just a big mass of blood and some of that dirty blond hair. Sorry, Kurt."

Gerd opened his mouth and laughed. His face seemed to suddenly split open like a cracked watermelon.

"No kidding," I said.

"Yeah, no kidding," Gerd said. "You ought to check it out sometime."

"Yeah, maybe."

"You like Kurt Cobain? I mean, did you like Kurt Cobain? Did you like Nirvana and all that?"

I nodded. "The greatest."

"Oh, come on," Gerd said. "Seriously? You seriously liked him?"

"Yeah, totally."

"Oh jeez," Gerd said. "One of those." He lowered his head, shook it, grinned, then looked up at me. "Really? I mean, come on, Kurt was a loser. He really was. You got to admit it. It was all hype. It wasn't that good. Then he shot himself. What a dork."

"Now wait a minute, Gerd…"

"No, I'm sorry," he said. "I mean it. I'm really sorry, but no, *non*, *nyet*. Kurt Cobain was loser. It was all media hype, man. Shoot, the music wasn't even any good. I mean, there were a couple of catchy songs, but it wasn't the ultimate greatest or anything, like you hear people say." Gerd shook his head again. "C'mon, most of it was pretty average, wasn't it? And some it was just bad – just banging around and noise, screaming his head off. Bad music, bad attitude, bad hair, bad everything. You got to admit. And then to kill yourself like that, right when you have a little daughter? I'm sorry, but that's not right, that's illness. And his wife, that Courtney? Oh jeez, that's another story altogether. Talentless, hysterical woman like that, taking all those drugs when she was pregnant? Junkie whore. And now they put her in movies? Please. *Please.* Give me a break." Gerd shook his head again. "The poor luck of that little girl, to wind up with parents like that."

Gerd scratched at his beard, then stared at his fingernails.

"You know," he said, looking at me again, "it's sort of funny, I guess, but I went to a Pearl Jam concert the night after they found Kurt's body. We had bought the tickets in advance, of course, but still, it was very strange, the timing of it. You know, Pearl Jam and Nirvana being from the same town and all, Seattle, some of the Pearl Jam guys probably even knew Kurt, or at least knew who he was…"

Gerd went on. I let him. I tuned him out, returned to my work, and let him. There's just no talking to some people about some subjects.

I heard Gerd calling my name.

"I'm sorry," he said, eyes twinkling. "So you don't agree with me. That's cool. I can't say I understand, but that's all right." He nodded. "Yeah, a lot of people really still like Kurt. They even put him up there with John Lennon, if you can believe. I've heard people say that."

Gerd was sort of smiling – a kind of maneuver with his lips and facial muscles that was veering awfully close to a smirk. I felt a sudden compulsion to get up and hit him. Or at least find a cream pie to mash in his face. A lemon meringue, perhaps.

I took a deep breath.

"I don't know how much you want to get into it," I said, "but sure, Kurt was important to me – I mean, as much as some distant rock star could ever be important to someone. He's still important to me. His music, who he was, what happened. I won't deny it. But if all you want to do is attack him and repeat news clips, nevermind. Let's forget it."

I turned back to my work.

"Well, wait a minute," he said. "You can't just say something like that. Explain. Come on, let's hear it. Now I'm interested."

I figured, for that quick moment, that it wouldn't hurt to try. This, of course, was a mistake.

"Well," I began, "it's like, it's like Kurt... Kurt... I don't know. The sound of his voice, jeez. It was like a raw nerve ending or something. The power of it... the power, well, maybe that's not exactly the right word... But yeah, the music, the energy of it... It was, how to say... it was hard and it you hard, but in a beautiful way – or, I mean, not *beautiful*, in the classic or cliché sense, but... beautiful in a totally incredibly rocking way, like nothing I ever heard before. You know? They nailed a perfect sound, especially on the one album, on all the albums really... Rock and roll perfection, the simple sound of it... Yeah, and what he was talking about in the lyrics, or seemed to be talking about... Yeah, and the drums, they were totally amazing drums..."

It was as if my tongue had suddenly disconnected itself from my brain. Yet onward I pushed.

"Shoot, it's like, it's like – I guess you could say Kurt was sort of my ambassador, in a way, in an ultimate sense. You know, for certain ways that I felt – that I still feel. I don't know – yeah, my ambassador, I guess... You could consider him that, in a way. A kind of representative, you know, for ways that I felt – or maybe, now that I think about it more, for ways that maybe I only wanted to feel, or want to feel, for whatever reason. Maybe for ways it seemed attractive to want to feel – that Kurt himself made seem attractive, the feelings..." I shrugged. "Ah, shit, what the hell. Does that make any sense? Do you know what I mean? Shit, it was just a great rock band. Maybe that's all."

Gerd's smile had gotten a lot bigger.

"Oh, *come on*," he said – and then a little laugh jumped out of his mouth. He wagged his head, struggling not to bust out in a bigger laugh. "No, I really don't know what you mean. I have no idea. I truly wish I did. But – well, that's interesting," he said, nodding and trying to make the smirk disappear. "Your ambassador. Never heard that one before. Nope. Your ambassador to billion-dollar corporate MTV rock and drugs and bad noise? Is that what you mean?"

He raised his voice and began a jokey kind of shouting at me – like he was playing the part of some crazed religious freak or political clown on a TV comedy-hour. "Fer crissakes, man! He was an entertainer, a friggin' guitar player. He wasn't some god. He wasn't bigger than life."

"All right, all right," I said. "Whatever you say, man. Shout it from the rooftops." I turned and looked at some papers on the desk.

Gerd made a few more attempts at the conversation, but they were unsuccessful. He kept saying he hadn't meant to cause a problem, and that he really respected my views. After a while I got up and went to the coffee machine. When I returned, Gerd was gone.

9

I came home that night very agitated. I tried to tell Dee what had happened, but wasn't very successful. She thought the whole exchange more humorous than anything else (Dee was purely ambivalent about Cobain, though she did like some of his songs). I was still frustrated, though, and the thought of a nice beer, or maybe a bottle of wine, was pretty alluring. But I didn't have that drink. Instead, I made a large pot of black coffee and sat down in front of our home computer.

I was still playing around with writing then, and it seemed I had a great many things I needed to come to terms with. However, matters were all jumbled in my head, and the going was rough, to say the least. After a few hours of typing a few words, deleting them, typing more, deleting, then walking out to the kitchen for more coffee, I suppose I was finally able to work out some of my consternation. Or maybe I just tired myself out. In any event, by one a.m. a goodly number of words were congealed on the screen. By three I had written the following:

FREEDOM IS A HARD-BOUGHT THING

They first laid eyes upon one another at a bookshop cafe, in a capital of what the analysts had taken to calling "The Other Europe." Sarah was old - she was in the second-guessing half of 34. Bryan was 25.

Sarah was a permanent temporary resident of the city, who earned her money handling legal documents for a large international firm of some repute. She initially observed Bryan from across the room, which was thick on this night, as on most evenings, with book-browsers and biscotti-munchers. But she didn't really think about him again - she wasn't forced to think of him again - until some 18 minutes later.

After all, Sarah had come with a man-friend, Joel, who was involved with western development-aid investment initiatives, and Joel needed his talking to. And besides, Bryan was in the corner on the stool, holding a worn guitar and singing songs. Or rather, he was in the corner on a stool, his stringy hair lashing about his face, holding a guitar, and singing songs - in the English language.

The novelty of English-singing guitar-players had worn off, at least in this particular capital, at least several months before. However, the city was still particularly bursting with the breed, and it would be several months more before any action was taken. In any case, young Bryan hardly registered with Sarah at all.

There was no great mystery in this. She'd seen his kind dozens of times before - who could miss them? The fellows in their long, tangly hair and crushed corduroy hats, slouched along every other street corner, singing their self-authored songs about fields of fresh peppermint and President Lyndon Baines Johnson, and the country-flavored one about the girl or the drug-fix (which was it?) which almost - but not quite - got away. In English. No, Sarah knew Bryan's kind, and she didn't care too much for it, no thank you.

One of the main things, of course, was that Bryan - just from the look of him - Sarah knew - she was willing to put 100 percent money on it - just from the little vacuous something in his watch-him-go grin - Sarah knew Bryan was another darned American.

And in the streets of eastern Europe could be heard the sound of the ever-present trams whining in the night, and the happy noises of a newly-freed people celebrating and writhing in their newfound unshackledness, amid the ancient art-deco and numerous history-enshrouded abutments.

Sarah herself was of course an American. Her man-friend Joel, however, was a second-generation ethnic Armenian citizen of Ireland. The couple had gone for supper at a recently established Thai eatery (operated by an ambitious, recently arrived family of Kurds), then headed over to the bookstore cafe for a nightcap. Lo and behold, some of Sarah's friends and many of her acquaintances were there.

As the group chatted and picked interestedly from a plate of unfrozen "cajun" chicken strips, Bryan re-entered the scene. He'd finished his performance and was now casting guitarless around the cafe. Call it "Brownian social motion," call it serendipity, call it too many like-minded people in too small a place, call it idiots - well, someone in the group sort of vaguely knew him.

What happened was that Bryan and Sarah exchanged a few words.

Not long later, Sarah was thinking of that moment, even as Joel flicked and flexed his tongue fairly deep inside her. Joel was a relatively small man, but he put up a pretty good fight. He groaned and wrassled Sarah, kicking and hawing - slow then fast, fast then slow once more. Joel was of the sort not adverse to a primer of cunnilingus - though he did expect the favor to be returned. But on this night, Joel's brand bored Sarah, and she knew it. It wasn't that he was unusually inept or particularly sloppy, in the context of the broad scheme of life, it was just… well, she was thinking of Bryan.

There had been something in the flash of the youthful guitarist's eyes. Or maybe - yes, the eyes, in conjunction with the toothily vacuous smile. Yes, that was it. The eyes and the toothiness, along with the healthy pallor of the skin - yes, and the long hair, lashingly mussed around the shoulders. And he really had said some funny things: A sly, condescending bit about the local customs, and an observation concerning the current international events, mixed in with what seemed to be some vague - but rather quite witty - "underground" cultural referencing.

Sarah gripped Joel's firm, pulsing penis and wrenched her mouth around it.

She'd seen Bryan exit the cafe with a few other (probably American) fellows - along with what looked to have been at least six young blonde girls. They were the whole pack of them carrying new green bottles of wine. And some of those girls - Sarah was willing to bet - why, they didn't look more than two days over 16 years old. Sarah seethed. These local girls - they didn't care who they gave it out to. They'd give it out to just about any foreigner who walked up - especially American men. These girls - they were so naive and stupid. They didn't have any respect for themselves.

Joel groaned and arched his back. It was getting close now. Sarah worked him. She worked it fast, but not sloppy-fast. She was aiming sharply now for that key split-second of slick frisson that would finally knock him down for good. Sarah wanted it over as soon as possible - so she could get back to thinking about Bryan.

But Sarah wasn't so lucky. Joel gently maneuvered her away, flipped her onto her back, and returned his medium-sized, somewhat swarthily-complected penis to her warm sopping pussy, kissing her deeply on the mouth as he did so. After a few minutes, Joel withdrew, whispered, and began flapping his tongue once more down between Sarah's legs. Oh jeez. Sarah supposed he was trying to "save" himself, to make it "last" a little longer. It went on like this, in various mutations, for another nine-and-a-half minutes.

Joel was almost asleep when Sarah realized she was bleeding from her back. Shit, she cried inwardly. It had happened again. It was always happening. The moles on her back - Sarah had tons of them. The doctors could only take away so many at one time, and new ones were always appearing. Nothing seemed to help. It the heat of his ardor, Joel's fingernails had succeeded in pricking open at least one of the moles, and perhaps several. Sarah knew she should get up, clean, treat and bandage the area. But she didn't. She didn't care. She'd wait until morning, when it had already scabbed over. Then she would have to tear away the scabbing to clean. But she didn't care. She would do it that way. She just didn't care any more.

And outside, the lonely night trams whined along their disparate tracks. The tram seats were filled with

slouching drunks, anthropology majors, imperturbable
early-morning cleaning women. The newly-freed city
celebrated and wriggled, frolicking about wildly in its
newfound unshackledness.

10

A day or two later I was going through my e-mail at work. There
was a message from Gerd:

DEAR MR. AMBASSADOR,

THANKS BUT NO THANKS ON THE DAY SWITCH. I'LL BE
HONEST WITH YOU. I COULD DO IT, BUT I JUST DON'T
WANT TO. IT WOULD FOUL UP MY SCHEDULE – I
ACTUALLY LIKE THE WAY IT IS THIS MONTH (FOR ONCE!).
DEBBIE WAS ALSO TALKING ABOUT MAYBE GOING OUT OF
TOWN ON THOSE DAYS (DEPENDING ON LANNY). MAYBE
YOU COULD STILL TRY SOMEONE ELSE. ANYWAY, JUST
TRYING TO BE HONEST WITH YOU. BEST OF LUCK
WORKING IT OUT SOME OTHER WAY. TALK TO YOU LATER
MAN.

MR. GERD

11

So we didn't go out to the cottage with Ivona and her husband.
Instead, Dee and I took a bus south and holed up at a hotel
overlooking a lakeside medieval village. It was a bit pricey, but we
rationalized a little splurge. It was time to be gone from work and
the city for a while.

The weather wasn't in our favor. The skies were overcast, the air damp and somewhat chilly. We spent quite an amount of time huddling on the bed, wrapped together like sausages in the blankets, sharing a special kind of feeling. The hotel resort had once been the exclusive reserve of the Communist hierarchy and its accomplices, we were told by the staff, and then the revolution occurred, and legislation was passed reverting it back to the original owners. The bed was wide and firm, the carpet short and ancient, the light fixtures festive, the room well-heated, clean and spacious. A large color television of contemporary vintage rested in the corner. We tuned to an international gymnastics competition and made love. The voices of the foreign-language sports commentators floated about and around us, the gymnasts whirled and kicked and flung themselves. Time raced by. We'd slip out for a meal, then return straight to the room. It was as good a vacation as any – perhaps, in some ways, better than most.

On the afternoon of the second day we felt obligated to at least take a close-up look at the lake and the trees. We moved across the main road, went down over some rocks, and came upon what looked like some sort of refugee camp. It turned out to be campers – mostly German and Danish families, but also a good number of the locals. They were spread out haphazardly, and there were too many of them – RVs smashed end-to-front next to tents; naked kids running every which way; the whole place smelling like meat burning over a campfire, combined with an overflowing latrine. The sun came out briefly, and so did the flies. Dee and I spotted a clearing and went for the shade.

This was adjacent to what looked like an unfenced tennis court. But the competitors weren't playing tennis. Far from it. It was a bunch of barefoot guys kicking a ball back and forth over a low net – a kind of soccer-cum-volleyball thing. I suppose there's a name for it, but to this day I don't know what it might be. A great many of the guys wore their hair in the style that is long in the back but short, in some cases razor-short, on the top and sides. More than a few of them seemed drunk. There was a lot of shouting, they seemed to be thoroughly enjoying themselves. We watched this action for a while, then decided to go in the lake.

The water was icy, to say the least, but the lakebed was smooth and hard, hardly any rocks or muck. We went out up to our necks, and then I stripped off Dee's bikini bottoms and entered her from behind – or so she confirmed. The water was amazing – it seemed like I could only barely feel the bottom half of my body. It was fine, though, rocking up and down out there, the sun spotting the water with gold and white flickers. It wasn't to last long, however. As we were returning to shore the clouds and overcast reappeared.

We hurried back to the hotel for showers, then headed out for an early dinner. We had chosen a different restaurant for each meal, but the menu choices were few and there hadn't been much variation; the chicken steaks always a tad too battered and fried, the boiled potatoes a bit too buttery. Even so, Dee and I generally cleared our plates, and this night was no exception. We had coffees afterwards, then went back to the room with a bottle of red wine from one of the handy liquor kiosks near the shore.

Within seconds of arriving, however, we had a fight – a real melee of a conflagration, as it turned out. Perhaps we had been spending too much time together. Things had been perfectly blissful for that first day and a half – and then, I guess, we had crossed an invisible threshold and things began to go the other way. It can work like that. As I say, it was a rough fight, too, nothing much in its favor. Some dark things were said, things designed to wound, and when Dee punched me in the back, I decided to leave.

I just don't accept it when people strike me. With Dee it was worse, since there was no option of hitting her back. We'd had plenty of these types of clashes during our time together, though I wouldn't say they were routine. But when Dee got violent, I had learned to run. Because the next thing was, she'd be biting. A punch is one thing, but a bite is another altogether, and I'd just as soon avoid it. It was a pity too, in some respects, because the sight of Dee in a filthy rage always got me excited – the look in her eyes that she got. It only appeared when she was really furious, or when something big would happen, such as on the few times we'd hit a nice score in Vegas or Reno. Her eyes would go big, and they'd sort of glaze over – but with this fire in them, a strange and dangerous kind of glint, tearing out the center of them.

It was about nine o'clock, I guess, and a light rain was falling. I walked down from the hotel to the row of pubs and restaurants by the lake. I went into a place, sat down and ordered a beer. After a few sips, I noticed a bank of slot machines – just about every other bar has these throughout Europe (they call them fruit machines over in England, apparently because of the symbolic use of cherries, pineapples, bananas, etc.). I got up and invested a few bucks worth of the local coin, losing it all in short order. I returned to my table and ordered another beer.

I had a few more. As I did, I grew extremely elated. Warmth, in the approximate shape of a sunflower, seemed to sprout between my shoulders. Despite everything, I loved Dee, I loved our life. It felt good to have been born. There were problems from time to time – granted. There would always be problems, of this I had no doubt. But so long as we had the will to fight through them, to take the bad straight in the face – with the assumption that good, also, lurked – well, it was all good if you looked at it like that. The future was out there. The things we would, the things we could, do. We'd been together a few years, but only now did it seem we were starting to really know one another – the full scope, the larger picture, as it were. All that had happened – all the fights and mistakes, the tears and tantrums, the guilt, blame and remorse – it was becoming part of a rich, solid, multi-layer foundation.

Dee, darn her – she was still the sexiest thing on two or four legs. Every encounter with her continued to yield some new insight: A taste, a texture, a scent. The qualities of her breath, as it rose and fell in a given moment. Her skin in a particular light, the lay of her hair on the pillow. I felt the urge to go back to the room and wrap her in my arms right then – to discuss and end the fight once and for all. I probably should have done that.

But my rhapsody was a good one, and I maybe I felt like riding it out a bit more. Even the bar itself somehow seemed blessed. The place was hardly special. But the lighting that night did indeed seem an unusually magnificent shade of amber. The clean-wiped wood surfaces appeared exceptionally golden and lustrous. The barkeep was humble and, to my thinking, most likely very wise. The few other patrons were bearded and noble. The beer was chilled to a benevolent pitch, well-frothed and bearing a most judicious edge. I drank and felt a sheath of wonderful heat slip over me. I suppose my cheeks grew very pink.

Amid my reverie, I was approached by a local man. He didn't suspect me as a foreigner at first – at least he seemed not to. But after he realized I didn't know much of the local tongue, it turned out he was acquainted with a fair amount of the English. We discussed our respective situations, in a general way, over a beer. When he suggested we add whisky shots to the next round, I didn't object.

It was sort of nice to have some company, and I extended, as best I could, my warm feeling to him. He seemed genuinely pleased to have found a new friend. He didn't have particularly interesting things to say, but I wasn't looking for, and didn't need, a bouncing and bantering buddy to shed more light and happiness over everything. I don't now recall the details of much of what we said to each other. I did notice he was wearing a pair of new white running shoes on his feet – somewhat of an odd choice, it seemed, to go with the dark blue sportscoat with the bright yellow hankie in the breast pocket.

At some point we left. I remember walking down a few drizzly, stony streets, then entering a new establishment. This one was considerably darker and more modern than the previous. It featured an "outer space" motif – glowing pastel designs of galaxies and star explosions covered the walls, etched out over a faux-velvet style material. The tables had beveled glass surfaces, and there was a greater variety of fruit machines. The place was also more crowded – a younger crowd, it appeared, though I also seem to recall a few middle-aged birds here and there. People were dancing on a small dance floor in the center. This was lit by rows of tiny flashing bulbs imbedded in the parquet-style floor tiles. Banging, chirping music from the hearts of machines burst forth from large speakers set in the ceiling corners.

My friend brought crisp new beers in tall glasses, along with whisky shots. I remember that part, clearly. And sometime after that, I remember the appearance of an actual whisky bottle on the table. And after that, I remember being surrounded by a number of women. Or maybe it only seemed like they were gathering about. Most of these were dressed in short skirts and shiny hose, lots of neck and wrist jewelry, high heels and so on. I recall being struck by the intensity of their perfumes, and they way the hair of some gushed down from their heads in elaborate waves and freshets.

The music was loud, it was very loud. It seemed to get more crowded in there. I remember people pushing against my back, pushing, at one point, my chest against the edge of the glass table. I remember it becoming hard to breath – the air thick and heavy.

I awoke down by the riverbank, lying in a patch of weeds next to an old wooden dock. I was completely soaked from the rain. Stuff from my nose was running down into my mouth and over my chin. My ears were roaring; in my chest I felt a painful throbbing. My mouth was dry and sticky, I struggled to swallow. It was still dark out, though a glow of morning purple was starting to peep over the hills.

I got up, seeking out the direction of the hotel. I checked my pockets – empty, both of them. A feeling of cold nothingness washed over me, followed by dizziness and a blast of nausea.

I staggered a step, eyes racing over the rough, weedy ground.

Then I saw the brave little shine – the keys. The hotel key and plastic yellow tag... and there, about a foot away, in a grassy tangle, my other keys.

I grabbed the two clumps. I shoved them in my pocket.

I was more than grateful; I was overjoyed, really. Here I was, with the keys. I reveled for a moment in the cool relief. No money, not a dime – but the keys. It was fine, it really was. It was better than that, it was the best thing I could think of. Lord, I thought. Dee could have been beaten, or raped or killed. I could have been killed. Maybe all of these.

It hit me then – it reared up, and for the first time really and for goodness hit me. Something akin to a shiver ripped down my back; my breath went short as my heart stampeded away. Dee had gone to the doctor two weeks earlier, and now it was confirmed: She was pregnant.

My recklessness horrified me. I could barely contemplate what could have happened.

I walked to the hotel, adding up the damage. I had either madly squandered or had taken from me somewhere in the neighborhood of seventy or eighty bucks, whatever it was I had been carrying. If Dee asked about the money, I would go ahead and tell her the whole story – every detail, nothing left out. She probably wouldn't be too angry. And if she was, that would be okay.

Thor Garcia was born in Long Beach, California, and has lived in Prague since the mid-1990s. His books include *The Citypoet & Other Stories*.